The Coventry Option

The Coventry Option

Anthony Burton

FOUNDED 1838

GPPS

G. P. Putnam's Sons
New York

*For my mother
and
for Tom Lipscomb*

I have turned my face
To this road before me,
To the deed that I see
And the death I shall die

—PADRIAC PEARSE, *Irish rebel*

Chapter 1

Coventry
November 14, 1940

THE railroad station where he had left the train was nearly a mile southwest of the grid of roads which formed Coventry's center. There were taxis in the station yard, but he had learned years ago to avoid taxi drivers. The man who had come to kill a city walked toward his target.

He went down the quiet tree-lined street purposefully but not hurriedly. Hundreds of miles away, across the Channel, they would be preparing now, he thought. They would be waking and shaving and thinking of a meal. His accomplices. They spoke a different language, but they were his accomplices as much as if they were walking at his side. Different reasons, same objective.

The tension was building in him, as it always did before the moment came to strike. He was conscious of something else: power. There was a feeling of great power. As he walked, carrying his suitcase, he looked at the city, and it was as if he controlled it and all the people in it: the stores, the shoppers, the offices, the policeman on his beat, the cars and the buses and the trams.

The cathedral, too. He could see the three spires—one of them belonging to the cathedral—that had symbolized the town for centuries, visible for twenty miles across the Midland plain. He owned them, but still they held no meaning other than as a target, the center of a killing ground. He supposed there were clergymen and worshipers to whom they meant something. But they were nothing to him.

Now, as he walked, there was something else. The tension

was building too high. It was like a graph showing the level of strain as clearly as black ink on paper. It was too high. He knew he was being watched. Asked why, he would have been unable to explain, but he knew. Behind him, almost certainly. He was being followed.

The urge to look over his shoulder beat through his head, through his whole body, like a demanding hunger, but he forced himself to ignore it. He was getting closer to the central complex of streets, and there were more stores. His tracker would be on the other side of the street, far enough back that he would be anonymous in the flow of pedestrians. It would be easy to lose him, but he couldn't be sure they weren't using a squad of men. There could be men ahead, standing and watching, ready to take over the chase, moving in a designed counterpoint with the man—the men?—behind.

He had to identify, separate, the men who watched. Discover how many. It didn't occur to him that he might be overwrought because of what he planned to do, that he might be unobserved. He knew.

He came to a pub. He went to the saloon bar and ordered a pint of bitter. Two men were standing with their drinks, looking silently out the window. He glanced at them, looked away. They could have been awaiting his approach down the street. A pub window was a good vantage point. He wasn't thirsty. He needed time to think. But then he found the beer was good, and he drank greedily. He had about seven hours. Then they would kill the city.

He thought about Dublin and about Donovan. Donovan had suspected betrayal because he had been part of the organization so long that he lived with betrayal and lies and deceit as if they were ill-favored pets. Donovan was a bastard, but an honorable bastard. He could trust Donovan, and he could trust the Germans because they needed him.

The pub was small, low-ceilinged. It smelled of cats. Nobody had followed him in. He went to the lavatory, and as he emptied his bladder, he saw there was a window, high in the

8

wall, through which he might clamber. He dismissed the thought as soon as it came. To escape one man outside and the two men in the bar would tell him nothing. If there were more waiting at the back, he would have gained nothing. They would have learned that he knew about the watchers.

Back in the bar, he finished his drink and left. He was a powerful man, but the suitcase felt heavier now. They couldn't know what he planned, he thought. And then the memories of other betrayals came to him, and for the first time he was afraid.

He began the routine that should tell him what he wanted to know. He went to a bus stop and waited behind two schoolgirls, prim in blue uniforms and wide-brimmed hats. The sign on the first bus showed it was going to Baginton. He went to the top deck and paid for the farthest point. He didn't look back or attempt to see who might have followed him on board.

Twenty minutes later, when the bus stopped at the gates of a modern khaki-camouflaged factory, he got off and approached the guard at the entrance. Still he did not look behind, showed no interest in anybody who might be watching.

"I'm looking for work, mate," he said to the guard.

The guard looked at him with the comfortable authority of his uniform. "Well," he said, "you won't find it here. The hiring's not done here. You'll have to go to the Ministry of Labor on Spon Street. Back in town."

"How do I get there, then?"

"Bus. Catch it on the other side of the street." The guard turned away, his duty done.

Now he saw the watcher, already moving across the street to the bus stop as if he had heard every word of the conversation. A nondescript man, heavy around the neck and shoulders. One man, he thought. Only one. There was no hiding place along the bleak fenced street for more. No cars, nothing. He could deal with one man. There was always the gun in his raincoat pocket.

A city-bound bus was approaching, and he had to run to

catch it. He let the other man get on first, saw him sit down-stairs just inside the entrance, and again went to the upper deck. He would move around the city a little as additional in-surance that there were no more followers. He might kill a couple of hours in a cinema. At his convenience he would lose the watcher.

The man downstairs, he thought, could be from London, but he doubted that. More likely a plainclothes copper as-signed to watch for newcomers at the station. A war factory town like this would be alive with such men, seeing a saboteur in every stranger. The tension eased, and he knew the danger of that.

As the bus rattled back into the city, he thought again about the other side of the Channel. Did they fly from Germany? Perhaps France or Holland. Over there, darkness would come earlier.

The pilots. They'd probably be walking toward the room where the weather experts would brief them. He stared up through the grimy windows, and beyond the haze of industri-al pollution he saw the sky was cloudless. Good flying weather. Good bombing weather. For a moment he wondered about the men who would be in the planes, the men who would re-lease the bombs. At his command. They were soldiers like him, except their weapons were bombs, not guns; high explo-sives, not bullets.

They would be bombing up, the bomb bays closing around the lethal loads. Mechanics would be testing the engines. He thought of all the effort and how much it depended on him, and his pulse beat faster.

Closer to the city center now, he could see the cathedral spire above its flying buttresses and the jumble of chimneys and roofs. He wasn't alone, he thought. Soon they would be on their way to join him. Destroyers, like him. The thought pleasured him.

He didn't allow himself to think about the last time he had seen German bombers overhead. That was in Spain, and that had nothing to do with this city that he was about to murder.

10

Chapter 2

AT this point in the line they faced west. The sun, now climbing, slowly flooded the ground with a brilliant white light, but it brought no warmth. Brock wondered if the cooks' fires would still be burning when they were relieved. The relief was always late.

"Death to the Fascist wind," Rafael said. It had become a joking phrase, applied to every discomfort and danger.

"Death to the Fascist cold," Brock said.

"It will destroy us before the Fascists can," the Spaniard agreed.

The snow-covered ground before them fell away into a huge saucer, the base of which looked smooth as porcelain from this distance. In reality it was pitted by gullies and craters. Staring through the barbed wire, Brock could see the tracks of a patrol from the night before. Everything else was familiar. To the left, the dismal huddle of buildings which was Teruel. In front, the open ground with the patches of frozen, unharvested corn. On the opposite edge of the saucer, the Fascist positions, marked by the red and yellow monarchist flag. To the right, far away, the immensity of the Pyrenees.

"They are late as usual," Rafael said. His face was windburned so badly that it was almost black. When he spoke, he made no attempt to hide his jagged, rotting teeth. There was no place for vanity in the line.

Brock took out the opera glasses that were his section's substitute for field glasses. The weak lenses were of little value, but Rafael looked hurt if he did not use them occasionally. The *centuria* was so short of equipment that the opera glasses had become a source of pride.

The enemy positions were about five hundred meters away, and Brock could see no movement behind the wire and sandbags. Farther south it was different. Directly across from Teruel he could see a column of vehicles maneuvering under an umbrella of black petroleum fumes. The distance made identification of the machines impossible, but a suspicion grew in Brock's mind. He said nothing to Rafael. The planes came shortly afterward.

They came from the south, high and fast. There were six Junkers and six Dorniers, glittering like shards of glass in the sun. Rafael raised his ancient Mauser and aimed at them. Brock knew he would have fired an absurdly ineffectual round but for the shortage of ammunition, just as they all had when they first came into the line and saw planes from the Condor Legion. Then each man had plenty of ammunition. Now they were down to twenty-five rounds per man.

"Bang, bang," Rafael said softly. He lowered his rifle and gazed up at the planes passing overhead. "They do not wish to visit us today," he said.

The Fascist guns began delivering their daily ration of shells. As it always did, the thumping of the guns died away after ten minutes. The rumor in the *centuria* was that the enemy was short of shells, but it was small consolation since the Loyalists did not seem to have any artillery on this front, let alone shells.

The relief guard, a Dutchman and another Spaniard, arrived as the guns fell silent. Brock and Rafael clambered out of the trench and stamped their feet while they took off their greatcoats and handed them to the newcomers.

Because of the shortage of clothing, only those on sentry duty could wear coats, which saw continuous front-line service. Brock swore as he felt the lice crawling about his crotch. Convention had it that parasites could not survive in the cold, but this didn't seem to apply to Brock's family of lice.

"They say the Fascists will attack soon," the Dutchman remarked. He was a small, rotund man, a Communist new to the International Brigade. Unlike Brock, whose boots and leggings were rotted, he wore thick new breeches and heavy, serviceable boots. It was said that he would soon be promoted to lieutenant. Brock did not trust him.

12

"Have any more supplies come up?" Brock asked.

"They are on their way," the Dutchman said.

"They're always on their way," Brock said.

"We have enough."

"If the Fascists attack now, they will walk through us. We have nothing."

"We have the workers behind us," the Dutchman said. "The whole socialist world is behind us."

"Well behind," Brock said.

"Let us not argue," Rafael said. "The enemy is over there, not here."

"This man talks like an Anarchist," the Dutchman said. "You know what happened in Barcelona."

Brock's leg, where he had been wounded, began to throb again. "Well, what happened in Barcelona?" he demanded.

The Dutchman, now down in the trench, would not look at Brock. "You will find out," he muttered. "You and your comrade Plunger." He pronounced it "*Ploon*jer."

"Is Plunger back?"

"He is eating, as usual."

The Dutchman turned to stare down into the gully. Brock and Rafael rolled their blankets bandolier-style over their shoulders and walked as swiftly as their chilled limbs would carry them down to the smell of the first food of the day. The fires were still alight.

This area was heavily trafficked, and the reek of decaying food and excrement was much worse than around the outpost. Plunger was standing close to one of the fires, eating lentil stew from his pan, shoveling the food into his mouth like a starveling. He winked at Brock but did not stop eating.

Brock unclipped his pannikin from his belt, filled it from the stew pot simmering over the embers of the fire, and began to eat. Once the Spanish cooks had been enthusiastic, but long ago they had given up any effort to make the eternal beans interesting. Brock thought of the warm kitchen in the house on Vicar Street when the money had been coming in, his mother at the stove, the thick bacon hissing in the frying pan, the pot of tea and the folded Dublin *Press* on the table, awaiting his father. The heat of the dying fire and the stew began to warm him. More men, relieved from the line, were gathering around the pot, filling their pans with the thin, steaming stew.

"Jesus, it's cold," Plunger said.

"That's because of the temperature," Brock said. He knew that when he talked to Plunger, his brogue reasserted itself.

Plunger grinned at him, wiping his mouth with his hand. "Don't be so bloody sardonic, my hard man," he said.

"All right, then. How did it go?"

"I helped kill an Englishman," Plunger said. Plunger was a big man, big at the shoulders and chest, with a big red face, nearly six feet three inches. He had innocent blue eyes and hair the color of December hay. A black cloak dangled from his shoulders, barely reaching his upper thighs, which were encased in threadbare riding breeches. A woolen cap was perched piratically over his right eye. The American major, a union organizer from Detroit, had sent him with reports to headquarters.

Brock said, "We're supposed to be killing Fascists."

"I know, hard man," Plunger said. His face lost its gaiety. He looked at the other men gathering around the fire.

"Come away a little, Michael," he said. "There's trouble, and I fear we may both be in it." They strolled, still eating, toward the farmhouse that was the *centuria*'s base post.

"What trouble?" Brock asked. The warmth of the fire had fully awakened the lice on his legs and genitals.

"You know where I had to go."

"Barcelona." Brock thought of the Dutchman in his greatcoat.

"Michael, there's a purge on. They're purging the Anarchists in Barcelona. There was a battle between them and the Communists for the telephone exchange. Holy Mother, this is a lunatic asylum. They're in the middle of a war, and here they are fighting among themselves like mongrels over a dirty bone."

He fell silent as a Spanish lieutenant, haggard and deathly white, stopped near them to empty his bladder. They moved farther on.

14

"Is it the wrong war we came to, then, Plunger?" Brock's voice was light, but he felt a chill that had nothing to do with the wind from the north.

"I tell you, they're killing each other, Michael. I saw it. And now the Communists have won, and they're throwing all their opponents into jail. They say the execution squads are being brought in."

"Rumors, Plunger." Brock said it without conviction.

"Rumors, is it? Well, now is it, then? Suppose I tell you that your old mate, your old Plunger, took part in a bit of it."

He hefted his Remington, the same one they had issued him in the Lenin Barracks in Barcelona when they both had arrived in Spain six months earlier. It had been one of the few weapons handed out that was less than ten years old. In Plunger's big hands, it looked like a toy.

"Suppose I tell you that the Englishman I just mentioned was an Anarchist, and suppose I tell you that I was part of the firing squad that sent him to kingdom come."

He lowered his rifle and said, "Ah, Michael, I'm not proud of it. I was on my way back when I got a ride in a truck heading for Teruel. We were about twenty miles out of Barcelona, me and this bunch of onion eaters, when a captain steps into the road and stops us. A hook-nosed whoremaster he was and no mistake. He had a sergeant with him, and he had a prisoner—this Englishman."

At the sound of plane engines they both turned and stared to the north. It was the same German squadron that had crossed the line earlier. It was heading southwest, its work completed.

"Where are the government fighters?" Plunger said. "Just once I'd like to see somebody take on those bastards." He dismissed the planes with a wave of his meaty fist.

"We all pile out of the truck, and the captain takes command. He jabbers at us, and the men line up, so I do the same. There's a couple of these fellows who speak a bit of English, and they say the prisoner is a deserter who's been spying for the Fascists."

"Was he in uniform?"

15

"Yes, a squirmy little runt. He could have stepped right out of a company of Black and Tans. There's no wall to put him up against, so they just stand him at the side of the road, him with his hands tied behind his back. He stands there, staring at us.

"He knows what's going to happen. He starts shouting. He shouts that he's no spy. He says he's an enlistee with the POUM. He says he was wounded on the Jarama front—where you got it, Michael. The captain tells him to be quiet, but he goes on shouting. Why shouldn't he, in his position?

"We bring our rifles up and he begins shouting, 'Long live the revolution.' That's when I know he's part of the purge, because that was what the argument was all about in Barcelona: whether to carry out the revolution now or wait until after the war, like the Communists want. They're getting rid of him because he fought with the Anarchists."

Brock said, "There were men from the POUM militia on the Jarama front."

"The captain orders us to fire," Plunger went on. "It was messy. You know these onion eaters and their aim, Michael. There were eight guns on that road, and two of them misfired. One bullet got him in the leg, and he fell. Another got him in the chest, and all the rest missed."

"What about your aim, Plunger?"

"I missed, too, Michael. But then I wanted to miss. The Englishman, he's lying at the side of the road, and even then he's still crying out, 'Long live the revolution.' There's blood coming out of his mouth, and his legs are kicking in the snow. He can't control them. He has a Cockney accent.

"Finally, the whoreson captain goes over to him and finishes him off with a revolver. They take his papers, and I get a look at them because nobody else can read English. He's with the POUM all right. He's a member of the Independent Labor Party in England. There are letters from his wife. And pictures of a couple of kids. He came from Battersea."

Brock shrugged. "These things happen," he said. "I'd rather mourn the dead in Ireland than an Englishman in Spain."

"But, Michael, don't you see, he was no spy. They killed him

16

just because he didn't happen to agree with the Communist way of running this damned war. They threw him in the ditch and left him there like a lump of bad meat."

Brock shifted his feet uneasily. "Perhaps there are no good wars anymore," he said. "Perhaps there never were. Perhaps we've been wasting our time here, Plunger. Perhaps we should be back in Ireland." He could see the American major at the field telephone, listening intently and then talking fast.

"It's not just the Englishman, Michael," Plunger said. "It's us as well." He looked around carefully. "Everybody knows the Communists have been holding back supplies and ammunition from this front because they want to make that war minister look bad. That fellow, Prieto, the one they're out to replace with their own man. But we're the only ones who've been talking out loud about it. Me mostly, but you, too."

Plunger pulled a length of red sausage from his pocket, dusted it off with his fingers, and began to chew at the end. Brock leaned down to pluck a frozen weed, which he used to clean his pannikin. Beyond the cooks' fires, the *centuria's* commissar was talking to the American major.

Nothing was as simple as you expected, Brock thought. There had been his mother's fury when she learned he was going to Spain with the Frank Ryan group. She was leaning against the sink when he told her.

"That business over there is nothing to do with us," she had said. Her arthritis had become so bad that she could only walk with the aid of a cane. "Michael, you're needed here," she said. "I'll not have you walking out on everything you've worked for."

"I'm going," he said. He was sick of the organization's internal squabbles. Sick of the petty aims. Sick of the lonely ambushes and sick of going on the run. Fifteen years and there seemed no end to it. Brock wanted something bigger. He was ambitious, not for himself but for his beliefs. In Spain it might be different: an uncomplicated assault on a notorious Fascist conspiracy, a conspiracy as bad as any London ever hatched. And Ireland—broken, betrayed Ireland—would always be waiting.

"You coward," his mother said. "You're running away from your father's murderers."

At that he had walked out of the house. Two weeks later he and Plunger were in Spain. But Spain proved no more simple than Ireland.

The Fascist guns were booming again. A boy, part of the flotsam of war who had attached themselves to the *centuria,* was running toward Brock and Plunger, and the major was shouting. "Come," the panting youngster said. Then, like a retriever, he turned and ran back toward the major.

When they reached the officer, he was back on the telephone. He was a chunky man with broad Slavic features topped by a khaki cap of the type worn by British army officers. He had a jagged scar down his nose, given him by company goons at the gates of an auto factory he had been trying to organize. He had other wounds, all of them won in American labor union wars, none of them in Spain.

He put down the telephone and looked at Brock and Plunger with the slightly maniacal grin of a man who had been too long in the line. "The Fascists are attacking," he said. "For you, it's just in time."

Brock stared at him. "Just in time?" he said.

"I shouldn't be telling you," the major said. "But the hell with them all. They were going to arrest you for treason. Both of you. They say you've been spreading subversive thoughts. Like that the Communists are deliberately keeping us short of supplies. We all know that rumor's nothing but a lot of crap, don't we?" He looked up at them from under the peak of his cap and closed one eye in a comically conspiratorial wink. He picked up a goatskin water bottle, held it at arm's length, and squirted red wine unerringly into his mouth.

The enemy guns now were firing with a steady thump, thump, thump. To the south a squadron of Dorniers was circling over Teruel as if pausing to relish the destruction they would cause.

Brock felt the sweat gathering in his armpits. For a moment, panic moved in on him like an insidious enemy always waiting for a weakness. He wanted to empty his bowels. It wasn't the

18

enemy attack. That was something he could understand and deal with. It was the thought of the little men plotting in dark corners while braver, more stupid soldiers took the bullets and shell fragments in the line. It was always the same, he thought desperately. It was how it had been in Ireland.

"Get up to the parapet," the major said. "I'm trying to reach Frank Ryan. We'll sort this out later. If we're still around later."

They started back toward the trenches. "They'll put us up against a wall," Plunger said. "Just like that poor English bastard."

"They won't touch us while the Fascists are attacking," Brock said. "We've got time to work it out."

"Should we take a walk, then, Michael? After the assault?"

"Desert?"

"It's better than a firing squad. These onion eaters are such awful shots. They could take all day killing you."

The position they took was protected by a jumble of limestone rocks and sandbags. All along the line they could see other Internationals tumbling into their positions, poking their weapons through or over the parapets.

"Look," Brock said. He had been right. From the Fascist lines facing Teruel, tanks were deploying across the saucer. At this distance they looked like evil black insects crawling over a white plate.

"The bastards," Plunger said.

Brock took out his opera glasses and studied the advancing tanks. Below the turrets, stubby guns were pointing up at extreme angles to give the greatest trajectories to their shells.

A machine gun began to fire from the Republican lines, but Brock knew the tanks were too far away, and bullets would not pierce their steel plating at any distance.

He focused on one tank which had rolled sideways into an arroyo and was struggling like a bound beast to extricate itself. The others came on.

The first shell from the tanks landed in front of the Republican parapets south of Brock and Plunger. It threw up a black burst of earth and rocks.

19

"Nineteen . . . twenty . . . twenty-one . . . twenty-two . . ." Brock said. "There's at least two dozen." Behind the tanks he could see hundreds of infantrymen. They were coming at a half crouch, loping across the snow to keep up with the tanks. He recognized the distinctive steel helmets.

"Italians," he said.

"Death to the Fascists," Plunger said. He was scowling down his rifle sights at the nearest infantrymen. He started to say something else when there was a sighing sound overhead, and a shell burst among the tanks.

"Thank Christ," Plunger said. "They've finally decided to do something about it."

"Russian seventy-five mm," Brock said.

"Holy Mother of God," Plunger shouted. "Will you look at that now." A second shell from behind the Loyalist lines had ripped apart one of the lead tanks. They could see the bodies of the crew flung about in the smoking wreckage. One man was trying to crawl away across the snow.

"We'll eat them for breakfast," Plunger shouted. "Come on, you bastards. Come on, and you'll all be shaking hands with St. Peter before you know it."

But there were no more shells from the Russian gun. The tanks had reached the incline up to the Republican parapets, and behind them came the Italian infantry.

Brock could see an officer, pistol in hand, shouting at his men, who were beginning to cluster behind the tanks for protection as they came within range of the Loyalist rifles. The rumbling scream of the tanks' tracks reached the ears of the defenders like a murderous threat. Brock realized he had not fixed his long bayonet, and he hastily clipped it into its slot.

"Sweet Mary, where's the artillery?" Plunger demanded.

Brock aimed at an aperture in the nearest tank. His old Remington, rusted and split at the stock, was an untrustworthy weapon, and he fired without hope. Plunger always joked that Brock had killed more men in Ireland than he had in the middle of a war. Up the line, the Loyalists had a captured mortar in action, but they could not get the range, and the mortar shells, the precious hoarded shells, were exploding harmlessly beyond the advancing tanks and infantry.

Plunger swore ferociously as he fired steadily at the infantry now in range. The Internationals could see the steel bellies of the tanks roaring up the slope, tilting, sliding, but always churning forward. The incline was so steep that the forward tanks, even with their guns depressed to the limit, could not hit the government trenches, but five had halted at the beginning of the slope and were pumping shells onto the rim of the hill. All up and down the line, the parapet was being demolished.

"Fall back! Fall back!" the cry was being passed down the trenches in English, Spanish, and French.

"Come on, hard man," Plunger shouted. "I'm out of ammo. Let's get away with us." They turned and ran to the left, looking for the communication trench. The noise from the tanks and the shells was overpowering.

"Here," Plunger screamed. "Down here." He stopped to make sure Brock was catching up and then ran into the communication trench.

Brock tripped over the body, grotesquely sprawled, of a man in a heavy greatcoat. He had time to see that it was the Dutchman, his back arched in agony, and then he was back on his feet. Brock was running hard when he felt a shattering pain.

It was as if a stick of dynamite had exploded in the back of his skull. He tottered, still upright for a moment, before he fell. For a moment, through the pain, he could hear the metallic screech of the tanks, the sounds of the Italian infantrymen shouting in triumph. But then there was no more pain, no more noise.

When consciousness returned, his eyes would not open. It was only later that he learned they were sealed with congealed blood. He heard voices, all speaking Italian. Sensing somebody at his side, he tried to sit up.

"Rejoice," a man said in Spanish. "There will be no more battles for you. Your war is over."

21

Chapter 3

Berlin
September 5, 1939

A SLIM, straight-backed army officer wearing civilian clothes walked briskly along the quay of the Landwehrkanal. He was Colonel Erwin von Lahousen, chief of the sabotage section of the Abwehr.

At 72–76 Tirpitz Ufer he entered a five-story gray-stone building, nodding acknowledgment to the salute of the uniformed sergeant standing inside the door. A small elevator took him to his office on the third floor, where he conferred briefly with subordinates. He made two telephone calls—one to his wife, who was vacationing with relatives in Düsseldorf—then gathered a red file from a wall safe and spent five minutes scanning the contents.

He glanced at the clock on his desk, a gift from his mistress, and saw that it was nine A.M. Lahousen tucked the file under his arm before bending down to speak to his secretary through the intercom.

"I'm going to see the admiral," he said. "Don't disturb us unless something vital comes up."

The elevator took him to the fourth floor, where another guard passed him through to a sparsely furnished anteroom. A naval commander greeted him. "The admiral is ready for you, Colonel," the commander said. "Go straight in."

Lahousen thanked him and walked through the open door. Admiral Wilhelm Franz Canaris, chief of the Third Reich's military espionage organization, smiled bleakly from his desk. Like Lahousen, he wore mufti. But his clothing fitted poorly, as if he were too impatient, too busy to bother with fittings by a good tailor. Canaris was not a man who indulged in small talk.

"It's good to see you back," he said. "Now, tell me, what is the status in Bavaria?" Lahousen had spent three days inspecting the saboteur training camp at Quenzsee.

22

"Not entirely satisfactory," the colonel said. He had not been invited to sit down, so he stood almost at attention in front of the admiral's desk. It was not a good sign. "We are straining the facilities. Too many students and not enough professors. There was that accident with the gelignite. . . ."

"You got rid of Dieckhoff?"

"He has been given a desk job in Hamburg. The problem was inexperience, nothing more. In spite of such incidents, the work proceeds. The shortage of instructors merely means there will be some delays in the training schedule. I will have a full report on your desk within the week."

They pursued the subject for several minutes before discussing the situation in Poland, where Canaris' agents were busily fomenting disorder behind the lines of the retreating Poles. Lahousen relaxed a little, noting the satisfaction in his chief's voice.

Canaris swung around in his chair to stare out the window at the canal below. Lahousen looked at the back of the admiral's gray head with something approaching affection. The old man was hard, but he was a professional; and so was his organization—the antithesis of the rival Sicherheitsdienst commanded by the young thug Heydrich.

"Let us move on to the English problem," Canaris said. "To be frank, I did not expect Chamberlain to stick in his heels over Poland. What is Poland to them? However, it is no good talking about what is past. They want war, and we must give it to them."

He turned back to his visitor and went on. "The English will be difficult. A small island. A tightly knit people with a class system that baffles me. Their counterespionage system is alert. They will present a formidable task. However, they will be your next priority concern."

"There has been some progress," Lahousen said. "There are people living in England who do not like the English."

"The Irish?" Canaris allowed a smile to crack his wintry features.

"They take themselves seriously," Lahousen said.

"And so do we all."

"They are not to be dismissed, Admiral. They won their independence, at least in the South, and historians will tell you that the Irish have been such an intractable problem for the English that a number of governments in London have fallen because of them."

"You think this IRA can bring down the Chamberlain government?"

Lahousen's voice quickened with enthusiasm. "The more I consider the matter," he said, "the more I'm convinced the IRA is a sharp weapon in the midst of the English, awaiting our use. The Irish travel freely between Ireland and England. They are accepted by the English as nobody from the Continent would be. They speak the same language. They work in the munitions plants, at airfields, around the docks. And they hate the English."

"The bombings they have recently committed—they have been inefficient, the work of amateurs."

"They need direction, Admiral."

"You mustn't misunderstand me, Lahousen. I don't oppose the concept by any means. It seems to me, too, that we have a ready-made espionage and sabotage system at hand. The question remains, How do we use it?"

"We are in touch with their headquarters in Dublin. They have already expressed an interest in working with us."

"What about their sections in England?"

"They are controlled from Dublin."

"Money?"

"Yes, Admiral, they want money. It's an organization noted for its poverty. We have already given them some as evidence of our interest and good faith. They're already asking for more."

"And what about MI Five?"

"Naturally London will be stepping up surveillance of Irish nationals in England, but there are so many that it is an impossible task. The British home secretary, Hoare, has brought in the Prevention of Violence Bill, which allows the government

24

to register all Irishmen and detain suspects. It was shortly afterwards that the IRA exploded those bombs at King's Cross Station and at Victoria Station in London. The Irish government also has been picking up suspects, for they fear the IRA as much as London does. But there will be enough Irish agents at large for our purposes."

The colonel was speaking with more optimism than he actually felt. He knew that the police pressure on both sides of the Irish Sea was hurting the IRA. Many of the most active gunmen and bombers were known to MI 5 and to the Free State police, who were busy picking them up or hunting them. The safest agents would be those unknown to the authorities, and these would be the less experienced men.

There was something else that worried him. From a brief study of the IRA he knew that it had been bedeviled by dissension, by incompetence and betrayal. Too many times its operations had suffered bad luck.

However, Lahousen was an ambitious man, and like most ambitious men, he preferred to give his superior encouraging news rather than risk displeasure with reality.

"How are you communicating with these men in Dublin?" Canaris asked.

"By radio," the colonel said, "and we have a courier system just going into operation. They are the ones who passed on the money."

"They signed for the cash?"

"Yes, Admiral." Not even the wizards of the Abwehr could escape the military bureaucracy which demanded an accounting of every pfennig.

"Very well. Now, I want a memorandum from you detailing the tasks that could be carried out by our Irish agents. If necessary, we can bring some of them over for training at Quenzsee. Perhaps you will have that in good order by then." The colonel noted that the Irishmen were now "our agents," but he did not miss the slight reproof in the reference to the Bavarian training camp.

"Yes, Admiral," he said.

25

"You should suggest targets. And you should confer with Colonel Piekenbrock to see what use he can make of the Irish in the gathering of intelligence."

Lahousen was well aware that the Abwehr was under continual pressure from the Luftwaffe and Kriegsmarine for information. Canaris' position depended on his satisfying their demands.

"Piekenbrock is familiar with our progress," Lahousen said.

"Good. Keep him informed. You must remember that we are interested in things other than sabotage, even though that is your field. There is feuding among the different sections. I want it to stop. I order that it stop. Competition is good; hostility is not."

"Yes, Admiral." The colonel was not used to such a scolding. Canaris must have heard about the squabble over the use of the radio network in Holland.

"You will cooperate with Piekenbrock, and he will cooperate with you, and there will be an end to this senseless bickering, you understand? We have no time for such childish games. I have already talked to him about this matter, and I shall expect to hear no more of it."

"Very well, Admiral."

Lahousen guessed that Piekenbrock had made the complaint about the sabotage section's use of the Dutch network. By raising the issue he had been able to advance his side of the petty dispute. He resisted the temptation to argue further. Nonetheless, he wondered uneasily if he had lost a point while his rival had gained one in Canaris' eyes.

Seeking recovery, he said, "You will be glad to know, Admiral, that one of the leaders of the IRA is coming to Berlin for discussions. He should be here in a couple of days."

"Who is this man?"

"His name is. . . . Excuse me." Lahousen flipped through his red file, then said, "His name is Donovan. Peter Donovan. He's an aide to their chief of staff, a man called Russell."

"I would like to meet him."

"Of course, Admiral. He should be able to tell us much

26

about their state of readiness. He will want money, of course."

"Our budget is not a cornucopia."

"The Irish are not ambitious in that respect, Admiral. A small amount satisfies them. I think they use it mostly to buy arms and to look after the families of men in jail."

"Very well, Lahousen. And let me have that report on Quenzsee as soon as possible."

Some hours later the sabotage chief arrived at the small apartment on the Reinerstrasse where a portion of his salary went to the support of a full-bosomed former secretary called Elsa Busch. She was pleased with his gifts from Bavaria and proudly modeled the folk costume he had bought, noting with satisfaction the way it emphasized the curve of her breasts.

Although he smiled at her posturing, she saw his thoughts were elsewhere, and she went to the kitchen to prepare the pork in the French way he preferred. Lahousen was wondering if he had made too much of the Irish agents with Canaris. Piekenbrock, damn him, would exult over his discomfiture if they let him down. When Elsa drew him to the big quilted bed, he was still brooding over the possibilities.

Peter Donovan was an inconspicuous man, especially in the cheap, worn raincoat he wore when he walked into Lahousen's office three days later.

The German officer noted with distaste that his visitor's shoes were cracked and muddy. There was a fuzz of stubble on Donovan's face. Lahousen's apprehensions about the Irish venture increased.

"Don't get up now," Donovan said, advancing with outstretched hand, his gait belying his years. "There's no need for formality between the two of us." There was surprising strength in his handshake.

"I'm glad you reached us safely, Mr. Donovan," Lahousen said, pointing to a chair.

"Ah, now I said there was to be no formality. Call me Peter."

"Very well," Lahousen said, wondering if Donovan planned to call him Erwin.

Closer now, he could see that Donovan's eyes behind wire-rimmed glasses were bright, even merry, above pouches of loose flesh.

"Would you care for some coffee?" he asked.

"I don't think so, Erwin," Donovan replied. "They gave me a good breakfast at that hotel. Most attentive they were. It reminds me of that joke about the old fellow who worked in the circus, looking after the elephants and cleaning out their stalls. Every so often he'd find himself in the wrong place, and one of the elephants would relieve himself on top of him and, Holy God, wouldn't that make a mess of him.

"Well, you can imagine that was a tough job, cleaning out all the leavings of a bunch of elephants and sometimes having all that shit landing on top of him. So somebody asked him why he didn't go out and find himself another, cleaner job." Donovan's eyes were dancing with amusement. Lahousen was smiling politely.

"The old fellow was shocked at the question," Donovan went on. "He says, 'Find another job? What, and leave show business?'"

Donovan rocked in his chair with mirth, while Lahousen summoned a laugh to hide his bewilderment. The Irishman, he saw, had very few teeth.

"What, and leave show business?" Donovan repeated, shaking his head at the beauty of it all. The German's thoughts were racing. He had expected a dedicated revolutionary, and they had sent him a comedian. He had wanted an ally from the enemy's midst, and they had sent him a clown.

"Very good," Lahousen said finally.

"Oh, Erwin, I have lots more like that," Donovan said. "But then, you don't want to hear my foolish jokes, I'm sure. We should get down to business, as the actress said to the bishop." He sat straighter in his chair and said, "We need arms and ammunition, and we need money. And we need them quickly."

Lahousen stared at him. The merry, winking eyes behind the spectacles had turned hard and purposeful. The voice, cracking with laughter seconds before, was now disconcerting-

28

ly cool and controlled. "We need them quickly," Donovan repeated.

"Of course. But there are other matters to be discussed," Lahousen said. He spoke unaccented English. "We have to be sure that the arms and the ammunition and the money are used in the best way. How many experienced men do you have?"

"We have units throughout Ireland, north and south, and in England, too. We have bomb experts, we have marksmen. We have men who know how to lay mines. We have men who learned their military trades in the British Army. But the most important thing about the Irish Republican Army is that our soldiers are dedicated to one belief—the belief that one day the English will be driven out and a free Ireland will arise."

Lahousen felt better. The clown had fled. He was now looking at the dedicated rebel he had expected. As a German, surrounded by Nazis but skeptical of their excesses, he thought he recognized a fanatic when he met one. This new Donovan—his eyes unblinking in resolution—this Donovan could have been a section leader at the Nuremberg rallies.

"Yes, a free Ireland will arise," Lahousen said. "That day will come." He was wondering how long the Führer and his chiefs of staff would tolerate an Ireland in the hands of such men. "If your colleagues are as determined and steely as you, then you could do great damage to the English," he said.

"There isn't a man among us who doesn't feel the same way," Donovan said. "We've fought the English for years, and we know them. We know how to deal with the bastards, all right: with bullets and bombs."

"I understood you were a professor in Dublin?"

"That's correct. Irish literature at Trinity College. But a way with the books doesn't mean you can't pick up a gun. There was a day when I took an English soldier's head clean off his shoulders with one burst of a tommy gun."

"Yet the English still control the northern section of your country."

"Aye," Donovan said. "But they're paying for it. Paying in

their own country to the tune of our bombs and bullets. And now—with the Germans against them as well—now is the time to strike until they are destroyed. We are ready."

Lahousen opened a box on his desk and offered his visitor a cigarette. Donovan shook his head and pulled out a blackened pipe.

"It is simple enough," Lahousen said. "We need agents in Britain. You need money and arms. There is no reason we cannot reach an accommodation that will suit us both."

He paused, watching Donovan stuff his pipe with tobacco from a battered tin. "We have the same aims," he went on, "the overthrow of the English. Naturally, German arms will accomplish that task eventually, but you could be of assistance in some ways." It would not do to exaggerate the importance of these Irishmen.

Donovan lowered his pipe, and when he looked at Lahousen, his eyes were hostile. "Give us what we need and we will do it," he said. "We will destroy them from within."

"Tell me what you need."

"Explosives, machine guns, rifles, and ammunition. We also need money."

"What are your targets?"

"I'm not authorized at this stage to detail such matters. But you may be sure that all your supplies will be put to good use against your enemies."

"There must be greater cooperation than that," Lahousen said. "There is a saying among the Irish, I believe, that he who pays the piper calls the tune. We're willing to support your efforts, but there has to be reciprocity in the form of action specifically required by the Reich."

"If it contributes to the downfall of the English, you will find we are more than willing to carry out the tasks suggested by your office. But, faith, that's something we can take up when we have what we need to act."

"Very well."

"There is the question of the delivery of the supplies to our units in Ireland. The De Valera government is maintaining

30

strict neutrality. In fact, it is cooperating with London in hunting down our men. The neutered bastards who claim leadership in Dublin are always ready to do the bidding of Whitehall. They will do anything to avoid what they call provocation."

"Then the deliveries must be surreptitious. It can be arranged."

"There is a place called Cobh on the southern coast."

"Very well. But that also is something that can be settled later."

"Colonel, we have waited a long time already. Too many years have passed. Too many brave men have died."

Lahousen's gray eyes lost their good humor. He stared at the little Irishman, and he said softly, "We have waited, too. Many Germans have died. We have starved and struggled and worked. We are not going to throw away our hand now because of impatience. We will act at the correct time, not before." It was a deliberate test of authority.

A spark glowed in Donovan's eyes for a moment, but then he said, "We can wait. But we need money."

Lahousen relaxed. "Yes, of course," he said. He opened his desk drawer and drew out an envelope bearing the stamp of the German Defense Ministry. He passed it to Donovan, who removed the bundle of marks it contained and counted them.

"This will buy food for some fatherless boys," he said. The remark was an acceptance of the amount.

"A good discussion, my friend," the colonel said with some relief. He had feared an argument over the money.

"We shall need more money later if we are to be effective," Donovan said.

"Of course, of course. When we know what your plans are. You're a deceptive man, Peter."

"Deceptive?"

Lahousen stubbed out his cigarette. "A professor and yet a soldier," he said. "They're a strange combination. Forgive me, but you look like neither."

The lines around Donovan's eyes deepened into a crinkle.

31

"You think I should be wearing a uniform or maybe an academic gown? If you knew Ireland, you would know that many things there are deceiving, hard to understand. It reminds me of the pilot who got a radio message from the airport down below. 'Give us your height and position,' they radioed to him."

Donovan was chuckling at what was to come. The clown was back.

"The pilot replied, 'I'm five foot ten inches, and I'm sitting at the front of the plane.'" Donovan rocked with mirth.

"Ah," Lahousen said, "very good, very good, indeed. Now let us go and see my chief, and then perhaps we can arrange some entertainment for you. A good meal, a few drinks, maybe some feminine companionship."

Donovan was wiping his eyes with a none-too-clean handkerchief, at the same time slipping the money into his pocket. "No, thank you all the same, Erwin," he said. "All I need is a bed and twelve hours' sleep. Then I'll be on my way back to Dublin. There's work to be done."

"Of course," the colonel said. "I will make the arrangements immediately. One thing first, though."

"Yes?"

"Perhaps you would be good enough to sign this slip. A mere formality. It's a receipt for the envelope."

Chapter 4

Dublin
February 4, 1940

SOMETIMES, always with a feeling of guilt, Brock wished that he had been born English. It would have been so easy then. Their battles were always fought in other countries. If they lost, then they simply returned home until they decided it was time to attack another land across the seas. If they won, they took over with cold, self-satisfied arrogance. They would begin to bleed their enemies, always, of course, talking about the twin glories of an incorruptible civil service and the gim-crack civilization which they were bestowing on the defeated. He could imagine the feelings of an English soldier returning to London—the satisfaction at the untouched solidity of the city, the heart of an empire, and never mind the blood that stained the flag that flew over palaces and town halls.

But he was not English, and London was not his city. This was. He looked at Dublin, smug and prim under the heavy gray clouds, the faces of pedestrians closed and self-satisfied. He could see no changes. Again the rage took hold, the fury at what had been thrown away by petty men of small ambitions. Swallowing his emotions like a poison, he walked toward home, a tall, thin figure still wearing the light-blue pants and ill-fitting jacket they had given him at the repatriation center in France.

His mother was dozing in her wheelchair in the kitchen, her crippled legs covered by a worn blanket. In the two years that he had been away she seemed to have aged ten. There were new creases at the sides of her thin mouth, and her skin was unhealthily pale. He kissed her and took her hand. Her eyes opened, and at first she stared at him without recognition. Then she knew him.

"Michael," she said. "Oh, my God, it's Michael."

"And who else would it be?" he said.

"Oh, Michael, Michael. And me so sure I'd never see you again." Her black eyes, the liveliest part of her wasted body, looked him over, and she began to rock herself as if with grief.

"But what have they done to you, Michael? You've no flesh on your bones. It's a skeleton you are."

"I was never a heavyweight," he said awkwardly. "A few of your potatoes, and I'll be back to my old self. They didn't serve boiled beef and cabbage in that prison camp. How are you, Mam?"

"Some tea. We must have a pot of tea." Both of them were

33

talking fast, as if speech could bandage the wounds of their parting.

He grinned down at her. "Now, you stay where you are," he said, "and I'll wet the tea." The pot was in the same place. Nothing had changed. The tea caddy was still on the window ledge, and through the window he saw the tiny concrete patch and the gate leading to the alley that ran behind the row of mean red-brick houses. But then he saw that a handrail had been set into the wall at an angle near the sink.

"I'm having more trouble with my legs," his mother said, noting his gaze. "Mr. Flynn, from upstairs, he put that in the wall to give me something to hold onto when I stand."

"Flynn?"

"The lodger," she said. "I have to get money from somewhere. You can't fish it out of the Liffey, Michael."

He sensed the cast of bitterness in her words, and he sighed as he turned up the gas. How long would it be before they were arguing again?

"I should have written more, but it wasn't always easy," he said, trying to extend the truce. "And then when I was captured. . . ."

"Ah, Michael, don't worry about that now," she said. "All I'm bothered with is, are you all right? Should you see a doctor?"

"No, Mam," he said. "The leg still hurts a bit sometimes, but the other thing was just a bit of shrapnel in my scalp. I've got a hard head like all the Brocks."

He poured boiling water into the pot, swirled it around to warm the inside, and then emptied the water into the sink. It was, he thought, the first time he had made a pot of tea since leaving Ireland.

"Have you heard anything of Plunger Cronin?" he asked.

"That great lout," she said scornfully. "Why would you want to find him?" Once his mother had seen Plunger very drunk. She did not consider him a serious man or worthy material for the organization. And there was the matter of his fondness for horses and bookmakers, the cause of his nickname. Casting around for reasons why Brock had gone to Spain instead of staying with the organization, she had settled the blame on the evil influence of Plunger.

"He saved me in Spain," Brock said angrily. "When I was first wounded. He carried me two miles to an aid station and risked a firing squad for leaving the line to do it. At Jarama, that was, when I still had some flesh on me."

His mother was unimpressed. "He didn't rescue you when the Eye-talians came at you with the tanks," she said. "He left you lying there and looked after his own skin."

"He did not," Brock said. "There was nothing he could do. The tanks were on top of us. He didn't know I'd been hit until he was out of the trenches, and by then the Italians were all around." Brock's hands were shaking. "If he'd come back, he'd have been killed. Would that have made you happy?"

"Don't you yell at me, Michael. Your own mother."

Brock turned away and stared out at the dismal concrete yard. It was useless.

"Plunger's up north," she said. "There was an ambush. An RUC man was killed. Plunger's on the run again."

So there it was. Plunger was back with the organization, already dodging from safe house to safe house.

"The General Army Convention had a meeting in Abbey Street," his mother said. "They've made Sean Russell chief of staff. You know what that means, Michael."

"I know," he said. It meant more bombing, more shooting, more funerals, more betrayals. "Russell's like the rest," he said. "They think they can throw out the English by blowing up customs posts."

"D'you not believe in it anymore, then?" His mother's lined face was taut.

"I do," he said. "But I tell you, Mam, we have to do more than ambush constables and take potshots at army barracks."

She drank her tea in silence. Then she said, "I didn't mean what I said when you left. I know you're no coward." It was the nearest she could come to an apology.

"It was said in the heat of the moment," he replied.

35

She wouldn't let it alone. "I was thinking about your father when I said it," she said.

"I know. But don't you see, Mam, I had to get away. All those years and all those good men lost and nobody seeming to believe in it anymore. Just a few of us."

"That's not true," she said sharply, her eyes bright. "The country would rise tomorrow if the word was given. Any house in Dublin would give shelter to one of the boys on the run."

"Giving shelter is not the same thing as revolution," he said. "The people here are content with their little lives and their bourgeois government and Mother England keeping an eye on us. In Spain I thought it would be different. It would be a straightforward fight between the Socialists and the Fascists. And it was at first. Then it got mixed up, like it is here."

"And what's mixed up about it here?" she demanded. "What's complicated about driving the English out of the Six Counties?"

"Ah, Mam, that's only part of it. D'you think things would be any different in Dublin if all the English soldier boys took ship back home? You'd still have the priests and the shopkeepers running everything. You'd still have the nuns in the schools. You'd still have the poverty and the youngsters catching the boat to America or England. Wild geese, you call them. Well, you won't tame those wild geese until we get what Wolfe Tone was after: a free socialist republic, out of the shadow of England. Aye, and out of the shadow of Rome, too."

"Wolfe Tone was no socialist," she said. Both knew the argument by heart.

"It was what he wanted," he said. "The factories and the farms and the shops and the schools in the hands of the people. Like it was in Catalonia until the Fascists came. No bowing and scraping. No 'yes, sir, no, sir.' They looked each other in the eye, and everybody was his own man."

"I'm sure you know more than I do," his mother said, secure in her own knowledge. "But that will come later, after the English have left the Six Counties."

It was the same argument, he thought, that had smashed

36

the alliance between the Anarchists and the Communists in Spain.

"After we've driven them out, Michael," she went on. "That's what your father, God love him, was about when he was taken."

His father. It always came back to his father. He remembered the feverishly bright eyes behind the bars, and he remembered the chill of the prison and the words of his father: "Look after your mother, Michael, for you're all she has now." They shook hands through the bars, and they both knew he didn't have long.

Brock's father had been a member of the Dublin Third Battalion, but he had been arrested while conducting a court-martial in Derry. He had been sent north to direct the affair as an outsider, free of bias against the suspect. There were ten of them: the three on the court-martial board, four witnesses, two guards, and the youngster suspected of informing. It was the classic offense against the IRA, and the penalty was death.

The Royal Ulster Constabulary swooped down on them before any evidence could be presented. The authorities charged the court-martial members and the guards and waiting witnesses with treason. Brock's father got seven years, and he was sent to Crumlin Road Prison. It was there that he died three months later. Cause of death: "heart failure."

"You'll take me to visit his grave," his mother said.

"I will."

"There'll be flowers to buy."

"We'll do it tomorrow. First I must see McGrath. Where is he?"

"I'll find out from Mary Brady."

"Oh, so Cumann na mBan is still at work?" Brock did not take the women's arm of Sinn Fein very seriously, though he admitted it had its uses. It was a Cumann na mBan girl, Elizabeth O'Farrell, who had taken the surrender message to the British after the Rising.

"Is Maggie still a member?" he asked.

"She is," his mother said. "The last I heard she was down in Cork."

"She never wrote to me."

"Did you ever write to her?"

"I sent a message."

"She'll come running when she knows you're back." She looked at him slyly. "Although I heard she was going to get married. She's not a girl anymore."

"She's only twenty-seven."

"She's twenty-eight," his mother said.

"How's her dad?"

"He's all right as long as the pubs don't run dry. You know your Uncle Matthew is dead."

"You said so in one of your letters."

"In his sleep. There was no pain, thanks be. He left us a bit of money in his will. You remember the bicycle?"

"I remember."

His Uncle Matthew had always been the one with a bit of money. One of the "wild geese," he had emigrated to America at the turn of the century, settled in Brooklyn, and opened a tavern near the docks. This had given him a steady income. He had flirted with politics, that favorite sport of the Irish in New York, and he had worked for Clan na Gael, the fundraising branch of Sinn Fein in America. To Brock he had been a figure touched with the glamor of distant places, a glamor enhanced by the money in his pocket. The bicycle had been a gift to his brother Patrick, older than Michael by four years.

Whenever Uncle Matthew arrived from America for a visit, he brought with him his heartiness, his cigars, his tales of the strange country across the sea. This time there was a watch for Michael, one which his mother made him keep at home for fear he might lose it. There was a cowboy outfit for Frank, who was to die of tuberculosis within the year. And there was the bicycle for Patrick.

"How's Pat?" Brock asked.

"Ah, Patrick is doing well," his mother said. "They've made him a sergeant now. He's in charge of the gambling in a place called Greenwich Village."

38

Brock laughed out loud. When he laughed, his saturnine features lightened, and he looked much younger.

"The police are supposed to *stop* gambling, Mam, not run it," he said.

"Oh, Michael, you know what I mean. He's talking about coming over for a visit."

Patrick was only sixteen when he ran away from home. The next they heard from him was a letter from New York. Brock always suspected his older brother had been encouraged by Uncle Matthew to take the boat to America—if not by words, then by example. There was nothing the family could do about it. Finally they gave permission for Patrick to stay, as long as he lived with his uncle. When he was twenty-one, he took the test for the police department, and now he was married and had two children.

But to Brock the chief significance of his brother's decision to find a new life lay in the bicycle. For with Frank dead, the bicycle passed to Michael, and to a twelve-year-old boy a bicycle meant freedom. Freedom to roam the city, even to ride out to Tallaght and into the country beyond. When he wasn't riding it, he was polishing it and oiling the chain and checking the pressure in the tires. It did not matter to Brock that it was an English bicycle. He made no connection between the English manufacture of the cycle and all the talk he heard at home of the English rulers in the castle and the way the country groaned under their heels.

His father had been a believer in the legacy of republicanism left by Tone, after whom he had named his last child, Michael Wolfe Brock. But, as always, the movement was riven by arguments about how, when, and where to act. The discussions had gone on and on in the same kitchen where Brock now sat, and he could remember many nights when he had fallen asleep at his father's feet while names like MacDiarmada and Pearse and Connolly flew about like ricocheting bullets.

The story of 1916 had been distorted into myth by exaggeration and fiction and time, but Brock, more than twenty years

39

later, could remember the events he had witnessed. He clung to the memories as if to the saddle on a bucking horse.

When they read the Proclamation of the Republic from the steps of the post office, he was cycling along Sackville Street. He saw the crowd, abandoned his machine against a wall, and pushed his way through the throng.

Standing in the sunshine in front of the Ionic pillars of the building was a group of men in the slouch hats and gray-green uniforms of the Volunteers. Padriac Pearse was still reading the Proclamation, while other men stuck copies to the walls of the post office. A scattered cheer, more defiant than victorious, came from the Republicans as a green flag appeared on the roof. Clerks and customers were leaving the building at the urging of armed men.

Brock was enthralled. When the reading was done he followed the rebels into the post office. One man, carrying a pistol, tried to block his path, but Brock dodged by him and scuttled into the hallway. He looked around at the scene of urgent chaos. Men were breaking windows and setting up lines of fire. Others were ripping down the bars that separated customers from post office workers. Every telephone, public and official, was in use. A first-aid station was being set up in one corner.

Behind the counter a red-faced man slammed down a telephone receiver and shouted, "They've taken the Four Courts." A cheer went up, and the red-faced man shouted, "Ireland forever!"

"Who are you and what d'you want?" Brock had felt a hand on his shoulder, and he turned around to see a muscular young man with a lock of black hair falling over a broad forehead.

"Michael Wolfe Brock, sir," he said.

"And what's your business here, young fella?"

"I want to help."

"Do you, now? And how could you help, a little fella like you?" The man was amused by the earnest white face of the boy. Brock, sensing sympathy, thought furiously.

"I've a bike," he said. "It's outside."

40

"Oh, you've a bike, have you? This is serious business we're at. How would your bike help us?"

"I could carry messages. I can ride very fast when I've a mind to."

The young man hesitated, and then he said, "Come with me, Michael Wolfe Brock. It would surely be a shame if a fella like you wasn't allowed to help on the day that Ireland gets its freedom."

He led the way to a small group of men who were talking off to one side. Brock guessed they were officers.

"Eamon," the young man said, "I've got a recruit for you. He wants to join up to fight for a free Ireland."

The man he addressed was small and sharp-featured, with dark, darting eyes. "Faith," he said, "you'll be bringing us babes in arms next, Michael. This is man's work we're at, and we've no place for a boy."

Brock saw his chance slipping away. "I can take messages for you, sir," he said quickly. "I've got a bike, and I know my way down every street in Dublin."

The little man stared at him and then burst into laughter. "You want to see your grave so early, then? How old are you, my brave boyo?"

"I'm fifteen, sir." Brock didn't look fifteen, but then he looked older than his twelve years.

"He's eager to help," the young man said.

The others were trying to get Eamon's attention. "All right," he said, starting to turn away. "You see that telephone over there, with the man talking? You go and wait there until we call you."

The young man grinned down at Brock. "You're a member of the Volunteers," he said. "Allow me to shake your hand and introduce myself. I'm a lover of poetry, a fighter for Ireland, helpless in the hands of a handsome woman, and my name is Michael Collins."

Nearby a man was swearing steadily at the telephone in his hand. "Dead as a kipper," he said finally, tossing it away in disgust.

"They still have the telephone exchange," Collins said. "Did you expect them to let you call up your best girl in the middle of an insurrection, then?"

From across the river the men in the post office could hear the boom of British guns. The sound of a commotion outside reached Brock. Running to one of the barricaded windows, he saw that the crowd, swirling like a whirlpool, was falling back. Within minutes it was a stampede.

Collins used his height to thrust his head above the barricade and crane toward the cause of the panic. When he reappeared, his face was grim.

"Well, boyos," he said, "this is it. The Lancers are coming."

Other men at other times would describe the advance of the Lancers on the post office as one in a long line of gallant stupidities committed by British arms. But the sight of the column of horsemen filled Brock with a strange mixture of fear and admiration.

They knew, these British soldiers, that armed and desperate men awaited them behind the broken windows. Yet they trotted forward, rising and falling in their saddles, their backs stiff with the hauteur of a hundred Lucifers, and their guns remained in their leather holsters. The crowd had gone now, and the only sound was the clatter of the horses' hooves and the gentle jingle of their accouterments. At their head an officer rode with easy grace, his saber slapping comfortably against his booted leg.

Suddenly Brock was thrust to one side, and one of the rebels took his place. In his hands was a rifle. Other men were rushing to take their places at the broken windows. Now Brock could see nothing but the backs of men peering out the windows along the lengths of their rifles.

He remembered the upper windows. He turned and scampered for the stairs, his heart thumping. When he reached the second floor, he found the windows there, too, were manned by armed men; but there were no barricades, and he would look down over their shoulders. He was just in time.

The Lancers, every man staring fixedly over his horse's head, were passing directly in front of the bulk of the post

42

office. Brock guessed they would halt, then turn to confront the rebels. To the English, engaged in the Flanders slaughter, this must have seemed no more than an inconsequential irritation.

"Fire! Fire!"

Immediately, every gun at every window blazed. It was as if the rebels were a firing squad, the cavalry the condemned. Brock was stunned by the noise. As soon as the sound of the guns died away, Sackville Street was filled with the screams and shouts of wounded men, the frantic neighing of their mounts, the clatter of men falling to the cobblestones. Within seconds the proud column had been reduced to a shambles of blood and death. Bodies littered the street. Wounded horses screamed in agony. One big bay went racing south, dragging its rider, whose foot was caught in the stirrup. Men were trying to crawl away. Brock watched in fascination as a trooper, one arm dangling uselessly, reached up to grasp the hand of an unscathed comrade still in the saddle. He tried desperately to pull himself up so that he could vault onto the horse's back, behind his fellow trooper.

For a moment it looked as if he would succeed. But then, half on the beast's back, his strength failed, and he toppled helplessly to the cobblestones. His head cracked against the stones, and there was a spurt of blood before he lay still. His fellow trooper hesitated for a moment, staring down in dazed horror, but then he collected himself and turned to obey a shouted command.

For the officer had survived, and he was re-forming his command. His back was as straight as it had been before the fusillade. He had drawn his saber, but his revolver remained in its holster. The insurgents watched in silence as the decimated column, back under discipline, began to withdraw.

"Why don't you shoot him?" Brock asked the man over whose shoulder he was staring. "He'll be back with more."

"We're under orders," the man said, but his sights were trained on the officer's back, and his trigger finger was curled.

43

No order came, and the Lancers trotted away to the south. Now it was impossible to hear the jingle of bridles and accouterments because the guns across the river were booming again. They sounded closer.

Brock was surprised that there was no sense of triumph in the post office. Nobody cheered. Nobody sang. When he returned down the stairs, he found the insurgents standing in groups, talking in low tones. "They'll be back, and next time they'll have their guns in their hands," he heard one man say.

He found Collins cleaning his gun. "They've gone," Brock said.

"Aye," Collins said. "We gave them a bloody nose."

He looked closely at the youngster. "Did you enjoy it, then, Michael Wolfe Brock?"

"It was good to see the English hit."

"Don't enjoy it too much," Collins said. "That's not what this is about."

The boy looked at him in puzzlement. "Isn't killing them the only way to get rid of them?" he asked.

"It may be," Collins said, his normally cheerful features suddenly somber. "But there are those who forget the goal and think only of the means. There is a evil that goes with the killings of men, whoever they may be. Some men, they do so much killing that it's all they have in their lives. Faith, they'd be unhappy if there was no longer any reason to kill."

Brock didn't understand. "Perhaps the soldiers won't come back," he said. "Perhaps they'll leave us alone."

"Perhaps," Collins said, the grin returning to his face.

"What will happen if the English leave?"

"Oh, Michael Wolfe Brock, there'll be dancing in the streets first, you can be sure of that. And the landlords of the pubs will become rich men, you can be sure of that, too. Soon, we'll all be speaking in the Gaelic and running our own country. We'll get rid of the bureaucrats and the priests who try to own our lives, and we'll have our own literature and our own music and to hell with what London says is fashionable.

44

"And the wild geese, they'll come back, Michael. They'll fly back with all the knowledge they've picked up in foreign countries, and we'll put it to good use in Ireland, where, by God, we need it. They'll bring their money, too, for we certainly need that. And those who can't come home for one reason or another, they'll give us their support whether they live in America or England or even down in Australia. Ah, Michael, we'll make a country you'll be proud to live in."

"Will they make you President, Mr. Collins?"

Collins roared with laughter. "Sure they will; but not right away, Michael. Perhaps they'll put me in charge of the treasury first, and then I can buy you a new bicycle. Except I don't like taxes, and without them there won't be much in the treasury, maybe not even enough to buy a bicycle."

"Can I stay with you, Mr. Collins?"

"Oh, so you want to make sure you get that new bike?"

"No, no." Brock was horrified. "It's not that at all, not at all. I want to help you get rid of the English. You said I could."

"Well, now, things are different from what they were a little while back. There's been bloodshed, and I fear there'll be more. The next time it won't be pretty soldier boys on horseback. It'll be artillery, and there's no fun in that sort of fighting." He paused and looked down at the eager boy.

"How old are you, Michael? The truth."

Brock stared down at his scuffed shoes. "Twelve," he said.

"That was about my guess," Collins said. "Now listen, Michael. Listen to me, and remember what I say. You've had your baptism of fire, and you were as brave as any Irishman, and that's why I'll tell you what I'm telling you now." He lowered his voice.

"The English will come, and they will destroy us. They'll kill us for rebelling against the Crown when they've got a tidy war on their hands in France. They'll call it treason, and those they don't kill here they'll hang, like they've hung others before. I know you'd march by my side to the gallows, but it'd make no sense. D'you know why?"

45

Brock stared up at Collins and shook his head. No adult had ever spoken to him like this before, and it was the most exciting thing that had ever happened to him. Except, perhaps, when the shots tore into the cavalry.

"Because Ireland needs you alive, Michael. When I'm gone and all these fine fellows in this fine post office, when we're all gone, there has to be someone to carry on what we were trying to do."

"But, Mr. Collins, why did you all come here if you knew you would be killed?"

"It's not easy answering that one. The best I can do is say that sometimes you know what you have to do. Besides, perhaps we won't be killed. Perhaps this uprising will have some effect. Ireland is a curious place, and curious things happen here. Now, away with you. Away home and look after yourself. And remember this day and this place."

Brock knew from the finality in Collins' voice that argument was pointless. He turned away and walked slowly across the hall to the main door. That was where his father found him.

"Your mother's out of her mind with worry," his father said, seizing him by an arm. "You'll come straight home, and you won't go out again until this is done with." He was very angry.

And so the young Volunteer was led ignominiously away. When they reached his bicycle, Brock turned and gazed at the post office. Looting had begun in the shops along Sackville Street. But the post office, with its barricaded windows, was silent and still.

"Come on, boy," his father said. "Pick up your bicycle, and let's be on our way before the British come."

Brock hesitated, for he had seen a tall figure standing in the shadows of the main door, a rifle slung over his broad shoulders. Above the sound of the looters breaking windows and their cries of excitement he could hear the man in the doorway shouting to him.

"Remember us, Michael Wolfe Brock," the man yelled. "And remember me."

Chapter 5

TOMMY O'BRIEN and his Five Shamrocks, all dressed in green pants and green jackets, were playing a tune that had reached Dublin from New York by way of London. It was catchy and energetic, and the dancers were sweating and laughing as they stamped around the floor. Above them a re-volving multifaceted chandelier cast a kaleidoscope of colors on the swirling bodies.

Brock watched them for a moment and then, as instructed, went to the door at the side of the cramped bandstand. A man, wearing a belted raincoat in spite of the heat, stood in front of the door, his restless eyes studying the crowd. Brock noted that his right hand was in the pocket of his rain coat.

"Is there any way I can help you?" the man said. His fore-head, below slicked-back red hair, was shiny with sweat.

"You look hot," Brock said.

"I'm all right. What d'you want?"

"I have to see McGrath."

"Who?" The man didn't move from the door.

"Jack McGrath."

"What's your name, then?"

"Brock. McGrath's expecting me."

"You're late," the guard said. He stepped to one side. "You can go in. No, wait a minute." He was staring across the dance floor.

"What's the matter?"

"Special Branch," the man said. "That joker in the tweed jacket. The bastards are everywhere." So the Special Branch, the creatures of the Dublin government, were still at work, hounding the Volunteers just as their British predecessors had, but with the extra viciousness men seem to reserve for their own kind.

"Who are they after?" Brock asked.

"They'll take anybody whose face they don't like. You've been away, have you?"

"I came back yesterday."

"All right, now, listen. You take a walk. Go to the bar and have a beer. Then come back. I doubt he'll stay long."

Ten minutes later, when Brock returned to the door, the man nodded at him silently and opened the door. "The bastard's gone," he said.

It was a small room, bare but for a table and some folding chairs. An unshaded bulb dangled from the flyblown ceiling. It was even warmer than the dance floor area, for there was hardly enough room for the eight men, who sat on chairs or stood against the walls.

Brock looked around. He knew some of the men from the old days. Paddy McGovern. O'Neill, who'd taken over from Ross as the gelignite expert. Rory Tobin. Joe O'Connor, who'd worked with his father. And McGrath, of course.

McGrath was sitting at the table, looking at Brock with a faint grin on his thin lips. As always he wore a cloth cap. Brock had never seen him bareheaded. McGrath did not rise, made no effort to shake his hand.

But Paddy did. "*Cead mile failte romhat abhaile.* It's good to see you again, Michael," he said. "It's good you got back in one piece." Then the others shook his hand as well. But not McGrath.

"We heard you were wounded, Michael," he said. "It doesn't show."

"Nothing serious," Brock said. "It's good to see you, too."

"Yes, well, we'll do the socializing later," McGrath said. "This is supposed to be an official meeting, so we'd best get on with it."

Brock leaned back against the door and folded his arms across his chest. "Who ordered the meeting?" he asked.

"Sean Russell," McGrath said. "He's chief of staff now, you know, Michael."

"I know."

"He wanted us to have a talk with you. To find out how you are and that sort of thing."

"To check me out?"

"Ah, Michael, we don't need to do that. We all know you and what you've done for the organization. There's nobody more loyal than Michael Brock."

"Except that I went to Spain. Is that it?"

"Now don't get on your high horse. A lot of boys went to Spain. Those who thought it more important than Ireland."

Brock stood up straight, away from the door. "If that's the way it's going to go, I'll be leaving right now," he said. His voice was harsh with anger.

Paddy McGovern hastily intervened. "Now, Michael," he said. "Jack didn't mean that the way it sounded. You and Cronin and the rest of them had every right to go to Spain. A lot of them never came back, although if you listen around the pubs, you'll find that more men came back from Spain than ever went."

"I'll tell you why I went to Spain," Brock said. "I went because I'd had a bellyful of doing the dirty work for men who think putting a bullet in a customs post is a victory. I'd had enough of following the orders of officers with ambitions as mean as their abilities. Officers who are frightened of Mother England, whatever they may say at Bodenstown or when they're standing each other drinks."

"You're angry, and who can blame you?" McGovern said. "You were right about a lot of things and some of us know it now."

"Anyway, you're back now, Michael," Rory Tobin said. "And things are going to be different with Sean Russell running the organization."

"How will they be different?"

McGrath cut in. "First we have to know if you've come back

49

to work with us," he said. "You did fine work before, and there's more to be done. Are you with us?"

"You know I am, McGrath. But I'm damned if I'll do any more shooting of constables when their backs are turned. I heard that Plunger Cronin's on the run again."

"He'll be in Dublin tomorrow," Rory Tobin said.

"What's Sean Russell up to, then?"

"You know he always wanted to take the fight to England. Like you."

"We were always overruled," Brock said bitterly.

"Have you not been reading the papers, then, Michael?" McGovern asked.

"They don't deliver the papers in a prison camp."

"That explains it, then," McGrath said. "You haven't heard about our boys in England. They've been livening things up with a bit of dynamite and such. Keeping the English on their toes. And there's more to come, much more. We'll blow up the houses of Parliament before we're finished. It's going to be a real campaign that will set England ablaze from north to south."

"Where's the money coming from?"

"That's one of our problems, Michael. It always has been. That's what we wanted to talk to you about."

"A bank job?"

"That's about the size of it."

"Where?"

"Are you willing?"

"Sure, I am. If the money's going to England."

"We have a nice one in mind, Michael. A nice English bank here in Dublin."

"See," Tobin grinned, "we use their own money to blow them sky high."

"You'll work with Plunger Cronin and the O'Bannon brothers. You remember Jamie O'Bannon, from Armagh?"

"He'll do."

"You'll be issued with machine guns and ammunition."

McGrath nodded toward a small, monkey-faced man in a black suit. "That's Jockey Hogan," he said. "He'll have a car, and he'll be at the wheel."

"Jockey knows how to drive a car better than he knows how to ride a horse," Tobin said.

"Who'll be in command?" Brock asked.

"It's your operation. Up to a point."

"What d'you mean?"

"After you've scouted the place, headquarters has to approve your plan. We're not gangsters."

"All right, that suits me. Which bank are we going to hit?"

"You'll be told later, Michael. The fewer people who know about it the better."

"I understand. Do you have a date in mind?"

"Yes, we do. But you'll be told that later, too."

Brock thought, So it starts again. He wondered if there would be any shooting. He thought sourly of other bank robberies that had gone wrong, and he wished for a moment that they had some of the expertise of Chicago gangsters.

"That's it, then," McGrath said. "We'll be in touch with you." And now he stood up, came around the table, and shook Brock's hand. "It's good to have you back with us, Michael," he said.

"Let's go and have a drink," Tobin said.

"One at a time," McGrath said. "The Special Branch bastards could still be hanging around."

The next day Plunger Cronin arrived in Dublin. Within three hours he and Brock were drinking in a pub on Francis Street. Brock's spirits lifted as he listened to Plunger's laughter. It seemed to fill the bleak saloon with warmth. But eventually Brock said, "They've got a job lined up for us, then, Plunger."

"Aye," Plunger said. "Just like old times, Michael. The O'Bannon boys are good. We should have no trouble."

"You sound as if you're looking forward to it."

"Well, it's what we wanted, isn't it? A go at England in her

51

own backyard. Did you hear what they've got lined up for me. They're talking about making me a member of the Army Council."

"They must be in a bad way."

Plunger grinned, and then he said, "Well, I'll tell you the truth, Michael. We're short of men. The youngsters don't come to the flag like they used to in the twenties. Do you remember what that English writer said about the young fellows, then? That they were haunted by the dream of dying for Ireland?"

"I remember," Brock said. "Some of them were."

"Well, they're not anymore. They're more interested in their football and their pints and their girls. The country is rampant with apathy."

"I don't believe it can be that bad. They're still Irishmen," Brock said. He felt depressed and tired.

"Now, Michael, don't let it pull you down. Let's have another drink." We walked over to the bar and called for the bartender.

When he returned with the drinks, he said, "The spirit's still there. The flame is low, but it'll burn bright given a chance. *Slainte!*"

Brock took his drink. "May the giving hand never falter," he said absently.

The only other occupant of the bar, an old man who had been talking to himself in a corner, stumbled to his feet and walked out. Plunger watched him go and then took Brock by his arm.

"Michael," he said, "there's something I can tell you that will lift your heart. We're on to something big. A real chance to get England's foot off our necks."

"Go on."

"You know Peter Donovan? The little professor-pal of Sean Russell?"

"I saw him only once. His brother worked with me up in the Six Counties."

"He's doing six years. The brother, I mean. Not Peter. Peter has been making some trips abroad, making friends with people who can help us. An alliance."

"That's an important word for a little man like Peter Donovan. Who's he made an alliance with?"

"The Germans, Michael. He's been to see them in Berlin, and they're going to help us. Money, arms, and ammunition. We're in radio contact with them, and big things are brewing."

Brock took a pull on his beer. After Spain he did not like the Germans. He remembered the day he had been marched through the streets of Saragossa, a member of a long column of prisoners. A group of pilots from the Condor Legion had been drinking on the sidewalk outside a café. As the column reached them, the pilots got to their feet and strolled forward until the prisoners were passing by within a few feet. They looked crisp and smart in their blue uniforms, and Brock could see the contempt on their faces as they watched the parade of beaten men, many bandaged, some on poorly made crutches.

One of the Germans, a trim-waisted dandy with a black and white terrier on a leash, turned to say something to his friends, and they roared with laughter. Brock felt sudden anger. These were the men responsible for Guernica and a hundred other atrocities.

As he approached the group, he straightened up, and he had to struggle with the temptation to throw himself at the laughing pilots. He stayed in line, but he glared at the dandy, and he shouted, "May you rot in the fires of hell, you bastard."

Instantly a Spanish guard was on him, jabbing him in the belly with the butt of his rifle.

"*Ein Engländer*," said one of the pilots in surprise. "Come here, you." The guard pushed him toward the fliers while the column marched on.

The German who had ordered him forward was large and corpulent, too big, Brock guessed, for the cockpit of a fighter plane. A bomber.

"Why does an Englishman fight with this rabble?" the German said, gesturing at the ragged column. "You're a Communist?"

Brock stood on splayed feet in front of the Germans, trying to regain the breath driven from his lungs by the guard's rifle.

"Why do you kill women and children?" he said at last. "Do you enjoy it?"

The German's fingers played with the holster securing a revolver to his hip. "Don't talk to a German officer like that," he said. Suddenly his fist shot out, connecting with Brock's already sore belly. As Brock doubled up, the German brought his knee up into his face.

The terrier was barking with excitement, straining at his leash in an effort to reach Brock, whose nose was streaming with blood. Finally, with a great effort, the Irishman straightened up.

"You'll still rot in hell," he muttered. "All of you."

The beefy German lifted the flap of his holster and took out his revolver. Brock suddenly realized the Germans were drunk.

"Gerhart," one of them said, "blow his Communist head off." He spoke in English to make sure that Brock would understand.

The German called Gerhart raised his revolver until it was pressing against Brock's throat. "Do you know who my favorite Spaniard is?" he said. His voice was thick, and Brock could smell brandy on his breath. Brock said nothing.

"A general who lived in the nineteenth century," Gerhart went on. "That's my favorite Spaniard, General Narváez. When he was on his deathbed, he was asked if he forgave his enemies. Do you know what he said? Do you, you Communist rat?" He pressed the revolver into his victim's neck until Brock winced with pain.

"No? Well, I'll tell you. He said, 'My enemies? I have none. I have had them all shot.'" Brock could not see the German's hand, but he sensed that the finger was tightening on the trigger. He clasped his hands in front of his groin and, whimpering with desperation, smashed them up against the German's hand.

It was impossible to tell if the German meant to pull the trigger or if it was Brock's action that caused the revolver to fire. The bullet sang away over Brock's head. The dog was barking louder than ever. A volley of words came from the pilots, but Brock could not understand any of them. He felt sick.

And then the fliers were turning away to look at the German officer who was walking toward them, shouting angry orders as he strode up.

In spite of their drunkenness, the group snapped to attention. Brock was ignored. He stood there, trying to stanch the flow of blood from his nose, until the guard pushed him back toward the tail of the column of prisoners. The last he saw of the German pilots, they were climbing into an open Mercedes tourer parked against the curb outside the café. The terrier was still barking.

Plunger said, "Ah, Michael, neither of us give a bucket of cold spit for the Germans, but we need them now."

"You don't have to persuade me," Brock said. "I'll take guns from Judas himself if it'll help Ireland get its freedom."

"That's right, Michael. A bullet's a bullet, whether it comes from America or from the Ruhr. And if the aim is true, the result is the same."

Brock looked around the dismal saloon, at the tawdry advertisements for Smith's Potato Crisps, at the bare wooden floor, at the cracked mirror which distorted everything it reflected. The popping gas fire under the mirror was too weak to banish the cold.

"We're a sad lot, the Irish," he said finally. "Will you look at this place? They should have a coffin in the corner, and then it would really be a jolly spot."

"It'll be different one day, Michael. Let the Irish bud come to full flower, and it'll all be different."

"Why do we have to pull off this bank job if the Germans are sending us supplies? Are they testing me, is that it?" Brock said. He said it without rancor.

"No, no, Michael. You mustn't think that. We're getting money, but the Army Council says it should go to the families of men who are locked up. And there's something of a problem about shipping in the arms and ammunition. We still need the money."

"When's it going to be?"

"Next Friday. Which means there's a lot to do."

"I'm ready, Plunger."

"But first there's something you'll be even more interested in."

"And what's that?"

"Maggie. She's back in Dublin."

The Gresham Hotel was in the center of Dublin. It boasted a top-hatted doorman, good service, and even better food. It was the favorite of fox-hunting families from the country who stayed there when they came into the city for horse shows and balls.

Plunger had given Brock the room number, so he went straight to the old elevator, which groaned its way up to the fifth floor. At the end of the corridor he knocked on the door. It was opened almost immediately.

"Hello, Maggie," he said.

She drew him inside, closed the door. "Oh, Michael," she said. "You're so thin." And then she went into his arms. Over her shoulder he saw that the room overlooked O'Connell Street. A lace curtain shifted gently in the wind coming through the half-open window, and the noise of traffic made a soft murmur. The room was spacious and comfortably furnished. To the left there was a bathroom. Hunting prints, gay and colorful, hung on the walls. Near the window, a big bed.

"Has somebody left you some money, then, Maggie?" he asked.

"Ah, no, Michael," she said, still holding him. "I've been saving every penny. Just so we'd have a nice place to be together in. Isn't it grand?"

"Not as grand as you, Maggie."

"Still the old Michael. A cartload of blarney and not to be trusted an inch." She went to the telephone, dialed, and grinned at Brock.

"This is Room Five oh Five," she said. Her voice had changed. Now it was upper-class English, high-pitched and touched with arrogance. "I want a bottle of French champagne," she said, winking at Brock. "Make sure it's chilled, and bring two champagne glasses, and be quick about it." She put down the receiver as Brock broke into laughter.

"You see," she said, reverting to her natural voice, "I'm not just your ordinary colleen. No, indeed, I can be as la-di-da as any of the old hags who spend their days bouncing up and down in the saddle and their nights bouncing up and down on any men they can get their hands on. Ah, Michael, let me look at you."

His hands on his hips, he grinned at her. She was as slim as ever, her black hair falling below her shoulders, her blue eyes shining as she looked directly at him. Below a loose gray sweater, her long legs were covered with black trousers.

"You look as if you're ready for the barricades," he said.

"I'm ready for something else first," she said. "Give me your mouth, Michael."

They were still kissing when the maid knocked on the door. She touched his nose with her lips and went to open it. The maid carried in a bottle and glasses on a tray and set it on a small table in the middle of the room.

"Will you be wanting anything else?" the maid said. She was no more than sixteen, a small creature with frightened eyes, awed, it seemed, by people who ordered champagne in the daytime.

"If there is, we'll ring," Maggie said. "Here," and she gave the girl a shilling before she scuttled out.

"Pour me some champagne, Michael," she said. "I'm going to take a bath." She left him.

57

Brock's hands shook slightly as he opened the bottle. It was a long time since he had had a woman. He had lived too long in a world of men. He remembered now the whores in Paris on his way home. After Spain and the prison camp they had looked like goddesses, but with his penury they were as unattainable.

"Won't you bring my glass of champagne to me, then, Michael?" Maggie called to him. "And bring your own in, as well."

A cold glass in each hand, he walked into the bathroom. It was warm and steamy. Maggie was stretched full-length in the big old-fashioned tub, smiling up at him. She had pinned up her long hair.

"How wonderfully decadent, me all naked and you fully dressed," she said, lifting a dripping hand to take her glass. Holding it carefully, she maneuvered herself into a sitting position so that she could drink. They sipped the wine, she smiling up at him, he gazing down over the rim of his glass. Her shoulders and her small, high breasts gleamed from their immersion. His eyes moved down her slightly rounded belly to the hair moving gently in the water like a tiny sea plant. She shifted her thighs and lifted a leg so that the water streamed from it.

"Are you not feeling like a bath, too, Michael?" she said. "I'll be glad to soap you down."

She talked while he undressed. "Did you have any women in Spain? Are they beautiful there? I bet they're no prettier than our Irish girls."

He stepped out of his trousers, and she stared at the mass of puckered skin where he had been hit, just below his groin. "Oh, Michael," she said. "Look what they did to you. Does it hurt?" She reached out and touched it with a soft, tentative finger.

"It plays me up a bit in damp weather," he said.

"That means all the time in Ireland. Come on and get in the water, and I'll bathe it for you."

Naked now, he stepped into the welcoming warmth of the bath. "At least you haven't lost any weight where it counts,"

58

she said with the throaty laughter that instantly brought back memories of other encounters. Perhaps, he thought, this time it will be different.

He sank down until he was sitting between her legs, his back to her. She put her arms around his chest, and he felt the twin thrust of her breasts and the grip of her thighs around his haunches. She soaped his back first, and he made a sound of sensuous pleasure.

"Do they train nurses how to do this?" he said. "Do all your patients get the same treatment?"

"Of course," she said lightly, still intent on her efforts. "But I think I'll give you some special treatment since you're a wounded soldier." Her hand moved around to his chest and then drifted down to his scar, the bar of soap in it sliding gently over the marred flesh. Her other hand took his phallus and held it firmly.

"It's getting in my way," she explained with the same remembered laughter. "Not that I'm complaining, you understand. In fact, I'm quite fond of the big fella." She played with him, murmuring, "Oh, Michael, I don't know whether to be angry with those Fascists for wounding you or grateful that they got you where they did. Another few inches . . . oh, my God."

She used her cupped hands to sluice him down.

"I want you," he said. Surely two years would make a difference.

Ignoring the big white towels lying on the cane laundry basket, they went dripping to the big bed, and Brock flung back the heavy quilt and the blankets and the white sheet. She lay on her back and stretched out her arms to him and said, "In me, Michael, in me."

Two years had made no difference. She whimpered and arched her back at the peak and then moaned and arched again as he went over the edge. But two years had made no difference to him. When they lay side by side, holding hands, her body was lax with satiation, but her eyes, seeking his, were wary, disquieted.

"You're a cold man, Michael," she said at length. "I thought

59

once it was me, but it's not, and you haven't changed. Has a woman ever satisfied you?"

Uaigneas gan ciuneas, he thought, loneliness without peace.

"You satisfy me, Maggie. You'd satisfy any man. It's just that I don't give of myself as easily as some. I can't throw myself into a relationship. I don't know. It's always as if I'm standing back a little, watching what's going on."

"Hold me, Michael," she said. He put an arm around her shoulders, and she rested her head on his chest. "Ah," she said, "it's a fine little hell we've made for ourselves. I think sometimes all the Irish are in it now. We've made it for ourselves on earth to be sure we go to heaven when we die."

She reached down and held his limp phallus. "You're man enough for me," she said, "but I'm not woman enough for you. I wonder what might be the answer to that riddle."

"Perhaps it was the years on the run," he said. "I don't know. But I couldn't trust anybody, and perhaps I still can't. Even you and even me." He thought of Michael Collins and the bicycle and what Michael Collins had become, and the old pain returned.

"I heard you were going to get married," he said.

"You heard that from your mother?"

"I did."

"Well, I'm not. There was a man, a doctor down in Cork, but we decided not to."

"*You* decided not to is my guess, Maggie."

"He was all right, but he's not one of us. He thinks it would be nice if the English left Ireland, but he doesn't really care. All he thinks about is the appendix and the tonsils and the boil on Mrs. Murphy's neck. If one of the boys came to him with a bullet in his side, courtesy of the Garda, he'd take it out, but he'd also report it because that's what the rules say he must do. A Castle Catholic."

"And how was he in bed?"

"That's none of your business, Michael Brock. But I'll tell you this, he had a warmth sometimes that wouldn't do you any harm at all."

60

He was silent for a moment, and then he rolled out of bed and walked naked to the window with its billowing lace curtain. "You can see the post office from here," he said. "You were just a baby, then, weren't you, Maggie?"

"You weren't much older," she said, reaching down to pull the sheet over her.

"How's that great rebel De Valera doing?" he asked.

"He's locking up the boys as fast as he can," she said. "He's scared stiff that he might lose his precious neutrality. He's scared that the English might invade, and he's scared that the Germans might invade. The IRA is provoking the English, he says, so he's trying to put them all behind bars."

"God rot that sanctimonious little clerk," Brock said.

"He has Boland as his minister for justice," Maggie said. "Some justice. Last year they declared the Army an illegal organization. And they brought in the Offences Against the State bill. Isn't that a lovely title? The Parliament in London couldn't think up a better title than that."

"They love their acts and their bills, I don't care what government it is," Brock said.

"They set up special courts, and they interned nearly a hundred of the boys," she said. "We went to court, and we got them all out, so they simply passed another law. In September the Special Branch lifted half the GHQ. Larry Grogan, Peadar O'Flaherty, and Willie McGuinness. And McGuinness with about eight thousand pounds on him."

"That'll be why they're so short of cash," Brock said, his voice so soft she could hardly hear him. He could feel the sweet breeze drying the sweat that had replaced the bathwater on his body.

"Some of them are on a hunger strike in Mountjoy Jail," she said. "De Valera's letting them die."

He felt the old anger and wondered at the pleasure it gave him. "Soon," he said, "if any Irishmen die, it'll not be in Ireland."

"England," she said.

"You know about that," he said.

"In Dublin everybody knows everything," she said. "Or nearly everything. Not about the bank job on Friday, though."

He turned and strode toward her. "Holy God," he shouted. "Is it still the same old nonsense, then? Everybody blabbing around the city so that I'll find every member of the Special Branch surrounding the place when we hit it. For Christ's sake, why don't they get a loudspeaker set up on St. Stephen's Green and announce it to the assembled populace?"

Before he had finished, she had thrown back the sheet and was on her feet, her hands on her slim hips.

"Who do you think I am?" she demanded. "Who? I'll tell you. You think I'm just a little nurse, always willing to run errands for the organization and to open my legs for you when you're in the mood for some physical relief. Not for love. For release of all your masculine tensions." She was shouting now, bending forward so that her flushed face was only a few inches from his.

"Well, you're wrong, Michael Brock. I'm not that at all. I work as a nurse because that allows me to move around the country, from hospital to hospital, wherever the organization wants me. But what I do, I do for Ireland.

"I've done enough work that the Army trusts me, probably more than they trust you, with your little side trips to Spain. And because they trust me, they tell me about missions like the robbery of banks. And in this particular case, the one on Friday, I happen to be able to give you some important information, and that's why I'm here, because I can tell you how much money there'll be in that bank and where you'll find it."

"Ah, come on now, Maggie," he said.

"As for opening my legs for you . . ."

"Maggie, my Maggie. Will you look at us? Both stark naked with our fists on our middles, hate pouring out of our eyes and shouting like fishwives." He was grinning at her.

She struggled to maintain her anger, and for a moment he thought she would hit him; but the laughter was already there in her, and it came out with a sound that was halfway between a whoop and a hiccup. He reached out for her.

62

"You think you can always get around me," she said, pushing her face against his shoulder. "You don't love me at all, and I love you, and I suppose there's nothing we can do about it."

His hands moved down her smooth, long back to cup her hard, muscled buttocks. "It'll work out, one way or another," he said. "Come on now, my Maggie, let's go back to bed, and you can tell me all about this bank that you've been spying on. We'll have a war council, you and me, under the sheets."

Chapter 6

Dublin
February 10, 1940

BY ten A.M. Jockey Hogan had stolen the car, a powerful black Wolseley similar to the models used by the police. It belonged to a solicitor who, unaware, had been trailed for three days by the diminutive Hogan. Every morning at eight-thirty A.M. he parked it outside his office, an office from which he did not emerge until after noon, when he walked to a restaurant for lunch.

Hogan did little more than park it elsewhere, against the curb only a few yards from the bank which was their target. It took him no more than twelve minutes from start to finish, he reported later. He used a wire to unlock the door on the driver's side. He already had a selection of ignition keys for Wolseley cars, and in two minutes he had found the right one. Then he drove it the mile to the bank.

Brock, Plunger, and the O'Bannon brothers were waiting in a safe house on Russell Street within five minutes' walking distance of the bank. It had been selected because of its proximity and because it had a telephone. When the phone rang, Brock answered.

"All set," Jockey said. "It's the Wolseley I told you about. Number LOP Two Seven Three. I have it about ten yards north of the bank, on the same side of the street."

"Where will you be?"

"At the wheel."

"No," Brock said. "Somebody who knows this fellow's car might see it. His wife or somebody like that. Once they start wondering what it's doing there and what you're doing in it, you're in trouble."

"All right, Michael, I'll be against the wall, within jumping distance of it."

"Hold tight, Jockey. We're on our way."

The front parlor, where they had been waiting behind drawn blinds, was thick with stale cigarette smoke. They looked up as he walked back in. The O'Bannon brothers exchanged glances, and one of them licked his lips. Plunger grinned and said, "Michael, my hard man, can we go and rob this bloody bank now? I'm tired of this little nook."

"Do we all know what we have to do?" Brock said, thinking that if they didn't it was too late now. "You first, Plunger. Off you go."

Plunger picked up a suitcase, stubbed out his cigarette, and walked towards the door. Big as he was, the case dragged at his shoulder. "I'll see you at the bank," he said, and then he was gone.

"You next, Dan," Brock said to one of the brothers. Brock studied Daniel O'Bannon, hoping that all the reports on hm had been accurate. He looked awfully young, he thought, no more than twenty. But the youngster nodded, shot an expressionless look at his brother, and then he, too, was gone.

"Give him a couple of minutes, Jamie," he said to the other brother. "Then you can be on your way, too." O'Bannon nodded and pulled his revolver from the pocket of his raincoat. He stared at it for a moment, then slipped it back. "I hope we don't have to use them," he said. His voice was steady, his blue eyes thoughtful.

"All right, Jamie, on your way," Brock said. "I'll be right behind you." Now he was alone. He picked up the cardboard box which once had contained flowers. The top was held down by black tape which would rip off in one pull.

He walked into the narrow hallway. "We're off now, then, Mrs. O'Neill," he called toward the kitchen.

The woman whose house they had used remained in the kitchen. "God bless you and keep you. All of you," she said. He could hardly hear her through the half-open door. "Please God, there'll be no blood-spilling spawned by whatever you're about."

"Thank you for the shelter you provided," he said.

"Ah, it's nothing," she said. "I know you're all patriots."

With the long box under his right arm, he left the mustiness of the hallway, with its garish picture of a sad-eyed saint, and stepped out into the street. Five minutes, he thought. Five minutes and it will begin. The day was clear, but high clouds hastened across the sky before a west wind. Two barefoot little boys were playing in the gutter. He heard their mother calling them from an upstairs window, but they ignored her. Rounding the corner of the street, he was in a busier area with shops and shoppers and buses and cars. A man pushed by him in such a hurry that the long box under his arm was jarred, and for a moment he feared he had lost it. He swore softly.

The bank stood on a corner, the entrance at the apex of the two roads. Almost immediately he spotted the black Wolseley. Jockey was lounging against the wall a few feet from it. Brock's eyes flickered to the boarded-up store one hundred yards from the bank. Plunger was just coming out. Brock saw him turn to lock the door behind him.

When he walked into the bank, he knew that Plunger was on his heels even before he heard the muttered words, "Everything's set." There were six customers. Two were standing at the counter. Behind the black bars, Brock could see three clerks at work. Four of the customers were standing at the walls writing checks or filling in deposit slips. All women.

At the farthest point from the door the O'Bannon brothers were standing together studying notices on a board with ear-

65

nest concentration. Brock went to one of the wall tables and picked up a deposit slip. At his side, Plunger said, "Any moment now, Michael." But the moments drifted by, and nothing happened. Two more depositors came in, one of them calling out a cheery "Good morning, Mary," to one of the girls behind the bars. Brock wondered whether she was the one who had passed on the information to Maggie. There was no sign of the bank manager. Sweating lightly, he looked at Plunger with the question in his eyes. Plunger shrugged and turned away. Perhaps the manager wasn't in, Brock thought. Jesus, Joseph, and Mary, he should have told Jockey to check.

He walked to the counter and looked into the blue eyes of a freckle-faced girl wearing a jumper the same color as her eyes. "Excuse me," he said. "I'd like to see the manager, please."

"Is it anything I can help you with?" she asked. "He's a busy man." Her features showed nothing more than pleasant helpfulness, and he decided she could not be Maggie's friend.

"I want to discuss a mortgage," he said.

"Usually he insists on an appointment," she said. "But I'll go and fetch him. Perhaps he'll see you."

Brock looked over his shoulder. The younger O'Bannon was walking toward the door. Plunger was still at the table. Now there were five customers in the bank. He was staring at the door through which the girl had gone when the first explosion came from the abandoned store. It was powerful enough to rock the bank building, and the noise from it seemed to come in waves.

Immediately Brock pulled at the tape securing the top of his long box. It peeled off with a sizzling sound, and the next moment he had the Thompson submachine gun in his hands. Everything began to happen with dizzying speed. Led by the redheaded girl, the bank manager appeared. He was a burly man with the raw red face of a Kerry farmer. At first he didn't see the Thompson.

"What the hell is going on?" he demanded angrily, as if the explosion were a personal insult. Then he saw the weapon Brock was carrying, and he fell silent, his eyes widening.

66

Brock leaped onto the counter and straddled one leg across the bars. One glance showed him that the O'Bannon brothers were in place, their revolvers out. Plunger was in his same position, his hands in his pockets, watching the proceedings with detached interest.

Another explosion from the boarded-up shop proved that O'Neill, the gelignite expert, had not lost his touch. There were supposed to be four separate explosions. Two more to come.

Brock pointed his Thompson down, swinging it in an easy arc between the frozen clerks and the bank manager, but it was to the customers that he spoke. "Everybody stay where they are and nobody get's hurt," he said. He was surprised at the level confidence in his voice. "This operation has been ordered by the Irish Republican Army, and the Army doesn't want to injure anybody unnecessarily."

The bank manager began to sputter. "Irish Republican Army, hell," he said. "You're just a bunch of bank robbers. Well, you won't get anything out of me."

One of the customers, an old woman in a shawl, had begun to cry. "Holy Mary, mother of God," she whimpered. "What will become of us?"

Daniel O'Bannon betrayed some of his tension. "Shut your mouth, you foolish old woman," he said. "Nobody's going to hurt you."

"The safe," Brock said to the bank manager. "We want what's in the safe."

"You'll not get it," the manager said. The third explosion that Brock had been awaiting came. It seemed even louder than the others. As the sound was dying away, Brock pointed the Thompson between the manager and the redheaded girl. He pressed the trigger briefly.

Bullets smashed into the wall behind them. The girl shrieked, clutching her breasts as if feeling the bullets ripping into her chest. The manager paled.

"The safe," Brock said. "You'll go into your office, and I'll be right behind you, and in there you'll open the safe. And

67

you'll be damn quick about it or you'll get some of these slugs."
He jumped down on the manager's side of the counter, the
Thompson pointed at the man's belly. He used his other hand
to pull down the canvas carryall which had been secured under his raincoat. "Catch," he said, tossing the bag at the manager, who almost dropped it in his confusion and fear but
then led the way into his office.

"Watch them," Brock called to the O'Bannon brothers. The
raid had been in progress for less than five minutes, and nobody had entered the bank during that time. Brock could
imagine the chaos in the street outside caused by the unnerv-
ing series of explosions. "Watch that big fellow particularly,"
he said, pointing at Plunger. "He looks as if he might like to
try and earn himself a medal." Plunger stared at him expres-
sionlessly, said nothing. Then Brock followed the manager
into his office.

"Let me make something clear," Brock said. "I'm a volunteer of the Irish Republican Army, and I've been assigned to
relieve you of some of your English money for the good of the
Republic. I don't know what your views of our organization
might be, and I don't particularly care. But you should know
that I've killed before as part of my duty, and doubtless I'll kill
again. It could be you this time."

The bank manager was staring at Brock as if he were some
vile creature revealed by a lifted stone. The manager wore
heavy tweeds and a high starched collar, and now the clothes
seemed too large for his sagging body.

"The key is on your key ring in your right jacket pocket,"
Brock said. "Take it out." The bank manager obeyed him.

"Good. Now go and open that safe, and if you delay I'll put
a slug in your back." The safe was on the floor in a corner of
the room near the barred window. It was black, and it looked
old enough to be a bank heirloom. While the manager knelt in
front of it, Brock lifted the curtain from the window and
peered out.

To the left, toward the blown-up store, he could see a crowd
had spilled into the road so that traffic was blocked. Police

were already at work holding them back. Even as Brock stared out, the fourth explosion shook the area, and the spectators shrank back. Some of them screamed, but others cheered as if at a fireworks exhibition.

"Hurry up, damn you," he said.

A moment later the bank manager swung the door of the safe open. Maggie's information had been correct. The shelves were lined with English bank notes.

"Fill the bag," Brock said. The bank manager turned to protest, but Brock pushed the muzzle of the machine gun against his forehead. "Fill it," he said. The manager began to transfer the notes, banded into piles, from the safe to the bag. Brock looked at his watch. "Hurry," he said. The manager's hands were shaking, but he accomplished the removal within two minutes.

"Give it to me," Brock said. He walked swiftly to the desk, put down the bag, and ripped the telephone wire from its connection on the wall.

The door key. He saw that it was in place, just as Maggie had promised. He backed toward the door, the Thompson still on the bank manager. "I'm going to lock you in," Brock said. "You can break the window and yell, but I doubt that anyone will take any notice of you for a while. Not with all that mess going on outside." The manager stared at him silently.

Then, as Brock took the key from the lock, he said, "I'll lose my job over this."

"Don't expect me to weep," Brock said. "You and your banks have been bleeding the poor people of Ireland for too long." He closed the door behind him, turned the key in the lock, and tossed it away.

"Have you got it all, then, Michael?" Jamie O'Bannon called.

"No names!" Brock said. Then, showing the bag, "Close to ten thousand pounds is my guess. Let's start getting out of here."

Just as he was about to jump back onto the counter, his eye caught one of the clerks. She was small and pinch-faced, and her thick spectacles did nothing for her. She looked more frightened than anybody else in the bank, but suddenly Brock knew she was the girl who had passed the vital information to Maggie.

Climbing back over the bars, he was encumbered by the canvas bag, and he tossed it down to Jamie O'Bannon. "Hold onto it for me," he said. Then he was down on the other side, and the three of them were moving toward the door, the O'Bannons' revolvers still pointing at the customers. The old woman was sniffling into her shawl.

"We're going to be outside for a few moments," Brock told the watching customers. "Anybody who comes out of this door in the next five minutes gets a bullet between the eyes. And remember, you'll be dying for England and its money, not for Ireland."

"The machine gun," Daniel O'Bannon said.

Brock had become so used to it in his hands that he had forgotten to put it away. "Christ," he said, "give me the box." He was very conscious now of the time draining away.

The younger O'Bannon kicked the box to him, and he dropped the Thompson into it. He found the lid. No time to replace the black tape. The brothers were already going through the door. The box under his arm, he went after them. Plunger was standing in the same spot he had occupied throughout the raid. Once they were clear he would drift away, with nothing to connect him to the robbers.

Outside the bells of police cars and ambulances were ringing. Police officers with linked arms were trying to push back the crowd that ringed the shattered building where O'Neill's bombs had gone off. Jockey's black Wolseley was away from the curb and reversing the few yards to the bank. He had the passenger door open on the bank side, and the O'Bannon brothers were swiftly climbing in.

Brock was moving fast over the pavement when he felt a hand on his arm. "Excuse me," he said "I'm in a hurry." But the hand maintained its grip. It belonged to a thickset man in a black overcoat. He wore a military mustache.

70

"I'm sure you're in a hurry," the man said. "Your lot always are. But I've a couple of questions for you. Special Branch."

Brock was contending with an icy paralysis when the window of the bank manager's office shattered. There was already so much noise that few people turned. "Stop them! They just robbed the bank. Good Christ, stop them." The bank manager was in full cry.

The Special Branch man turned to look, and for a moment Brock thought he could break free. But the hand remained firm on his arm.

Jockey was shouting something. In the back of the Wolseley Brock could see the O'Bannon brothers' white faces staring at him through the open door. And then there was a revolver in the fist of the Special Branch man.

"You're under arrest," he said. "You give me any trouble, my boyo, and I'll kill you like the thug you are." Brock looked over his shoulder and saw Plunger coming through the door. The Special Branch man, confused by the swiftness of events, had not yet connected the car with his captive.

Brock screamed at Jockey. "Get away," he shouted. "I'll deal with this. Jesus Christ, go on!"

Jockey pressed the accelerator, and the car surged off, narrowly missing an approaching police car. The rear door, still open, swung wildly as the Wolseley sped away.

"Don't worry, we'll get them," the Special Branch man said. "Into the bank with you." But there was no way they could get into the bank, because Plunger's broad shoulders barred the way.

Plunger shot through the material of his raincoat pocket. A giant black scorch mark appeared as the gun roared. The bullet hit the Special Branch man in the belly. He groaned, and his hands went to the wound. His revolver dropped to the pavement. Brock was free of the insistent hand, but for a moment he just stared at the man from the Castle. Blood was spurting from his stomach, seeping through the material of his coat and onto his hands. He was gazing down in disbelief. Then he fell.

71

"Come on," Plunger shouted. He ran to Brock. "Come on," he said again. Then they both turned away from the crowd and ran as if trying to catch the Wolseley.

"Down here," Brock shouted, turning into an alley. They pounded along the cobblestones, the sound of their frantic passage echoing off the red brick walls. The machine gun, poorly concealed by the box, slowed Brock down, and once he almost lost it. At the other end of the alley he gasped, "All right, Plunger. Slow it down. Walk." When they came out into a quiet back street, both were gulping air into their laboring lungs.

The old Austin was there, Paddy McGovern at the wheel. Brock and Plunger jumped into the back, and McGovern immediately let out the clutch and accelerated away. It had been McGovern's idea to have the backup car, and he had volunteered to drive his own machine. By the time they had told him the story, the car was on the other side of the city.

"We've got to see McGrath," McGovern said. "Somebody talked, and we know exactly who it is. There'll be a court-martial."

Chapter 7

County Kildare
February 18, 1940

BROCK lay on the short, coarse grass on the hill above the cottage. To the east the heavy dark clouds seemed to touch the sullen-looking waters of the ocean so that it was difficult to see the line of the horizon. Inland the rough stone walls bordering the small fields formed a crazy network, like veins showing through the belly of some green beast.

The others were waiting inside the cottage, but Brock, oppressed by the thought of what was to come, had walked away up the hill. He could see the small meandering road along which they would bring the accused.

It was always the same, he thought. The planning, the effort, the action, and then the betrayal. What was different this time was that the betrayer had been trapped into revealing himself. Always, eventually, they were unmasked. Why did they do it? he wondered. What did this man have to gain?

In the case of Michael Collins it had been easy to see the reward. Power, prominence, a place in the history books. Evidently that had been enough for him. He had gone to London, and he had met and talked with the men who controlled an empire, and they had listened to him and nodded their heads at his words and congratulated him on his rhetoric and entertained him at their great houses. And it had been too much of a temptation for a man who had once cycled around Dublin with a price on his head, a man who had given orders for the deaths of other men while the English brought in their own gunmen to find him and kill him.

It was strange, Brock thought. Almost every time he had met Collins, a bicycle had been involved in their encounter. At the Dublin post office it had been Brock's cycle. He remembered Collins' joking promise to buy him another one from the treasury of the Republic. Then the young Brock had been led home, and the British shells had come crashing into the beleaguered defenders' midst, and the fire had burned downward from the shattered roof. The Rising lasted less than a week. One by one the defenses were crushed under the weight of the British arms.

It was inevitable, the way it happened, he thought, staring over the cottage to the hills beyond. The message of surrender. The white flag. The column of exhausted survivors being marched under guard into captivity. The good citizens of Dublin turning away from the rebels who had failed, giving tea and food to the British soldiers.

And yet, he thought, plucking a thick blade of grass to chew, there could have been another way. They could have refused to surrender, and for some, at least, the fatal result

73

would have been the same. Who could tell what might have been the fruit of that defiance?

Collins had not died. Not then, at least. He had been among the weary survivors herded along the streets. Brock did not want to think of the surrender, but he found the picture in his mind once again. Released at last from the house, he had gone down to the green in front of the Rotunda Hospital, where the captives were assembled inside a forest of British bayonets. Many of the rebels were still bleeding from their wounds, their eyes sunken, stubble on their chins. A steady drizzle added to their misery of defeat, but the British had not finished with them.

There was a captain in charge of the prisoners, Lee Wilson, born in Ireland but a British regimental officer. He was enjoying himself. As Brock watched through the gaps in the surrounding khaki and as nurses stared down from the hospital windows, the rebels were brought before Wilson one by one.

They were forced to strip naked in front of him and then endure his contemptuous taunts and mockery.

"Look, now, at this fine example of Irish manhood," he shouted at a potbellied middle-aged man whose thin hair was plastered against his gleaming-wet skull. "By God, it seems to me he would be a lot handier with a pot of ale than with a rifle. Did you manage to kill any British soldiers, Paddy? You probably did, yes, you probably did. Firing your rifle from the safety of buildings is about your mark.

"Ah, so we're shivering, are we? Well, I'll tell you Paddy, there are a lot of men in Flanders who are shivering right now. But they are men. They fight like men. In the trenches, with no women to bring them tea and lie down on their dirty backs for them. Get away from me, you filthy mick. You make me want to vomit. Next."

The rebels took his vicious mockery silently—Tom Clarke and Sean MacDiarmada and Michael Collins, all of them— until they were marched off to Richmond Barracks, where the G-detectives, the men of the political division of the city police, were waiting to select candidates for courts-martial. Brock thought he saw Collins for a moment, but he could not be sure. He did not know then whether the big Irishman had survived. Neither could he have known the eventual fate of Captain Lee Wilson, ambushed and shot dead in County Wexford.

Lying on the hill above the cottage more than twenty years later, Brock imagined the shaming thoughts that must have filled the heads of the men on the Rotunda green. The brave adventure ending with them standing like animals, the objects of sneers and laughter.

There were those who said that the 1916 defeat led to victory in 1921, the signing of the Free State treaty. But Brock and the men waiting in the cottage were not among them. For them it had been a betrayal as treasonous as any committed by the informer who would soon be brought along the dusty road from Dublin. The English still in the Six Counties, the Free State still part of Britain's economy, existing under London's sufferance.

Collins, Brock thought, could have pushed it either way. He pushed for the treaty. There were those among his comrades who said that Collins had been trapped by the politicians, but Brock did not believe it. The transformation had been too basic.

It had been as basic as his father's and that of most Irishmen when they heard the British were executing the leaders of the rebellion. Fifteen Irishmen were shot, including the wounded James Connolly, who was tied to a chair. And suddenly, all across Ireland, the men of the Rising were no longer seen as fools suffering from delusions of grandeur but as martyrs, men who carried the honor of their country into English prisons.

Brock's father, out of work for much of his life, picking up a few shillings from casual work at the docks or cutting peat, found a purpose in life that had never been there before. He joined the Irish Republican Brotherhood, and by the time the rebels who had escaped the execution squads began to return from internment, he was a section master. It was a time of ferment, excitement, danger, and above all, consuming hatred for the British, who had turned the country into a garrison state. General Sir John Maxwell had forty thousand troops under his command, and at first there was little the Fenians could do except sing the songs that were being composed about Easter Week and read the poems that were being written about the men of the Rising.

Then Michael Collins came home from the internment camp in Wales.

At first he worked as secretary to the National Aid Association, a group set up specifically to raise funds for victims of the Rising. But his leadership had been recognized at the end of the rebellion and in the Frongoch internment camp, and soon he became director of organization of the Volunteers. It was about to begin: the ambushes, the killings, the Black and Tans, the weeping women, the legend of the gunman.

Brock's father was part of it all. He would be away from the house for days at a time. He would return exhausted and silent about where he had been. He referred to his absences as "my little journeys."

Brock was fifteen years old when his father brought the revolvers and the Mills grenades home for the first time. They were in a shopping basket, an innocent-looking old basket until the loaves of bread and the brown paper were pulled aside to show the deadliness of the weapons.

With one brother dead and the other in America, Brock had his own room, and it was there that his father went. "You'll sleep on the guns of Ireland tonight, Michael," he said, and he pulled the covers from the boy's bed. He took out a knife and carefully cut a slit in the mattress.

"I doubt you'll feel them, but you'd best not roll about too much in your sleep."

"You're not putting those bombs in the boy's bed, Patrick," Brock's mother said. "Holy Mother of God, what if they go off in the middle of the night?"

"He'll know nothing about it if they do," his father said, winking at Brock in male conspiracy.

She was not amused. "I'm telling you, Patrick. You'll not leave them in that mattress. Jesus, no wonder this family's land is all in window boxes. Have you no sense whatsoever? I have an idea. We'll put the bombs up the chimney. Then we'll start a fire, and if the soldiers come, they'll never think of looking there."

The bombs, after the pins had been taped into security, ended up in young Brock's mattress. The next day his father called him from the backyard into the kitchen. When Brock walked in, his father was busy scribbling on a piece of paper.

"It's time for us to talk, Michael," he said, putting down the stub of pencil. "You're nearly sixteen, and that's old enough."

"Old enough for what?" he asked, excitement growing in his belly.

"You listen to me for a moment and then ask your questions. Here, pour yourself some tea and be still. Now, Michael, I haven't been the best father in the world to you. We've had our troubles, and there've been times, I know, when you've gone to bed hungry. Many times. And you've gone without shoes, and your clothes have been hand-me-downs."

"It was the same for all the children around here," Michael said. He felt uncomfortable now, for it had been part of the family's pride to ignore their poverty. After all, he had been given a bicycle, and few of his friends could even afford a tram fare.

"Your mother had it worst of all," his father said heavily. "She went without so you could eat, all of you, and now there's no reward, for her arthritis seems to get worse every day. When she lost Frank. . . ." He shook his head.

"It could all have been different," he said. "Different for everybody if we'd been given the chance. Perhaps we should have taken it in 1916. Perhaps I was wrong to hold back.

"But now there's another chance, and this time the Brock family will take it. D'you know what I mean?"

"The Volunteers," Michael said excitedly. "Up the Republic!"

"It's not a question of hoorays and flags and cheers," his father said. "There's hard work to be done and dangers to be faced, and anybody who thinks it's banners in the breeze soon learns different."

"They say the English are offering ten thousand pounds for Michael Collins," young Brock said. "They're bringing men over from London especially to look for him. Are you working for him, Father?"

"Another thing you learn with the Volunteers is that a word spoken is a word too many. Can you keep your silence, Son? This is no game that's being played."

"I can be silent," Brock said. "Remember when the soldiers came and twisted my arms and hit me in the face?"

"I remember, Son. You're a good young fella, even with your mischief." He folded the piece of paper on which he had been writing and kept folding it until it was a tiny square. "I want you to take a message," he said. "Put this in your shoe and take your bicycle and go along to Number Six Harcourt Street. You'll find a fella there that you'll recognize. Give him the note, and then come back and report."

"I will, Father. I know the quickest way."

It was growing dark when Brock left the house. He could afford no lamp for his bicycle, but he sped off over the cobblestones, glad that he had just cleaned and oiled the machine. At the address on Harcourt Street he leaned his cycle against the wall and knocked on the door. He heard movement behind it, bolts being pulled back, but the door did not open.

"Who is it out there?" a voice called.

He looked up and down the silent street and replied, "I have a message."

"Who is it?" the voice repeated.

"My name is Michael Brock," he said.

He heard another bolt being drawn back, and then the door opened. The hallway was in darkness, but he could see the bulk of a large man standing inside.

"Come inside quickly," the man said.

When he was inside, the door was closed and bolted behind him. "Come this way," the man said. They walked into a room illuminated by a candle burning on a paper-strewn desk.

"You've put on some height but not much weight," the man said. The yellow light from the desk caught his face, and Brock stared.

"Mr. Collins," he said.

"You have a good memory," Collins said. "Shake my hand as a fellow Volunteer, and give me the message. Your father told me you'd be coming."

Brock reached down into his shoe and took out the square of paper. Collins unfolded it carefully and took it to the light.

"Six revolvers and four grenades and they're all in your bed, Michael Wolfe Brock," he said. "It's a lumpy mattress you must have these nights."

"Ah, I don't feel them, Mr. Collins," he said. Suddenly he felt shy, overcome at meeting the director, the man hunted by soldiers and spies and informers, the man leading the fight against the British. Only the chief of staff, Cathal Brugha, stood above him in the hierarchy of the guerrilla army, for De Valera was still in America trying to raise funds.

Gravely Collins shook his hand. "It's different times that we meet in," he said.

"They are," Brock said. "But I remembered you, Mr. Collins. Like you told me to."

Collins tossed back the lock of hair dangling over his forehead and gave a full-throated laugh. "Let's steal a moment from our arduous duties, and let's you and me talk, Michael. Take a seat in that old armchair."

Taller himself now, Brock realized that Collins was not as big a man as he had thought at the post office. It was the graceful athletic build that increased his stature. That and his forceful personality. There was an openness to his features, a frankness to his gray eyes, a lively intelligence that would have drawn the gaze to him in any crowd. When he spoke it was in the accent of County Cork.

"Many things have happened since the Rising," he said. "For one thing, we're both older."

Brock, sitting upright in the battered old chair, realized that

79

Collins looked considerably older. Some of the boyishness had fled his features. There were new lines of maturity around his full lips.

"Did they hurt you, the English, when they took you from the post office?" Brock asked.

"Nothing but my pride was damaged," Collins said. "And I learned a lot. About the English and about the Irish. You taught me something, too, Michael Brock." He nodded toward a corner of the room. A bicycle stood there, bigger than Brock's but much dirtier.

"You were right," Collins said. "There's nothing like a bicycle for getting around Dublin. And, as I remember, I still owe you a new machine."

Brock flashed a grin, and the next moment they were both laughing. Sitting there with Collins, Brock suddenly felt grown-up, as if the very presence and personality of the guerrilla leader had made him an adult.

"What are you dong with yourself these days?" Collins wanted to know. Brock realized later that part of the man's charm lay in his intense curiosity about those he met. He would talk to them and question them about their lives out of a genuine curiosity that flattered and drew them out in a way few men could. Brock, a boy, was treated as an adult, on even terms, with no reference by word or attitude to their different ages, different status.

"I can't get work," Brock said. "I wanted to be a flier, a pilot, but we have no money for education, and I can't even get a laboring job. The best I can do is make a bit of pocket money helping out at Mrs. Regan's store on the corner of our street."

"Have you thought of going to America?" Collins asked. "I nearly went there a few years ago. But I changed my mind. Perhaps if you went you could find a way to go to college, and then perhaps you could fly the aeroplanes."

"My mam doesn't want me to go," Brock said. "I have a brother over there, and I'm the only one left at home, and she doesn't want me to leave." He hesitated a moment, then burst out:

"Mr. Collins, I want to help Ireland get its freedom. I don't think it helps Ireland to run off to America. I want to be here when we get rid of the English and have the sort of Ireland you talked about when we first met. I want to be like my father. I want to work for the Volunteers. I want to work for you, Mr. Collins." He fell silent, abashed at his vehemence.

"Your father's a fine man, Michael," Collins said. He was sitting at ease in the chair at his desk, one leg dangling over its arm. "So are all the Volunteers. They have a vision of the way it will be one day, and they're working for it, aye, and dying for it."

He looked at the papers on his desk and tapped a pencil against his teeth.

"Do you know what they call us in England, Michael? The English newspapers? They call us killers, gunmen who shoot policemen and soldiers and Black and Tans and Auxiliaries in the back." A cloud passed over his broad features. "They call me the chief gunman, a murderer who delights in seeing blood flow. Oh, Michael, if they only knew how I hate the killing and the bitterness that grows and grows.

"And in America, where they don't know the truth any better, they write that I'm the will-o'-the-wisp Scarlet Pimpernel who goes out into the dark and dangerous streets with a gun in the pocket of my trench coat. Me, who never carries a gun and rides all over Dublin on my bicycle in broad daylight." He shook his head in disgust. "They try to make it a glamorous thing, this awful killing and the betrayals and mothers weeping over lonely graves."

"The killings have to be done," Brock ventured.

"Some of them, Michael, but not all of them. There's so much blood I fear we all may drown in it."

"Why don't the English go, then? Why did they come in the first place?"

"Ah, the English. They're a strange race. As strange as the Irish, Michael, and that's strange enough. They cannot understand why we shouldn't be happy to live under the Crown, happy to take our orders from London. We'll never understand them and they'll never understand us."

"They're evil," Brock said, parroting words once used by his mother."

Collins shook his head slowly. "No race is all evil," he said. "There are evil Englishmen just as there are evil Irishmen. The trouble is that they seem to ship their worst cases over to poor old Ireland."

"The Black and Tans, they're evil," Brock said.

"They are. But even so, we're beating them." Collins glanced down at his papers, and Brock wondered if he should leave. But the director began to speak again.

"The same nation that recruited the Black and Tans produced Milton and Shakespeare and Dickens," Collins said. "It's a contradiction, but there it is. Do you read at all, young Michael?"

"I go to the public library. I like adventure books, though most of them are English. I'm starting to read some history. History of Ireland. I've read about Cromwell, and I've read about the famines."

"Would you like to write, then?"

"No, Mr. Collins. I want to do things."

"Ah, I long for all this to be over and done with. When that day dawns, I will pick up my books, and I will go away, and I will spend my life reading. Maybe a bit of writing as well. There's no pleasure in this sort of life we're leading now. The bombs and the bullets and the killings and the betrayals."

"If I had a gun, I'd go and shoot the first British soldier I saw," Brock blurted.

Collins tensed and pointed a finger at Brock, and now the boy felt the power of authority in the man. "Never say that. Never say that again, Michael Brock. The Army doesn't kill for the sake of killing. We do it because we have to. Because it's the only way to gain our freedom. Too many Volunteers and too many of the English kill because they enjoy it."

"I'm sorry, sir," Brock muttered.

Collins sighed and reached into his pocket. He brought out a folded piece of paper, worn and grimy from much handling. Carefully he smoothed it out, and Brock saw that it bore lines of writing, the penmanship small and neat.

"I keep this with me always," Collins said. "I read it sometimes when I have to give orders that I know will result in the deaths of Englishmen. It helps, for it's one of the most terrible stories ever committed to paper."

"Is it a true story?"

"It's true enough," Collins said. "You've read about Cromwell, that great Protestant, how he tried to destroy us by the sword. Later, in the eighteen forties, the English almost succeeded. Their weapons were callousness and greed, famine and pestilence.

"There was a magistrate in Cork called Nicholas Cummins, and in 1846 he visited Skibbereen, which is not far from where I was born in West Cork. He wrote about what he had seen, and he sent the writing to the Duke of Wellington with a copy to the London *Times*, which published it December twenty-fourth, Christmas Eve, 1846. I'll read it to you."

Collins began to read, at times lifting his eyes from the page, so well did he know the words.

"My Lord Duke, without apology or preface, I presume so far to trespass on your Grace as to state to you, and by the use of your illustrious name, to present to the British public the following statement of what I have myself seen within the last three days.

"Having for many years been intimately connected with the western portion of the County of Cork, and possessing some small property there, I thought it right personally to investigate the truth of several lamentable accounts which had reached me, of the appalling state of misery to which that part of the country was reduced. I accordingly went on the 15th instant to Skibbereen, and to give the instance of one townland which I visited, as an example of the entire coast district, I shall state simply what I there saw.

"Being aware that I should have to witness scenes of frightful hunger, I provided myself with as much bread as five men could carry, and on reaching the spot I was surprised to find the wretched hamlet apparently deserted. I entered some of the hovels to ascertain the cause, and the scenes which presented themselves were such as no tongue or pen can convey

83

the slightest idea of. In the first, six famished and ghastly skeletons, to all appearances dead, were huddled in a corner on some filthy straw, their sole covering what seemed a ragged horsecloth, their wretched legs hanging about, naked above the knees.

"I approached with horror, and found by a low moaning they were alive—they were in fever, four children, a woman and what had once been a man. It is impossible to go through the detail. Suffice it to say that in a few minutes I was surrounded by at least 200 such phantoms, such frightful spectres as no words can describe, either from famine or from fever. Their demoniac yells are still ringing in my ears, and their horrible images are fixed upon my brain. My heart sickens at the recital, but I must go on.

"In another case, decency would forbid what follows, but it must be told. My clothes were nearly torn off in my endeavour to escape from the throng of pestilence around, when my neckcloth was seized from behind by a grip which compelled me to turn, I found myself grasped by a woman with an infant just born in her arms and the remains of a filthy sack across her loins—the sole covering of herself and baby. The same morning the police opened a house on the adjoining lands, which was observed shut for many days and two frozen corpses were found, lying upon the mud floor, half devoured by rats.

"A mother, herself in a fever, was seen the same day to drag out the corpse of her child, a girl about 12, perfectly naked, and leave it half covered with stones.

"In another house, within 500 yards of the cavalry station at Skibbereen, the dispensary doctor found seven wretches lying unable to move, under the same cloak. One had been dead many hours, but the others were unable to move either themselves or the corpse."

Collins fell silent. Brock felt angry tears burning his eyelids.

"You read that before sending guns against the English," Collins said, "and it helps. That's what they reduced us to with their civilization, their rule of law and justice, their doctrine of laissez-faire. And while more than a million were dying, the landlords and the English were shipping wheat, oats, cattle, pigs, eggs, and butter down the Shannon to Britain. Under armed guard."

"I don't care what you say, Mr. Collins. They should be killed."

"It's not that simple, Michael Brock. We have to act with intelligence and fortitude and daring if we are to reach our goals. We cannot take on the British Army at full tilt. But we can make ourselves such a damnable nuisance that London will get rid of us like a burr from under its crotch. One day we will have to sit down and talk with them, and there will be an agreement, and then the future will lie in your hands, Michael Brock, yours and other young men like you."

Collins folded the paper and slipped it back into his pocket. "You must be off to tell your father you've delivered the message," he said.

"I want to work with the Volunteers, Mr. Collins."

"How old are you?"

"I'm nearly sixteen."

"Very well, Michael Brock. Your father will tell you what to do. There'll be the oath to take and other things."

Brock stood up, his heart beating fast. "Will I work for you, Mr. Collins?"

"You'll work for Ireland, not for me. But remember, don't enjoy it if you have to do terrible things. Now be off with you, and be careful. It's past curfew time."

Brock was already on the street when Collins, standing at the door, called him back. "Here," he said, handing over the folded paper which told of the 1846 famine. "Keep this, Michael Brock, and read it sometimes. I don't think I'll need it anymore."

Brock cycled home, alert for the armored cars and Crossley tenders and the sudden stab of searchlights which would mean the Tommies or the Black and Tans were on the prowl. The piece of paper lay tucked in Brock's wallet for years, and sometimes he read it. It was taken from him when he was captured in Spain.

85

Lying on the grass above the cottage, Brock found his thoughts would not concentrate on the years after Collins had accepted him and he had taken the oath. The assaults on customs posts, the grenade attacks on truckloads of soldiers, the street fighting after the treaty was signed, the bombings, the lonely years crossing the border into the Six Counties, hunted by both sides . . . they all merged into one, like a film run at an absurd speed. The time he spent arguing with the priest in a church where he had taken refuge, a priest who had offered to take his confession while Brock had asked about the value of a religion that endorsed murder and executions. That time was of no more significance in his mind than the moment six months later when he saw Cathal Brugha run out of the blazing ruins of the Hammam Building into the bullets of a Lewis gun fired by a free stater, a man who had once followed Brugha.

From the south he heard the sound of an engine, and sitting up, he saw a car traveling toward the cottage. They were bringing the accused.

By the time Brock reached the muddy yard outside the cottage, the car had stopped in the road, and two men were bringing the suspect toward him. Brock walked through the front door, ducking his head under the low lintel. It was little more than one room with a tiny scullery at the back. The members of the court were already in their places.

McGrath, his face as cold as that of any bewigged judge, sat at a table set up in front of the empty fireplace, flanked by Rory Tobin and Joe O'Connor. Not even for a court-martial would McGrath remove his cap. He pointed to a wooden chair, and Brock sat down. Other men were sitting or standing against the walls. All their eyes turned toward the door as the accused was escorted in.

Brock knew him. It was the redheaded man who had guarded the side room in the dance hall. His hands were tied behind his back. His tie hung crookedly, as if other hands than his had tied it. His face was sullen, whether from anger or fear Brock could not tell. The two men behind him pushed him until he was standing facing McGrath.

86

"Release him," McGrath said. One of the men produced a knife and slashed the bonds.

"This is an illegal proceeding," the redheaded man said. "I will not take part in it. I do not accept it."

"You will accept the sentence, nonetheless," McGrath said without humor. "Whether you take part in it or not. I advise you to cooperate." McGrath looked around the silent room, crowded now with the panel, guards, witnesses, and the accused. Brock thought, Ah, McGrath, this is where you love it best, not out among the bullets and the bombs but in small rooms where men have to listen to you.

McGrath straightened his shoulders and sat upright. "This court-martial has been convened by orders of the Dublin Brigade of the Army of the Irish Republic," he said. "The accused, Patrick Monroe, here present, is charged with treason in that he did spy on the secret councils of the Army and did pass information to the Special Branch, which is a creature of the illegal Dublin government. If found guilty, the penalty is death. What do you plead, Patrick Monroe?"

The redheaded man said nothing. He stared down at McGrath, rubbing the marks on his unbound hands, and now Brock decided it was anger that darkened his face.

"We will hear the evidence," McGrath said, leaning back into his habitual slouch. One of the men against the walls stepped forward, put his hand on a Bible on McGrath's desk, and took the oath. As soon as he finished his testimony, guided by McGrath and the two others on the panel, he stood up and left the cottage to join the guards on the road outside. Another witness took his place.

It was an old, sad story, Brock thought. A man torn by different loyalties, first believing one thing, then another. Brock did not doubt that when Monroe joined the Volunteers and took the oath, he would have gone to his death for his comrades. But then the years passed and the doubts took hold, doubts born of the lack of progress, and the faith in the eventual victory of the Army withered until Monroe was ripe for plucking by the men in the Castle, ever vigilant for the potential informer, experts at turning a man against his friends.

Word had gone to commanders of the Brigade that Monroe should be watched, for the Army had its informers inside the Castle, too. Too many times information about operations had reached the Special Branch. Too many times Monroe had come under suspicion.

He had not been told about the plans to rob the bank. But he had been allowed to know that Brock would be outside the bank between nine-fifteen and nine-thirty on the morning of the raid.

"Our information from inside the Castle is that the Special Branch badly wants Brock," one witness said. "They still want him for that ambush outside Limerick more than two years ago, and they suspect him of leading the action squad which dealt with the admiral, Henry Somerville, down in Cork in 1936."

So, taking the bait, the redheaded man had telephoned his masters with the Special Branch and told them that if they wanted Michael Brock they would find him outside the bank. Instead, one Special Branch man had been killed, and the raiders had got away with thousands of pounds, and now the informer was in the hands of those he would have betrayed.

After his stubborn silence it was a surprise when the accused suddenly burst into speech. "You will all be hunted down," he said. "You can kill me, and I don't doubt you will, but you will be signing your death warrants, for it's murder you're about to commit. You are all chasing a phantom, all of you. Don't you know you're living in the Republic they fought for in Dublin in 1916? Don't you know? We have achieved nearly all our aims: independence, our own government, freedom from England."

"Do you call it independence when London still controls the Six Counties?" McGrath demanded.

"That will come," Monroe said. "You all know it will come in time."

"It will only come by our efforts, by our bleeding and dying to achieve it. And it will only happen if we get rid of vermin like you who would betray us."

88

"De Valera is gaining more than you can with all your bombs and your bullets."

"De Valera is letting patriots die in his prisons," Tobin cut in angrily.

The court was so intent on the sudden argument that few in the little room had noticed the door open to allow a small man in a raincoat to slip in. But now he spoke and every eye swung to him.

"This is supposed to be an official court-martial, not a meeting of the Kilkenny debating society," the newcomer said. He walked to the center of the room, and now Brock could see the crinkled face, the cold, unforgiving eyes behind the spectacles. For a moment there was no connection, and then he realized it was Peter Donovan, assistant to the chief of staff, maker of alliances with the Germans.

"We've nearly finished, Peter," McGrath said. Now he was sitting upright. "The prisoner has admitted his treason. He is one of De Valera's men. He is guilty as charged."

"Then let's be done with it," Donovan said.

As he spoke, the accused swung around and began to shout at the men lining the walls. "You bloody fools, " he cried, "do you not see what kind of men these are? These are not the men of the Rising, the heroes of the Tan War. They're malignant failures who've taken over the Army for their own crazy purposes."

"Tie him up and gag him," Donovan said, unmoved. "He should never have been untied." The escort went swiftly to the prisoner.

"You can gag me, but you'll not alter the truth of what I say. Kill me and you're all murderers." The men around the walls, Brock among them, began to file out of the room. By the time he reached the fresh air the prisoner had been silenced, his hands bound behind his back. Brock turned up his collar against the drizzle that had started during the court-martial. There was no need for him to have come. He hadn't been called as a witness. He wondered where Plunger was, why he hadn't been called.

"I'm glad to see you back." Brock realized that Donovan had joined him. The voice was soft now, heavy with brogue.

"You know me?" Brock said.

"I know you. There's nothing you've done for the Army that I've not known about. Your father was a friend of mine."

"Then I'm happy to meet you properly. Though there's no pleasure attached to the proceedings we've just witnessed."

"It has to be done," Donovan said. "He took the oath like all of us, and he broke it."

"Did you . . . did the Council know he was being set up for a trap?"

"We did."

Suddenly Brock's anger could not be held down. "Did you know I could have been killed outside that bank? Or at the very least arrested? Did that thought ever enter your heads?"

"It did."

"It was a test?"

"Ah, Michael, I don't like the word. But if you insist, yes, it was."

They were bringing him out now in a small procession. The prisoner was in the middle, his hands behind his back, his eyes staring wildly over the black gag in his mouth. It looked to Brock like a scarf. While the judges and the witnesses watched, scattered around the muddy yard, the convicted man was led to the wall of a tumbledown outhouse. He stumbled once and had to be held until he regained his balance.

"He's a shameful man," Donovan said.

"He had his beliefs," Brock replied.

"He believed in the money they were paying him, that's true enough."

A member of the escorting party had a bucket in his hand. He lifted it above the prisoner, then lowered it, open end down, until it covered Monroe's head and rested on his shoulders.

"The English like to use buckets," Donovan said.

Four men with rifles formed a tight group ten yards from the prisoner, and Brock remembered Plunger's description of

90

the execution of the Englishman on the road in Spain. He hoped this would not be so belabored. He found himself remembering the prisoner's last desperate words and realized they had lodged unwanted in his mind.

"I want to talk to you, Michael," Donovan said.

The four men raised their rifles. A strangled mumbling issued from inside the gray-metal bucket. McGrath was standing alongside the execution squad, waiting for the rifle barrels to steady. In his right hand, dangling at his side, was a revolver.

"Fire!"

The rifles crackled unevenly, and half a dozen starlings took off in chaotic flight from the roof of the outhouse. The metal-shrouded head jerked back, smashed into the red-brick wall. For a moment the body leaned against the wall, and then it collapsed as if somebody had kicked the legs from under it. The squad lowered its arms, and McGrath stumped forward, his revolver at the ready. He looked down at the heap of crumpled clothing, then fired one bullet into the upper left part of the chest.

"What will they do with him?" Brock asked.

"Who? Monroe?" Donovan sounded surprised, as if the trial and the execution had happened long ago, as if they were no longer of interest. "I don't know. They'll probably dump him in a ditch. They might even deliver him back to his friends at the Castle."

Brock turned away, his depression deepening. How many times had similar scenes been enacted? How many more would there be? Again he remembered the anger of the prisoner, fury when there should have been fear, shouts when there should have been pleas for mercy.

"Come with me," Donovan said. "I'll drive you back to Dublin."

The cars and the motorcycles had been left in a village more than a mile away so that no attention would be drawn to the scene of the court-martial.

"Go in ones and twos, boys," McGrath ordered. "We have

91

no need of the Special Branch smelling around here today."
He sounded pleased with the proceedings, as if they had completed a successful picnic.

"He delights in all this," Brock said as he and Donovan struck out across the damp fields. "To him it's as good as a victory."

Donovan had squashed a shapeless hat on his head to shield his unruly gray hair from the rain. An unlit pipe protruded aggressively from his lips.

"You're not fond of him, I know, Michael," Donovan said. "But we're all in the same family, and we have to get along together or we hang together. It reminds me of my brothers and sisters. We didn't always like each other, but we had to get on with each other. I come from a large family: six boys, five girls, and one stork."

"A stork?" Brock asked in puzzlement.

"Yes, he liked to be close to his work." Donovan was grinning impishly up at him, and Brock laughed, not at the joke but at the puckish expression on the older man's face.

"Some people say I remind them of that actor at the Abbey Theater, Barry Fitzgerald," Donovan said. "The one who went to Hollywood." He was smiling as if the thought diverted him. "Do you find any similarity now, Michael?"

Brock laughed. "You like the idea of playing the stage Irishman?"

"Sometimes it helps."

"Tell me about my father. Did you work with him?"

"Yes, I did. He was a fine man, one of the martyrs we seem to breed in Ireland."

"He would never tell me what he was doing. He never even mentioned that he knew you."

"He wasn't a talker," Donovan said. "He did what he had to do, but he didn't talk about it. But he asked me once to keep an eye on you. That was in the jail up north, when he knew he didn't have long."

"Were you in jail with him?"

"Aye, they took me at the same time. But they didn't torture

92

him, Michael. I want you to know that. He wouldn't have told them anything, though, any more than I did."

"They tortured you?"

"Oh, yes. They tried to open my mouth."

"It's not easy to be brave at such moments." Brock could not imagine the little man in the hands of the RUC bullies. He seemed too insignificant a person to win their attentions. Brock was breathing deeply, glad to be away from the cottage and the body sprawled in the muddy yard. He wondered how they would move it.

"What did they do to you?"

"They take their time," Donovan said, his voice almost too soft for Brock to hear. "They kept me in darkness for two days. At least I think it was two days. They had taken my watch, so I had no way of telling. You couldn't see your hand in front of you. It has an effect on you, that. As if you're dead but still alive to suffer it."

"They're bastards," Brock said. He wondered how he would stand up to such treatment.

"They opened the door, finally, and pulled me out. You can imagine the effect of light after all that darkness, Michael. I couldn't see. I tried to cover my eyes with my hands, but they took my arms behind my back, and they pulled up my eyelids to keep my eyes open. They asked me how I felt. 'Begorra,' I said, 'If I felt any better, I couldn't stand it.' They didn't like that. They kicked me. They made me lean against the wall, resting all my weight on my fingertips."

Brock and Donovan had reached the crest of a hill. They paused and looked down at the village where the cars had been left. There was no sign of movement on the roads in and out of the village.

"Let's sit down for a moment, Michael," Donovan said, "and I'll finish my story. They put a bucket on my head, just like we did with that traitor back there. Then they bounced sticks off it until I thought my head would split open like a cut orange. One of them lifted it off and asked me if I wanted to talk. They were after Tom MacDonagh, and of course they wanted

93

evidence against your father. All I could do was shake my head. So they put the bucket back and began to hit it again. Every time they took off the bucket they'd ask about Mac-Donagh and other things, and every time I'd not say anything, and every time they'd put the bucket back on and hit it.

"I didn't tell them anything. Not then, not at any time." Donovan had told his story without emotion, but now there was a deep-running pride beneath his words. He was sitting on a stone wall, staring down at the village, his pipe still unlit. He looked like a bespectacled elf, Brock thought, not a victim of the Constabulary's torture chambers.

"They did it to my father, too, didn't they?" he said. He knew it was true, whatever Donovan might say.

"No, they didn't, Michael," Donovan said angrily. "I told you they didn't. He was too sick, even for them."

"They would love to hurt a man who's already sick."

"They didn't touch him."

"You have kind intentions," Brock said. He walked away a few yards and stood, kicking at a tuft of grass.

After a few moments Donovan joined him. "I shouldn't have talked about it," he said. "There's no profit in looking back. We have to look forward. To the smashing of England and its puppets in the North. The day I see London beg for mercy, that's the day I'll be happy. And it's coming."

"I heard you were in Germany."

"Where did you hear that?" Donovan's voice was sharp.

"It's all right. It was from somebody who had the right to tell me."

"Sometimes I think we have more wagging tongues than brains."

They began to walk down to the village. "Earlier," Brock said, "we were talking about me taking a test. Outside that bank."

"It was you that called it a test."

"Did I pass?"

"You made a mistake or two, but we'll pass you." Donovan's voice was light and whimsical, and Brock felt another surge of anger.

" 'You made a mistake or two, but we'll pass you,' " he mimicked. "What mistake? What mistake did I make that was bigger than you and your Council setting a trap for a man in the middle of a bank robbery ordered by the Army?"

"You're a likable fellow, Michael Brock," Donovan said, his voice colder now. "You're dedicated to the cause, and I believe you'd do anything for it. If you have a sin, it's an intellectual arrogance. You see things a certain way, and you'll not tolerate any other way of seeing them. Now, under the umbrella of the Army we've gathered all types, socialists and Catholics and atheists, the old and the young, even a few Englishmen. They all take the oath; they all agree to follow their orders."

Donovan took the pipe from his mouth and pointed the stem at Brock.

"You have always followed orders, Michael," he went on. "But, underneath, you sometimes believe you know better than those above you. You have to understand that there is always a reason for those orders, and sometimes you can't be allowed to know the reason."

"Theirs is not to reason why? Is that it?"

"Something like that. This is an Army you're in, and in an Army you do what you're told."

"You objected to my going to Spain."

"We didn't object. It was a cause that drew a lot of young men like you, and we understood that. But now you're back, and you're still subject to the oath, and you must sometimes do things for which you can see no reason. Now, as to the bank, well, it was a sort of test. We had to know about you, Michael. How you reacted in a crisis. If you were still the same Michael Brock."

"The mistakes?"

"I was there, outside the bank, in the crowd. I saw it all. When that Special Branch man grabbed you, you froze. You just stood there, isn't that right?"

"I suppose it is. I wasn't ready for it."

"Plunger had to kill a man because of it. And now you're both on the run. D'you see what I mean?"

"I see."

95

"Ah, Michael, don't be downcast. It happened, and maybe it'll happen again. It's not a natural life we're leading. But I want you to open your eyes to your own failings as well as those of others. I can say all this because I'm an old man and a teacher and because one day it could mean your life as well as that of others. Will you think about it?"

"I'll think about it."

"Good. It reminds me of an old joke. The one about the fellow who walked into the pub and asked for . . ."

"I'll think about it," Brock cut in, "if you'll make me a promise."

"What promise?"

"Not to tell any more jokes." Donovan looked hurt for a moment, his little mouth almost pouting, but then he laughed.

"Very well, no more jokes," he said. "Although it's a shame, for I have some good ones."

They walked into the village. Behind them came three other men from the court-martial. A dog barked, but the streets were empty and the doors closed. Brock guessed that the villagers knew the meaning of the influx of men who had gone across the fields. He caught a glimpse of a face behind a lifted curtain which swiftly fell back into place. Donovan's car was a small black Morris, now parked outside a grim-looking pub.

"Get in," Donovan said. "The sooner we're away the better." He started the engine and turned the car toward Dublin.

"The Army Council wants you to go to England," he said, turning on the windshield wipers. The dirt on the glass turned into a smear of mud, then cleared as more rain washed it down.

"What for?" Brock asked, but he already knew enough to guess the answer.

"There's work to be done there," Donovan said. He smiled briefly, as if the thought gave him pleasure. "Besides you're not much use in Dublin while the Special Branch is after you. You'll be safer with Mother England. You're been there before, haven't you?"

"I have," Brock said. He thought of the times he had

crossed over, nearly always to escape the attentions of the Special Branch after some incident. It was strange, he thought, that England, the enemy, had become his haven, the place where he could relax, secure in the knowledge that nobody was hunting him.

"Are we going to attack the English at home, then?" he asked.

"We're going to do more than that. We're going to smash them. We're going to bring down their Parliament and their Buckingham Palace and their Tower of London, and we're going to destroy their industries and their shops and their houses until they bleed like we have bled, and their heads will be ringing like mine did when they had that bucket on it, and their farms will be as deserted as ours during the famines, and they will know how it feels to be a conquered people, living on the sufferance of their masters."

His relish in his tumbling words was a palpable thing, as satisfying to Donovan as a meal to a hungry man, a woman to a long-celibate prisoner. In fact, Brock thought, there was something almost sensuous in the pleasure that Donovan drew from his words.

"And you'll have a part in it, Brock. Your efforts can help the final overthrow of the people who have held us down for eight hundred years. You can help pay them back for all the cruelties, the callousness, the contempt they have made us endure."

"With the Germans?"

"Yes, with the Germans. They are going to destroy England, and we are going to help them do it. The English, they're a decadent people, and they deserve to be finished."

"There are disturbing things about the Germans, the Nazis."

"I won't try to blink it away. I've been there, and I've seen them. They're not like us. But we need them just as they need us."

"You would sup with the devil, then?"

"I would."

97

"So would I if it means freedom for Ireland."

"I'm glad you say that, Michael, for we can make use of your experience, your dedication. The Germans, they have the money, the arms, the power to do what we cannot alone."

"I'm ready."

"Plunger Cronin and others will be going over, too. To join Volunteers already working there. This could be the beginning of glorious things, Michael."

They reached the outskirts of the city. The drizzle had turned into a downpour which filled the gutters and reflected the few electric signs from the shining pavement.

"D'you want me to take you to your safe house?" Donovan asked.

"No," Brock replied. "Best to drop me at a bus stop. Best not to have your car seen there. I'll take a bus, and then I can slip in the back way. When do I go to England?

"Arrangements are being made. You'll hear when it's time."

The car pulled up to the curb near a bus stop, and Brock climbed out, flinching at the intensity of the rain.

Chapter 8

Berlin
April 12, 1940

FROM a distance, from London or New York or Tokyo, the invasion of Norway appeared a marvel of ruthless efficiency in which every objective was seized according to a carefully orchestrated timetable. There were those in Germany who knew the truth.

Canaris sat in his office above the Landwehrkanal reading the reports from his agents aboard the freighters *Widar* and *Adar,* vessels which he had dispatched to Oslo harbor three days before the projected invasion. He made a mental note to radio congratulations, personal congratulations. But for them, the operation might well have foundered.

Not only had the Norwegian shore batteries sunk the *Blücher* in Oslo fjord, but they had damaged the *Emden* and forced the invasion transports to retreat. The campaign had stalled before it started. But then came the message from the Abwehr chief's agents aboard those innocent-looking freighters. A small force of German troops, they radioed, had managed to take control of the airfield at Fornebu. Airborne troops could be landed there in safety. Within hours a hurriedly assembled division was being shuttled into Fornebu and was sending patrols out toward the capital. Nine hours after the agents radioed from the harbor, Oslo was in German hands.

Because of lack of foresight, the German high command had failed to establish essential communications. Because of foresight, Canaris had once again come to their rescue. Now his mind was already turning to the future. He looked at his watch. Lahousen and Piekenbrock were late. Canaris disliked unpunctuality.

When his two lieutenants arrived shortly thereafter, discussion turned first to the network of agents which had been created in the Low Countries and in France. As in Poland, it would be their duty to spread confusion and fear before the thrust of the Panzers. Some had hidden German uniforms which they would don at the tactical moment before setting out to seize bridges and other strategic points, giving the impression that the Nazi spearheads were far ahead of their actual advance. Others would wear enemy uniforms to further engender chaos.

Canaris then broached the subject of Britain. Because of Hitler's embargo on the infiltration of agents into Britain, aimed at lulling British fears of the Reich, espionage there had been at a minimum. Not until shortly before the outbreak of war in the West did the Führer relax his edict and allow Canaris to dispatch his agents. Except for the successful mapping of airfields, the effort had been notably ineffectual.

"They were ill-prepared," Canaris said. He did not waste time apportioning blame. Instead he looked at Lahousen, who had not been overwhelmed by the failure of the German agents. They were Piekenbrock's responsibility. The cutback in espionage in Britain left the IRA as the most potent weapon in the midst of the enemy, and the IRA was Lahousen's responsibility, his idea.

"We have had to increase the funds allotted to the Irish," Lahousen said smoothly, "but I think it will be worth it. Dublin is already moving more men into England, and at the moment our rapport with the IRA Army Council is good. They are insisting on some of their own projects, but they're also ready to follow our wishes."

"If it suits them, no doubt," Piekenbrock said.

"My dear Piekenbrock, over there they have a saying, 'England's difficulty is Ireland's opportunity.' Thus, if they help us, they know they are increasing England's difficulties. I foresee no problems in that area." His relations with Piekenbrock were worsening daily.

"Communications?" Canaris said, looking at Piekenbrock.

"The radio system is satisfactory."

"They're using the *Afu?*" Canaris' reference was to a small transmitter weighing only four pounds. Consisting of one tube operated by four tiny batteries, it could be heard at the Abwehr radio station outside Hamburg but was virtually inaudible elsewhere.

"Yes, Admiral. We have already trained some of the Irish in their use at Quenzsee. Women among them. They're quick to learn." A jovial Rhinelander, Piekenbrock had a shrewd brain behind his bluff exterior. He raised a topic now that had already occurred to his chief.

"These Irish," he said. "We shall be dealing with them as if they are our agents. And yet we have no way of verifying their reliability or their expertise."

"You are right, my dear Piekenbrock," Canaris said. "But there is no time to investigate. We have to rely on Lahousen's reading of their leaders, in particular this man . . ." He paused and looked at the sabotage chief.

"Donovan," Lahousen said. "Like you, I am concerned about this aspect. There is only one way to approach it. The Irish must be excluded from all knowledge of our other agents. They must be considered a separate arm of the Abwehr. All communication must be by radio, and there must be no contact between them and the agents already installed. Nor must they be brought in touch with agents who will go over at a later date. In that way they cannot endanger our espionage operations if they should prove unreliable. As for their expertise, we shall see. So far they have carried out some small sabotage assignments with efficiency."

"They should be used only for sabotage," Canaris said. "As time goes on I can foresee great possibilities for them."

"I am sorry, but I don't trust them," Piekenbrock said. "How do we know that they aren't in touch with the British? It must have occurred to MI Five that the IRA is an obvious ally for us. How do we know that the British haven't set up this whole operation?"

"Whatever happens, they couldn't be as untrustworthy, as incompetent, as the agents we have sent over," Lahousen said waspishly. "They have been a disaster."

"There is no need for that," Canaris said. "That is over and done with. As for the Irish, they will be tested. If they carry out the more important assignments that lie ahead, then we can assume their independence of London. Personally I do not think that British counterespionage is cunning enough to try to use the Irish in the way you suggest, Piekenbrock. They have suffered failure after failure. That foolishness at The Hague. . . . Anyway, Lahousen is right. There is no danger of betrayal so long as the Irish are partitioned from the rest of our operations in Britain. If they fail, then we have merely lost one of our possibilities, nothing more." He paused and gazed reflectively at a little statue of the three monkeys who see, hear, and speak no evil, the only touch of humor in the somber office.

"Now we come to something else," he said finally. "The Luftwaffe and Göring." He wrinkled his nose in distaste. "They have developed a bombing aid which they say overcomes all problems of weather. They claim it will lead planes directly to their target in spite of darkness, cloud cover, and storms. Put simply, it is a radio beam which the pilot uses to home in on his target. As the bomber flies along the beam, it reaches intersecting beams which tell the pilot how far he is from the target. The last intersecting beam tells the pilot that he is in the general area where he must drop his bombs.

"The scientists are very proud of this new control system. There is only one difficulty: so far they haven't been able to put the pilot in the exact slice of air that he needs to be in to hit his target accurately."

"They need help from the ground?" Lahousen ventured.

"That's exactly what they need," Canaris said. "And, of course, they turn to the Abwehr. Without ground guidance the bombers could unload five to ten miles from their specified target. When they want to hit an aircraft factory, they might be bombing a big field. When they're trying to destroy a port facility, they might well be bombing a farmhouse."

"Clearly, some sort of signal from the target area is needed," Piekenbrock said.

"A radio signal from the ground, perhaps," Lahousen suggested.

"Perhaps," Canaris said. "Perhaps a radio transmission of such simplicity that even your Irishmen could manage it efficiently."

Chapter 9

Dublin
May 27, 1940

THE man's name was Sharp, Alan Sharp. Brock looked at him and thought that he seemed to take himself and the newspaper he worked for very seriously. True to his name, he had an angular face, all tangents and planes, as if a cubist had put him together. Even his black hair looked geometric in its well-greased arrangement. He wore a heavy overcoat, but he still appeared cold as he sat in the room over the Dublin pub.

"I expect they told you," he said, "I'm a foreign correspondent for a New York newspaper which is very interested in the activities of the IRA." He imbued the words "foreign correspondent" with an aura of reverence and consequence. Brock looked across the room at Maggie, who raised an eyebrow infinitesimally.

"That's nice," Brock said.

"Yes, well, my editors thought it would be a good idea if I talked to a member of the IRA so that we could get a first hand human story. Perhaps we could start with your name?"

"No," Brock said.

"I understand. That's all right, we'll call you Sean X. D'you have a rank?"

"I'm just a soldier in the Republican Army."

Sharp took a notebook from the pocket of his topcoat. "Just a soldier," he said. "I like that. And what are your duties?"

"To carry out orders," Brock said.

"Michael!" Maggie was not amused.

Emboldened by her support, the reporter said, "You're not being very helpful. Your chiefs said you were a good representative of the IRA, and they said you would talk to me, and here you are giving me answers as if I'm a policeman engaged in interrogation."

"I'm not very good at talking," Brock said.

"A man of action, eh?"

"I do what I'm told."

"Well, I'll tell you something. I'm not without influence in the States. My stories are read in the homes of important people who could help the IRA. Your Army Council agreed that it would be valuable to have the right sort of story in my paper, but you don't seem to agree with them. It almost seems as though you're disobeying orders, not obeying them."

"Does it, indeed?" Brock said, an edge of anger in his voice.

"Listen, I'm a soldier, and I'm afraid I don't have much time for your 'important people' in America who might be able to help us. I'm sure they enjoy reading your stories over their breakfast tables, and I'm sure the Irish-Americans think about us all the time, especially when they're having a drink or two and singing a song or two about the old country. But that doesn't do us much good over here, does it?"

Maggie stood up and walked towards them. "Why don't you go downstairs for a moment and have a drink," she said to Sharp. "Have a drop of good Irish whiskey. There's been a bit of a misunderstanding. We'll clear it up in a few minutes, and when you come back we'll start over again."

"Well, okay," Sharp said. "But just remember. The Army Council, your chiefs, set this thing up, and I don't think they'll be very pleased if nothing comes of it. I'll be back in a few minutes." He stood up, pulled his coat closer around him, and left the room.

For a moment they were silent, looking at each other. Then he grinned. "I'm being very naughty, aren't I?" he said.

"You'll not get around me like that, Michael Brock," she said, unsmiling. "Do I have to go through it all again? Are you that slow to understand?"

"Let's go to bed," he said.

"You won't take it seriously, will you? All you think of is the bombings and the shootings and the killings. You don't see that money is needed, that we need help from other people."

"We'll get all the money we need. We'll get it ourselves. We don't have to deal with scribblers, pompous writers who think they're doing us a favor listening to us. Ah, to hell with him."

She went to the window, parted the curtains, and stared out at the gray day. He saw that her back was stiff with tension.

"Sometimes," she said, "sometimes I don't love you at all. Like today. Because it seems to me you're being stupid just to raise my hackles. I have no more time than you for that American, but I know that we need him. Guns are not enough in our war. Dedication is not enough. Faith is not enough. There has to be politics and propaganda. We have to conduct our war on every front we can find."

He felt a weariness seeping into his soul. Over the years he had heard it all before. The sloganeering by men with blazing eyes and bitter lips. The dicta of the organization on badly printed pamphlets handed out at meetings, on street corners. Now he was getting it again, this time from a girl who had been playing with dolls when he first picked up a gun. He felt like a muddy veteran straight out of the front line who is sent, unfed and unbathed, the smell of sweat and death still on him, directly into a classroom to listen to a lecture from a crisply uniformed recruiting sergeant. Somewhere in the weariness a spurt of anger touched him.

"Don't tell me," he said. "I've read that book. I helped write it, Maggie. So don't you preach to me. You're a nice young girl, all neatly clothed in your beliefs. You look splendid. But I'm too frayed around the edges. I've been wearing the uniform of obedience a long time now, and there are bullet holes in it."

"It sounds as though it's letting in some doubts," she said. "Are you feeling the winds of disbelief, Michael?"

Oh, yes, he thought, even the young ones, the beginners, were always sniffing around for the heresy, the first sign of skepticism. He, too. It was an organization of paranoia, an attitude spawned by all the betrayals, the informers, the secrecy that cloaked the words and deeds. He ignored her question.

"Politics," he said. "I've had a taste of politics. I know what politics can do to good men. Look what it did to Michael Collins and those other brave fighters who went to London and sold us out. They talked to reporters, and they talked to politicians, and look what that gave us."

She let the curtain drop back into place and turned. With the light behind her he could not see the expression on her face.

"They made a mistake, an awful mistake," she said. "But sometimes I think you're glad they did. It gives you a bitterness that you hold on to like a life raft. Without it you wouldn't know what to do with yourself."

"Oh, certainly," he said. "I love it. I love being chased around the countryside, hiding in ditches, eating whatever I

105

can find, always looking over my shoulder. Oh, certainly, I just love that. How I would hate it if the Special Branch was no longer hunting me, if I could live in peace and quiet with no more killing and no more danger of being killed."

"You don't know whether you would or you wouldn't," she said. "Because you've never lived any other way."

He was silent. It was true. He couldn't imagine what it would be like to have no gun at hand, no more fear of death. It had begun, really, with the Rising, and it hadn't stopped.

"Ah, come on, Maggie," he said. "We're both right. Let's not go at each other with our heads down just because of some American reporter."

"Will you talk to him, then?"

"It'll do no good."

"Do you really think that's up to you to decide, Michael? He was right, you know. You're a soldier, and you're disobeying orders. The Army Council arranged all this. Sean Russell himself gave the okay. It's an order to a Volunteer."

"I'll talk to him."

"Will you be a little more pleasant?"

"I'll try. If you'll take me to your bed afterwards."

Now she laughed, and she went to him and took his head in her hands, and she looked down at him and said, "Oh, Michael, we've been messed up so badly. Don't you sometimes wonder how we'd have been together if we'd been living normal lives? I do. Maybe a home and a family and the whole of green Ireland to play in." She bent and kissed him on the top of his head, pulling him into the cradle of her belly and thighs.

"It'll happen one day," he said, but as he said it, he realized he had no faith it would. "Go and get the great writer," he said.

When Sharp reappeared, he carried three glasses filled to the brim with whiskey. "A peace offering," he said. "All on expenses."

"The problem has been cleared up," Maggie said. "Michael didn't understand everything."

They drank the unwatered liquor, and Sharp pulled out his

106

notebook. "Perhaps you could tell me something about your background," he suggested. "Human stuff always goes down well."

Now Brock talked, and Sharp scribbled. Brock talked about the poverty of Dublin's back streets and the ache for freedom that grew in them. About the Rising and the Black and Tans and the gunmen and how he joined them, and inevitably it came to Michael Collins.

"The British wanted Collins so badly they could taste him," Brock said. "They knew that he was leading the Army, that his was the mind behind all the rebel activities, that without him the guts would go out of the movement. So they tried everything to get him. They tried informers, and they swooped on houses, and they put up roadblocks, but none of it was any good. Finally, they looked to Cairo."

"Cairo in Egypt?"

"Why there, I don't know. But they gathered sixteen British officers in Cairo, and these sixteen were given the assignment of finding Collins, of killing him. They were given new names, forged identity documents; in fact, new identities. I suppose the point of it was that they would be safe from Collins' informers inside the Castle. And he had them. From Cairo the sixteen traveled to Dublin wearing mufti and all posing as commercial travelers. They arrived singly and on different dates, taking up residence in rented flats, some in Pembroke Street, some in Mount Street, and others in various hotels."

"This seems to be getting away from you," Sharp said.

"We'll get back to me in a minute. Collins' intelligence operation was better than the British thought. Among other things, a spy for the English broke down under IRA interrogation and told the story of the sixteen who had come looking for Collins. He said some of them were Irish, and he described where they were living. But the sixteen won the first round. They caught one of Collins' lieutenants, Frank Thornton. Then they made a mistake: after interrogation they let Thornton go."

"They didn't realize who he was?"

"They thought he was just another Volunteer, of no particular importance. Then they doubled up on their blunder. They caught two more men close to Collins and then allowed them to go, too. Collins knew the mistakes wouldn't continue. Something had to be done about these spies. And it was. After a series of conferences, it was decided they must be wiped out."

"You mean killed."

"I mean executed."

"It was war," Maggie said.

"The date was November twentieth, 1920. 'Bloody Sunday.' Squads of Volunteers were dispatched to the lodgings of the sixteen. I was in one of the squads, assigned to dealing with two men named Watson and Jones, who were sharing a flat in Mount Street.

"How old were you?"

"I was eighteen."

"My God, and they made you part of an execution squad?"

"I was glad to be a member. It was a mighty blow for Ireland, and I was privileged to take part."

"Tell me about it."

"Our orders were to strike at nine A.M. There were eight of us in my squad. Our leader was Billy McMahon, who was himself executed later by the Free State government."

"There's an awful lot of blood around Ireland."

"There is. Jones and Watson were in a second floor flat. We'd had them watched, so we knew they were both at home. Having a Sunday morning lie-in, we reckoned, and we were right." Brock rose and began to pace the room.

"There was no trouble getting in the front door. They weren't very clever. No security. Three men went around to the back in case they tried to get away there. Me and Billy McMahon and three others went up the stairs. It was a green door. I'll always remember that green door. We had three Thompson machine guns and two revolvers.

"We listened for a moment, but there was no sound except a bit of noise that could have been somebody snoring. Mc-

Mahon told us to get ready, and then he used one of the Thompsons on the door, around the lock. We kicked it in and poured inside. We started shooting even before we could see everything.

"They had two separate single beds, and both of them were asleep when we came in. One of them never stirred. The bullets went through the bedclothes into him, and he probably never did wake up. The other one was different. He was out of his bed in a flash. Wearing blue and white striped pajamas, he was. A hatchet-faced man with cropped white hair, although we couldn't see too well because they had the curtains drawn and it was dark in the room. The noise, with all that firing in a small room, was tremendous. The white-haired fellow was fast, as if he'd made preparations for just such an incident. He threw himself towards the window which faced out over the backyards. I'm telling you, his feet didn't seem to touch the ground. When he got to the window, he flung himself against it, right at the curtains."

Pacing about the small, bare room above the pub, Brock felt a sense of dissociation. What was he doing here, talking to this American about events that had taken place years before and that no longer had any significance, certainly not to newspaper readers in a foreign country? They meant something to him, but he couldn't be sure what. He looked at Maggie, who had heard the story before, and she was watching him with something hidden in her face. He realized he had fallen silent.

"Was the man wounded?" Sharp asked, looking up from his notebook.

"He was," Brock said. "There was blood all over his pajamas, but it didn't seem to stop him."

"Did he get through the window?"

"What? Oh, no. He couldn't fight his way through the curtains. They were as good as a brick wall. It happened so quickly. The others were pulling the bedclothes off the man who hadn't stirred. McMahon's gun had jammed. He shouted, 'Shoot, Michael. For the love of God, shoot.'

Brock went and picked up his glass from a table and

finished off the last of the whiskey. "The Englishman, he was clawing at the curtains, his back to us. I hesitated, I suppose, for McMahon shouted again, 'Shoot the bastard.' So I did. I shot him between the shoulder blades. With my revolver. He gave a great gasp, as if the air had been kicked out of his lungs, and he fell down, bringing the curtains with him. I could see where the bullets had gone into him. It finished him."

"Fascinating," Sharp said. "Did you know his name? Was it Jones or the other fellow you mentioned?"

"I don't know," Brock said shortly. "It wasn't the moment to try to find out. We had to get out of there."

"Was that the first Englishman you killed?"

"There always has to be a first, doesn't there?"

"I didn't mean to upset you."

"I'll go and get some more drinks," Maggie said. She went out with a warning look at Brock.

"It was the first," Brock said.

"But not the last?"

"Not the last. Strangely enough, when you're a soldier, you're expected to fight and to kill. Don't they do that in your army?"

"With us it's different. We've no experience in ambushes and execution teams and raiding houses."

"It's just a different form of warfare. D'you expect us to stand up in front of them, the whole bloody British Army, and take them on with our revolvers and shotguns?"

"The British Army isn't doing too well in France right now."

"If we had as many soldiers as the Germans, we could destroy them, too," Brock said.

"I believe the Germans worked with the Irish in the nineteen fourteen-to-eighteen war. Isn't that true?"

"England's difficulty is Ireland's opportunity," Brock said.

"It doesn't make the Irish any more popular in America. The sympathy there is with the British."

"We'll manage without the Americans. The British are very good at propaganda."

"Did your execution teams kill all the sixteen British

agents?" Sharp heard Maggie at the door and went to open it for her.

"We got fourteen of them," Brock said.

"Did they catch any of you?"

"Oh, no, they didn't bother. Not at first, anyway. They simply put a lot of Auxiliaries into lorries and sent them out to Croke Park, where there was a Gaelic football match that afternoon. The Auxiliaries got out their guns, pointed them into the crowd, and pulled the triggers. Point-blank into the crowd."

"My God."

"They killed fourteen men, women, and children, including one of the football players. That's their idea of warfare. Later on they picked up Dick McKee, Peadar Clancy, and a young fellow who had nothing to do with the executions, Conor Clune. They took them to the Castle, tortured them, and then they shot them."

The interview continued, but now Brock's voice was a monotone, as if the description of Bloody Sunday had exhausted all his emotion. It had been a long time, before Spain, since he had talked of that day, and he realized now that he had deliberately pushed it to the back of his thoughts. If the Rising hadn't been the beginning of the killing for him, then it had been Bloody Sunday. He wondered how many more people he would have to kill. With a sudden sense of shock he began to tick off mentally the names of the young men who had gone into the hills with the flying columns or into the streets with him to fire their guns and throw their bombs. They were nearly all gone, either to De Valera's side or to America, or they had just put down their guns and accepted that they had failed. Or they had been killed. Most of them had been killed either by the British or by the Free State, which had learned from the British how to kill and then improved on it. There were just himself and Plunger and a handful of other men led by an aging executive whose dreams now were tinged with bitterness. Again he remembered the words of the redheaded man who had been court-martialed at the cottage.

"What happened to Collins?" Sharp asked.

"After he sold us out, he was a minister in the Free State government," Brock said. "Before the treaty had been ratified, he went before the Dail, and he said, 'If I am a traitor, let the Irish people decide it or not.'

"Well, they decided. Collins was on a tour in his own County Cork. Just like the British, he was, with a Crossley tender and an armored car as escort and plenty of soldiers. But it didn't do him any good. He went through a place called Skibbereen, and he was driving through the valley of Beal na mBlath when they ambushed him. They killed him in the road there, and some said it was a shame, especially at his funeral. But there were others who said he got what he deserved, and I won't argue with them. But that's all in the history books; it's not what you want from me."

"It all affected you, though? Helped make you into what you are?" Sharp's eyes were shrewd, probing.

"Not at all," Brock said with a touch of anger. "I'm what I am because I believe in what I believe. Collins was one of many I worked with. Some of them have kept their beliefs, some haven't. That's all there is to it." He knew Maggie was watching him with that same impenetrable expression.

"Why do you think your Army Council selected you as the man I should interview?"

"You know as much as I do," Brock said, shrugging. He thought without mirth that it was probably because they had so few to select from.

"What would you say is the worst sin of the De Valera government?"

"Apart from the men they've hunted and killed and allowed to die in prison? Isn't that enough?"

"The Church seems to support him."

"Aye, the priests would warm his bed for him. They feared the true republic we were after because to them it carried the seeds of anticlericalism. So they support him, and he gives them the license to judge our books, our behavior, our plays, our schools. Do you know the poem that was written about the Rising? It talked about a terrible beauty being born. Well, I

112

have a question. Where is this terrible beauty now? Is it in the smug middle class, the church-haunted state, the dependence on Mother England? It's all dreams ending in mediocrity, with the Six Counties still held by a tyranny directed from London."

"They say the IRA is allying itself with the Nazis."

"Do they?"

"Would you work with the Germans against the English?"

"It's an interesting question," Brock said, rising. "But I think we've talked enough. You must have all the material you need for your story."

Sharp folded his notebook and slipped it into his pocket. "Will you have a drink with me downstairs?" he asked. "I owe you another drink for your time."

"You don't owe me anything but a promise of accuracy in what you write," Brock replied.

"My paper is famous for its accuracy," Sharp said with a return to his earlier loftiness. "As a foreign correspondent, it's important I get things straight because my stories are read in the State Department. You don't have to worry."

"I'll come down with you," Maggie said, leading him to the door. "They should have a taxi waiting by now." She looked back at Brock. "Wait here, Michael," she said. "There's something else."

When they had gone, Brock went to the window and stared out, but he quickly tired of the view of slate roofs and red-brick walls and grimy streets. It was raining again. Hands in pockets, he walked slowly about the room until he found himself in front of an old mirror hanging lopsided on the wall. Absently, he straightened it and then paused to stare at his gaunt face. The lines running from the corners of his nose to the corners of his mouth were deep and permanent. It was, he thought, a forlorn sort of face, the sort of face that had seen much, and much of what it had seen it had not liked. Well, he thought, that had been his own choice, nobody else's. And in spite of it all, at thirty-seven he was still alive, still outside the jails, still moving forward on his course. Already he had lived

113

to be five years older than Michael Collins, and he wasn't finished yet.

The door opened and Brock turned, expecting Maggie. It was Donovan. Behind him came Sean Russell, the chief of staff, and behind him, Maggie. It was the first time since his return from Spain that Brock had seen Russell.

The IRA chief looked tired and sick, his once-ruddy face wan and wasted. His clothes hung on him loosely, showing cruelly how his muscular body had degenerated. They shook hands. Brock could feel an almost repulsive clamminess in Russell's palm.

"You don't know the good it does me to see you again, Michael," Russell said. "We've all missed you, and me more than most."

"It's good to be home," Brock said. He wondered if his shock at Russell's appearance showed through the platitude.

"Let's all sit down," Russell said, sinking wearily into a chair. "We must talk briefly, and then I must be on my way.

"Can I fetch you a drink?" Maggie asked.

"No, no, I haven't the time, much as I'd love a hooley with Michael. We'll do it one day."

"Did the interview with the American reporter go off all right?" Donovan asked.

"I think so. I answered all his questions," Brock said, looking across at Maggie, who was standing at the window, dividing her attention between the men in the room and the street outside.

"I know reporters," Donovan said. "Most of his story will be about himself, about how he made contact with us, how he had to go under cover, how he was passed from man to man, how he came here blindfolded and left the same way. But we'll get enough of what we want across."

"Let's get on with it," Russell said, and Brock realized that in spite of his sickness he was still the man in command.

"What is it?" Brock asked.

"You're to go to England tonight. There's a fishing boat that

114

will take you across, you and Plunger Cronin. But there are some things we must tell you first. You know about the Germans?"

"I know."

"Very well. I'll put it to you frankly. You're going to be working for them. We have an alliance, which is to our advantage, but they're insisting that some of our best men in England must follow their instructions, must obey their orders as if they were German agents. It will mean that although you're still a Volunteer, with the loyalties of a Volunteer, you will be under the direct control in England of the German Secret Service." Russell paused and pulled out a handkerchief as a bout of coughing overcame him. He wiped his mouth.

"In return we're getting money and arms. And we're getting the best of the deal anyway because the Germans want to destroy England, and you will help them, and that is our aim, too."

Brock nodded. He wondered how long Russell would last, who would take his place.

"Suppose the Germans win," he said. "Why wouldn't they become to Ireland what the English are now?"

"We have an agreement. Freedom. Ireland for nobody but the Irish."

"The Nazis have broken agreements before. We might exchange one lot of masters for worse."

"It could happen," Russell agreed softly. "But we have no alternative. I'll be honest with you, Michael. We're a dying organization. The young men aren't coming to us anymore." For a moment a look of bafflement settled on his white face. "The old call doesn't seem to be there now, not like it was once. I don't know whether it's because the young men nowadays are different or whether it's because we don't make them understand. But the fact is that we have to move strongly now or, we can't blink it, the Army will dissipate into a bunch of old men with more memories than strength. This is our chance, and we must seize it." Again he was wracked by a fit of coughing, and again he wiped his mouth with his handkerchief.

115

Donovan was looking away from his chief as if embarrassed.

"You must tell us now," Russell went on. "If you will not work for the Germans, then you must tell us, because once you're in England it will be too late. Tell us you can't do it and there will be no recriminations, no hostility against you. We will find another man, and you can continue your efforts here in Ireland."

"You have always talked of striking England," Donovan said.

"Let him talk, Peter," Russell said. "It's his decision."

They were all watching him, Russell and Donovan and Maggie, her back now against the window.

"There's nothing to discuss," Brock said. "I'll go, and I'll do what they tell me. It's what we've both always wanted, Sean, to take the action and the killing and grief to England."

"Good," Russell said. "Now listen to me. You'll go over with Cronin, but in England you'll split up for different tasks. Arrangements have been made for both of you. Identification papers, ration books, clothes coupons, and so on."

"Forged?"

"Aye, forged. We have a good man for that. Now, our units in England are in touch with Berlin by radio. However, you need not bother about that. To ensure security, you will deal with only one contact, who will bring you your instructions. Come here, Maggie."

She walked to Russell's side, and he took her hand. "This fine girl will be your contact, Michael," he said. "We have no greater patriot in all the thirty-two counties. Did you know she had been to Germany?"

Brock looked at her in surprise and shook his head. Maggie smiled slightly at him. "Ah, there's so much he doesn't know about me," she said to Russell.

"She went for training in the use of their radios," the chief of staff said. "They tell me she's very good, better than most of the men who've gone over."

"Will you be coming over with Plunger and me?" Brock asked her.

"No," Russell said. "She will be in touch with you later, when

116

you're established over there." He looked at Donovan. "Is there anything else?" he said.

"The money."

"Oh, yes, the money. You'll be given enough money to live on for some time. But it will be best for you to take a job so that you fit into the background. Arrangements are being made for that." He stood up, and the other men rose with him.

"I'll wish you the best of luck," Russell said, reaching out to take Brock's hand.

"It's time it ran with us," Brock said, feeling again the cold dampness of Russell's palm.

"I'll say no more than this, Michael: All the patriots of the past, Tone and Parnell and Pearse and Connolly, none of them did more than you will if you help bring down England and so lift the occupation of the Six Counties and return Ireland to her native sons. Our thoughts and prayers will be with you."

Russell nodded at Donovan, who pulled an envelope from his pocket and handed it to Brock. "Maggie will tell you what you must do," he said. Then Donovan opened the door for him, and he was gone, Donovan after him.

"How long has he been sick like that?" Brock said.

"A year or more," she said. "He's getting worse."

"He'll not live to see Ireland free."

"Sometimes I wonder if any of us will." There was an uncharacteristic note of pessimism in her voice, but Brock hardly heard her. He was opening the envelope. They were mostly five-pound notes.

"That'll pay for a lot of wine, women, and song in London," she said, watching him count them.

"London, is it, then?" he said. "The heart of the beast."

There were nearly five hundred pounds in his hands. Brand new notes, he thought, probably from the bank he'd robbed.

"Tuck that away in your pockets, my Michael," she said. "There are things to do if we're going to get you on that fishing boat tonight."

Chapter 10

COLONEL Francis Edward Blood called out, "Come in." The door opened, and a cartload of file folders appeared, pushed by a young woman, her face pleasantly flushed from her exertions. Like him, she wore civilian clothes.

"The files you wanted, Colonel," she said.

"I don't know that I do, now I see how many there are," he said. "Put them over there by the window."

She eased them over to the required place, finally standing upright and brushing her fair hair back from her forehead. "Is there anything else, sir?"

"No, you run along and get yourself a cup of tea." As the door closed behind her, he stood up and walked over to survey the brown cardboard files all neatly tied with red ribbon. He didn't like the look of them. Picking one at random, he saw it was marked JOHN O'GRADY, ALIAS PETER STONEHAM, ALIAS DONALD CAMPBELL. The papers inside amounted to a biography, starting with a date and place of birth, continuing with schooling and the jobs John O'Grady had held.

Blood's eye fell on one paragraph: "Believed to have been recruited to the IRA in Wexford around the month of June, 1928. He left his job as a plasterer almost immediately and did not receive further official recognizance until December, 1931, when he was given a sentence of three years in Londonderry for an attack on a night watchman during an unsuccessful attempt to steal dynamite from a blasting site."

Blood read on. O'Grady, it seemed, had served his time without any remittance. He had been a recalcitrant prisoner, surly and showing no signs of remorse over his misdeeds. Flipping through the pages of the file, Blood saw that it was a catalogue of crime and punishment, supplemented at times by information which could only have come from an informer within the IRA. He turned thankfully to the last page.

"O'Grady was last seen in Londonderry in the autumn of 1939. At that time, it is known, he had not deviated from his loyalty to the IRA. It is believed that he crossed over to England shortly after the decision of the IRA Army Council to spread terrorism to these shores. Understood to have taken part in the unsuccessful attempt to explode a bomb in a Birmingham cinema in February, 1940. STILL AT LARGE."

Blood scowled absently and tossed the file back among the others. All would tell the same sort of story, though some would conclude with the capital-lettered words DEAD, JAILED, or NEUTRALISED. He stared through the window at the H-shaped goalposts in the park below. Neutralized, he thought, was a hopefully all-encompassing word, the sort of word vague enough to appeal to bureaucrats. It could mean anything. The subject could have turned informer. He could have emigrated to Australia or America or anywhere else, for that matter. He could have dropped out of active participation in terrorism. He could have. At the same time, there was no way to be sure that the informer was not still working for the IRA, that the émigré had not returned, that the inactive had not become active. If such proved to be the case, the bureaucrats would merely alter the epilogue on the files.

Blood wondered if any of the men named in the files were lodged in the cell block he could see to his left. He no longer drew any amusement from the irony of spending his working days in His Majesty's Prison, Wormwood Scrubs, London W. 12.

Certainly it would tickle his old colleagues at the Yard, colleagues who knew how many men he had sent here. How the villains might feel was another matter. But Blood was not a man to linger over ironies. He accepted them and moved on.

At Scotland Yard he had been known as a thorough, plodding detective who sometimes enjoyed the fruits of an intuitive perception. Those envious of his steady climb through the upper levels of the Metropolitan Police called him lucky, but his superiors, who could follow his thought processes with the intimacy of authority, discerned a brilliance too frequent to be called luck.

119

At the age of forty-nine, he had been promoted to detective chief inspector. Even then they did not know his secret. Blood's vice was innocent enough, and if it had been discovered it would have produced little more than a few chuckles along the corridors; but he guarded it, for he was a private man.

He was a painter, a watercolorist. His family knew it, but few others did. He would take his wife and son to the seaside for vacations, and while they sported on the sands he would take his paints and his canvases and retreat into a world of delicate flowers and fluffy clouds and, there, lose himself.

Blood had been a DCI for less than six months when his wife died. A chill turned into a cold, which became pneumonia, and there it was. His first thought was resignation. The work which he had once enjoyed turned into a tedious routine. He knew it was partly because he could no longer involve himself in specific cases, following them through from start to finish. But also there was a lack of relish in living. All that seemed to have gone with Yvonne. So his second thought was also resignation, and he left the Yard.

He had enough money. His wife came from a moderately wealthy family, and they had invested her money wisely. Together with his pension, the proceeds would allow him to live comfortably, for he had simple tastes. His son was already away from home, working as a deck officer on a transatlantic freighter.

So Blood went down to Polperro, in Cornwall, and found a cottage and began to paint. It healed him. He enjoyed the sea air, and he walked when he wasn't painting. He was a good cook, and he put on some weight and even managed a tan. The trouble was that he discovered he was not a painter. Not a full-time painter. Within four months he was bored. Perhaps it had something to do with the certainty that war was close. Perhaps he was at an age when the last restlessness shows the battle flags to approaching dotage. The fact was he was bored.

Thus he was when the call came, telling him to report to an import-export office on Baker Street. It was, he quickly learned, one of the tentacles of MI 5, which seemed to delight in setting up shop in the dingiest of offices in the grimiest of buildings. The interview, conducted by a harassed little man who had been an Oxford don before the war, was brief; and Blood quickly realized that either they had already decided to recruit him purely on the basis of his record or that they would take anybody who wasn't actually bedridden. Blood was delighted to be back at work but less delighted with the place of work, which was Wormwood Scrubs Prison, lost in the wastes between East Acton, Shepherds Bush, and North Kensington. He was given an office in the reception block and awarded the title of colonel, which, he surmised, was their fuzzy approximation of a DCI in the military.

More important, Blood was made a control officer.

MI 5 had seized a number of German agents operating in England. All had been offered the opportunity to become double agents, ostensibly continuing their work for Berlin but in reality acting under the direct control of MI 5. Some had accepted their situations; others had been executed. Each double agent was put in the care of a control officer who became the alter ego. Just as the agent had to live two lives, so did the control officer, who had to try to enter the mind of his charge, watchful for the triple-cross, caring for the agent's psyche, concerned above all that the Germans believed the false messages their agent was radioing to a relay station aboard a vessel sailing up and down the Norwegian coast, thence to Hamburg.

Blood was fascinated by the concept. No murder case, no manhunt had engrossed him as much. As a result he was deeply disturbed when he was told that somebody else would be taking over his duties. He had grown to like and enjoy his Czech agent, code name Skylark, and he feared a newcomer would not understand him so well. Blood, however, was trained in discipline, and after an initial protest he turned over his agent with the deepest briefing he could command.

Now he faced his next task: the IRA. Blood had no experience with the strange phantom army, but his philosophy was that they were criminals, and he knew how to catch criminals whether they acted from greed, laziness, or political fanaticism.

Standing at the window, consciously ignoring the files, he wondered briefly whether different goals might produce different types of villains, but just as swiftly he dismissed the thought. Motivation was merely a factor which had to be considered. The crime was still what mattered, and if the IRA had decided to work for the Germans, well, that was a crime, and like any other it could be countered.

Again a knock on the door. He turned from the window and called out, "Come in."

The man who walked in had the thick shoulders and wrists and the scarred features of a boxer. Nestor Bryant had done some of that in South Africa. Amateur stuff, but he had enjoyed it. His official reputation, however, was built on his skills as an interrogator. He was known for these skills in Johannesburg and in Durban, in Nairobi and in Hong Kong; in fact, wherever the colonial power needed information about the activities of its nationalist enemies, the men who worked to usurp control.

His services were in demand wherever the Union Jack flew over foreign lands, and he was happy to go where the call was strongest. He was a man who enjoyed his work.

Inevitably his calling had taken him to Ulster, where he had spent nearly four years extracting the facts needed by his masters. That was where MI 5 had found him.

"Good morning, sir," he said, eyeing the cartload of files. "I see you have them."

"Yes, the Yard sent them over last night. It's going to be a hard slog, but it's got to be done."

"It'll be a pleasure, sir, meeting my old friends again. I bet I know most of them, one way or another."

"I hope so. Did they tell you downstairs what this is all about?"

"Pretty much, although there are a few blank spaces. They said you would fill them in."

"Very well. Now, let's see. When did you leave Belfast?"

"No more than a month ago, sir."

"Then you're as familiar as we are with the IRA shift of focus. To England."

"I am. The bastards. They should round up all the Irish in this country and sling them into jail. I don't know why we let them run free. Not at a time like this. Did you hear the news from France this morning?"

"I know. It's pretty bad."

"The bastards. They'll stab us in the back, I know it."

Blood stood up and walked to the window. A lone man with a black spaniel was walking across the playing field toward Hammersmith Hospital to the right. Blood watched silently as the dog pulled its master to the goalposts and raised an elegant leg.

"I know something of your history, Bryant," he said finally. "So I can understand your feelings about the IRA. It can't be pleasant to be accused of brutality toward a prisoner."

"It was lies from start to finish," Bryant said to Blood's back. "The inquiry cleared me completely."

"It didn't do your career with the RUC any good, though, did it?"

"It did not, sir. I was on the point of resigning at one time. Then I thought, To hell with those fucking terrorists; that's just what they want. So I stayed." Bryant's face was red and angry.

Blood turned away from the window. "Yes, I think you were wise. However, there's something I must bring up, and then we'll say no more about it. This is very serious business we're engaged in, and we can't afford any emotionalism. In my experience, the worst detective is the one who takes things personally, creates his own vendetta against criminals."

Bryant started to speak, but Blood raised his hand. "No, let me finish," he said. "Because of your experiences with the IRA in Ulster, you have good reason to feel belligerent toward them. It would be odd if you didn't. But too much hostility can cloud judgment, and that could be fatal. Therefore I am ask-

123

ing you to put all that behind you. If we're going to track down these men, we need to be cooler and smarter than they are. If you think your deductive faculties will be affected by your emotions, I want you to tell me now. I don't want to find we're making mistakes when it's too late. Do you understand?"

Bryant looked at Blood, glanced at the files, then looked back at Blood. "I understand, sir," he said. "You don't have to worry. I don't think my work has been harmed by my feelings, and I don't think it will be in the future."

"Very well, we'll say no more about it. Take a seat, and we'll get down to business. First of all, it's no secret that the IRA has been moving men into Britain."

"They boast about it in Dublin."

"I know. It's not an organization that's noted for its security. On the other hand they may have their reasons for telling the world what they're up to. At first we had a suspicion that they might be planning to work with the Germans. Now, as a result of various pieces of information falling into place, we know it to be a certainty."

"They tried to do it in the other war."

"Right. Now, Bryant, you've been cleared for some secret information, but I must emphasize that what I'm about to tell you is so significant that it could mean the difference between winning and losing the war. I know that may sound melodramatic, but nonetheless it's perfectly true."

"I'm not one to open my mouth."

"All right. I can tell you that some very clever young men, many of them from the universities, have joined us. Some of them think they're smarter than they really are, but that's another story. What's important is that one group has cracked the radio code which the Germans are using to direct their agents over here."

"They've cracked it? Sweet Jesus Christ. You mean you're plugged into their network over here?"

"To all intents and purposes, yes. We don't know where all their agents are operating, but we do know what they're being told to do because most of their orders come by radio, and the

124

code is blown. There are other encouraging aspects to the counterespionage scene, but it's the radio system that concerns us."

"Where do we come in, sir?"

Blood walked over to the files and looked down at them with distaste. There were far too many, he thought.

"As far as we can make out," he said, "about half of the radio messages are directed to IRA men in this country. That doesn't mean that all the terrorists use radios. It seems that the radio operators here have the duty of passing on directions to agents who probably have no other contacts."

"Then there should be no difficulty hunting down the agents. We merely note what their orders are and then grab them when they try to carry them out."

"It's not that simple," Blood said. "The fact is that so far, the IRA doesn't seem to be doing anything. The radio messages have all been routine stuff: keeping in touch with the agents, sometimes telling them to move from one city to another, but not directing them to any specific action. It seems to me they're waiting for something."

"Invasion?"

"It could be. They could be waiting to act as a fifth column. We just don't know. We have fairly nebulous stuff that doesn't really help us zero in on them. Code names, that sort of thing."

Bryant looked at the files. "So we have to examine that lot to see who might be the likeliest lads to be over here?"

"Exactly. It's needle in a haystack stuff, but we have to hunt through those files, extracting those which seem most dangerous."

"It could be any of them."

"It could be. But your job is to use your expertise, your knowledge, to select the possibilities. They tell me you have more information on IRA men than anybody else in the country. That's why you were detached here from the Constabulary."

"And promoted to major?"

125

"We'll make you a general if you spot the people we want. I suggest we do a preliminary run-through of the files first to weed out those we can dismiss completely."

Bryant joined Blood at the cart with its load of brown files. "All right," Blood said. "Let's make a start."

Chapter 11

The Irish Sea
May 28, 1940

PLUNGER was strangely somber. When Brock remarked on it, he said, "It's the bloody sea. I know I'll be seasick. I always am. Particularly in the dark like this, when you can't see a thing and the bloody boat keeps going up and down. Up and down."

"We'll be ashore by dawn. It won't take long."

"Long enough," Plunger said disconsolately. He was leaning against the stern, staring back at the lights of Dunleary, his big shoulders hunched against the wind.

"There's something else that doesn't help," he said. "Maureen. She didn't want me to come. It's the first time she's ever tried to stop me. She was shouting at me, and the kids were grabbing my legs. A proper scene, I can tell you."

"Women," Brock said.

"I think I'll marry her when we get back."

"That's not the first time you've said that."

"I know. But when it comes to pinch. . . ."

"The kids need a proper father."

"I send her money. They're looked after all right."

"She's a good woman."

"She is, at that. She's never once complained when I've gone off on jobs. Not even when we went to Spain. I don't know what's come over her."

"Women," Brock said again. Maureen was a big, lusty woman who had produced three children for Plunger. She drank as heartily as Plunger and almost matched him in size, with muscles bigger than most men. Her children promised to develop a similar bulk. Brock sometimes tried to imagine the Homeric meetings of Plunger and his woman in the bed in her terrace house. It should, he thought, be accompanied by the clash of cymbals, the blaring of trumpets.

"Has she never suggested you should get married?"

"Not once," Plunger said, but Brock doubted him. He knew something of Plunger's background. A militantly disciplined education at the hands of the Christian Brothers. The inevitable truancy ending with the equally inevitable theft and the juvenile court. He had been dispatched for three years to the reformatory at Daingean in County Offaly. Behind the high walls he had suffered the efforts of the priests, the oblates of Mary Immaculate, to reclaim his mortal soul from the grasp of the Devil. Education took the form of constant beatings, sometimes floggings in front of the massed inmates.

To erase any misplaced ambitions for sumptuous living, the menu offered porridge, bread and dripping, bad potatoes in cabbage water, and unsweetened tea. The high point of the year came at Christmas, when meat was served. Plunger had been in rebellion against any form of conformity ever since, and that included marriage.

The boat was moving away from the shelter of the land now, pitching more, and Plunger was leaning over the side.

"It's worse at the stern," Brock said. "Let's move up a bit." But Plunger was already vomiting.

He continued throughout the night until he was pale and shaking, looking somehow shrunken from his normal size. A little after midnight the wind changed, giving the old boat a smoother motion, and Plunger was able to sink wearily onto the deck, retching only occasionally. Almost immediately the engine spluttered, surged back into life, spluttered again, and then died.

Dawn was coming up by the time they had cleared the

127

blocked fuel line. The boat's blunt snout was turning back toward the lightening sky when Brock saw it. He stared across the heaving, metallic-looking waters for a few moments, lost sight of it, and then saw it even closer. He went to the ramshackle affair of wood and glass which served as meager shelter to the captain at the wheel.

"Something in the water," he said, pointing. "About one hundred yards and to the right."

"Ah, there's lots of things in these waters," the skipper said. "We're already late." But he stared in the direction of Brock's extended finger. He was an old man whose years of hardship at sea seemed to have reduced him to nothing more than the essentials of bone and weathered skin.

"Probably from one of those freighters they've been sinking," he said. "Still might be worth taking a look at. It's going to be full daylight by the time we get you over there, anyway." Indeed Brock could see the English coastline, a line of darker gray on the horizon.

The thing in the water was white. A swell lifted it, as if offering it to the chalky dawn. "Jesus, Mary, and Joseph, it's a body," the captain said. "Jim, Peter, get up there!" The man and the boy who were his crew went forward and leaned over the gunwale. Brock joined them to stare down at the body.

It was sprawled over a wooden hatch which floated a few inches below the water. One hand was lashed by cord to a spar of the hatch; the other arm was floating uselessly, gently lifting up and down in a curiously fastidious gesture.

The man was naked but for a pair of pants which had slid halfway down his buttocks. He was on his belly, his head resting on the outstretched arm keeping his nose and mouth clear of the water. The captain shut down the engines, and the boat drifted until it was bumping delicately against the side of the hatch.

"You'll have to go in after him," the captain shouted. "One of you go over the side and cut him clear."

Brock stripped off his jacket and shirt. "I'm a good swimmer," he said. "I'll go." The next moment his shoes were off, and he was over the side.

The shock of the cold water made him gasp. In the water the swells appeared much higher than they had from the deck, and for a moment he could not see the hatch with its helpless cargo. He followed the line of the boat's hull until he was within reach of the hatch.

"Is he dead?" the boy shouted.

"Get me a knife. Quick." He had to tread water until the boy reappeared, a knife in his hand. Once he thought he would be crushed between the hatch and the peeling hull of the boat. The boy leaned over the side, holding the knife by its tip. The handle went into Brock's hand and slipped. Just in time, Brock grasped the blade as it slithered downward. He swore as he felt the naked edge penetrate the skin of his palm.

"Is he dead?" the boy shouted again.

Brock concentrated on sawing away at the cord. He was holding the man's arm as he worked, and the flesh was cold.

"Get a rope over the side," he called. Before completely severing the cord, he clambered halfway onto the hatch, kicking his legs to maintain his position. The rope came over, and he grabbed it. The hatch was moving more jerkily now, and he realized the wind must be getting up.

It took him nearly five minutes to get the rope around the man's middle and secure it. Then he slashed the remaining fibers of the cord. The wrist, he saw, was badly swollen.

"Pull him up slow and easy," he called. Kneeling on the water-smoothed hatch, he guided the burden away from the hull as they pulled away. He could hear the boy asking, for the third time, "Is he dead?" He waited, still kneeling on the swaying hatch, until the rope came over the side again. He grabbed it with hands so chilled he could scarcely feel it and somehow managed to scramble back aboard.

They had the body flat on the deck, Plunger steadily pumping the walls of his diaphragm. The captain was watching. "Start her up, and head due east," he said to the older crewman. A few minutes later the deck was shuddering to the thud of the engine pistons, and the grimy fishing boat was bucking into the swells again.

Plunger was tiring. "Here," Brock said, "let me take over. It'll warm me up."

"Make some hot coffee, and get the brandy," the captain shouted to the boy.

Brock had hardly touched the figure on the deck before the eyelids began to flutter. "He's alive," Plunger shouted. Brock continued the artificial respiration, feeling some warmth returning to his own limbs. When they lifted the man's head and forced his lips open to pour down some brandy, his eyes opened completely. He jerked his head away from the upended bottle. "Give . . . water," he mumbled. "Water."

All four of them now were kneeling around his head. "Be easy," the captain said. "Take a drop of the brandy, and then you'll have some coffee."

"Water," the man mumbled again. Brock could see that his tongue was dehydrated and swollen. After a moment the man seemed to understand. He allowed a few drops of brandy to pass his lips, his tongue working against the liquid.

"Let's get him out of the wind," the captain said. They made a nest of blankets in the lee of the wheelhouse, then carefully carried him over and wrapped him up. By then the coffee was ready, and the man had begun to shake uncontrollably.

"Put more milk in it," the captain said, and glancing at Brock, "You'd better get into some clothes." The wind and the exertion had dried him off as well as any towel. Offered the lukewarm coffee, the man swallowed it in such gulps that they had to pull the cup from his lips.

"Slowly, slowly," the crewman said, speaking softly as if to a baby. Brock, back in his clothes, went to the captain.

"What are we going to do?" he asked.

"That man belongs in a hospital."

"I know."

"We can be in Liverpool in less than an hour. There are hospitals there."

"If we go into Liverpool, they'll check our papers. They'll want to know what a bartender from Belfast is doing aboard a fishing vessel registered with the Republic of Ireland."

"It's complicated things, sure enough," the captain said. "And we have to make up our minds quickly."

Brock stared over the bow toward the English coast, illuminated now by long beams of sunshine which had broken through the clouds.

Always the unexpected, he thought. If the engine hadn't broken down, they could have been ashore well before daybreak. If he hadn't spotted the body on the hatch, they still could have slipped into the River Dee and gone ashore at an isolated spot.

"He has to be seen by a doctor," he said. "We'll have to go into Liverpool. Is your radio working?"

"After a fashion."

"All right, tell them to have an ambulance waiting. We might still pull it off. There'll be some confusion getting him ashore. With any luck we can help carry him off, and nobody'll think to ask about us."

The captain went to put in the radio message, and Brock returned to the lee of the wheelhouse. "He was torpedoed," Plunger said. "He's off an English freighter, the *Maria Fairclough*. A deckhand."

"How long ago?" Brock asked the man.

"Three days," he said painfully. He was still shivering, but there was a trace of color in his stubbled cheeks. "My hand hurts," he said.

Brock pulled away the blanket and reached for the man's arm. They had forgotten to remove the cord which attached his wrist to the hatch spar.

"Jesus," Brock said. The flesh was swollen and livid. The cord was buried so deep that only the frayed end which Brock had cut gave any indication that the purple effusion concealed a bracelet of cord. "Do you have any morphine?" he asked the crewman. When the man shook his head, Brock swore. "Aspirin, you must have aspirin."

131

Again Jim shook his head. "Brandy is all we've got," he said. "And there's not much of that left."

"Well, give it to him," Brock said, hiding the horror of the hand under the blanket. He suspected it would have to come off when the survivor reached a hospital.

Plunger was smiling. "I feel better," he said. "Must be having something to do."

"We're going to have to put in to Liverpool, Plunger. That man's going to die if we don't get him to a doctor."

"You're out of your mind." His voice was high with astonishment. "He's an English seaman. For Christ's sake , my hard man, we haven't come over to rescue the English. We've come to destroy them. They can take him to a doctor after we've dropped off."

"He'll die, Plunger."

"I don't give a flying fuck if he dies. He's English. What's the matter with you, Michael?"

"I just don't want to go to the trouble of fishing him out of the sea only to let him die. He's been torpedoed and spent days floating around the ocean. I think he deserves a chance."

"What are you, God or something? We have orders to follow, and those orders are that we get into England without a brass band announcing our arrival."

"We can still do it."

"Not in the middle of Liverpool, we can't."

"Nobody will be looking at us. They'll all be fussing around the Englishman. We can slip away in the confusion."

"And suppose we can't. Suppose they grab us. What d'you think they'll say about us in Dublin when they hear we threw up the whole thing to save some bloody Englishman?"

"It's my responsibility."

"It'll be my body sitting in an English jail."

"Dublin put me in charge, at least until we get ashore."

"Jésus, Mary, and Joseph."

"I doubt that the skipper would let us do it your way, Plunger. He's a sailor, too, and he's got his feelings."

132

Plunger touched his coat pocket. "I've got something here that would change his mind for him," he said. "Very quick, too."

"Don't be a fool," Brock said. "He's a Volunteer. His son is in jail right now in Dublin."

Plunger's surrender, when it came, was complete. "All right, my hard man," he said. "The two of us will help carry him ashore, and then we slip away. But I tell you, if anybody tries to grab me, there'll be some shooting."

"We're not wanted in England."

"Ah, Michael, you know we're on their lists. The best we could hope for is to be shipped back to Dublin, and there's a couple of murder charges awaiting us there." He suddenly grinned. "You know something, I don't feel sick anymore."

"The boat's not tossing like it was."

"It's not that. Now I've got worse things to think about."

In the Mersey a naval launch came alongside. It was all brass and white decks and coiled ropes and neat uniforms aboard, an absurd contrast to the sloppiness of the battered old boat that had brought them across the Irish Sea. A young lieutenant sporting a neat beard stepped aboard, followed by an older man carrying a brown leather bag.

"Where is he?" the lieutenant asked.

They led the naval officers to the lee of the wheelhouse, where the seaman was lying, eyes closed, in the pile of blankets. The older officer, evidently a doctor, busied himself for a few moments, making a wry face when he saw the swollen wrist.

"We must get him into the hospital at once," he said. At the lieutenant's order, four ABs came aboard and carefully lifted the merchant seaman, still in the blankets, into their launch.

"Come on," Brock muttered to Plunger, and they both stepped over into the launch.

"Hey, what's this?" the lieutenant said.

"We're going with him," Brock said.

"There's no need. We'll look after him now."

133

"We saved him," Brock said. "We want to make sure he's all right."

"He went into the water after him," Plunger said, nodding toward Brock. "Nearly drowned getting him out, he did."

The lieutenant hesitated, and Plunger added, "We've sort of got a personal interest, Lieutenant." He smiled disarmingly.

"Well, I suppose there's no harm in it," the young officer said, accepting their presence, and a few moments later the launch was speeding toward shore. An ambulance was waiting on the dock, and as the launch tied up, a stretcher was handed down. Across the water Brock could see the fishing boat turning back toward the open sea. He looked to see if the lieutenant had noticed that they were being abandoned by their vessel, but he was too busy supervising the removal of the patient.

The doctor followed the stretcher into the ambulance. Brock and Plunger climbed in after him before the doors could be closed. Almost immediately the ambulance moved off.

"Will he be all right?" Brock asked the doctor, who was taking his patient's pulse.

"He's young and he's strong. He's got a good chance. I don't know about his wrist, though . . ."

"It's a nasty one," Plunger ventured.

"Aye, well, I've seen nastier. There's worse things happening at Dunkirk, they say. At least this one's back in England."

"Dunkirk?"

"Haven't you heard the news?"

"We've been at sea."

"Half the British Army's on the beaches at Dunkirk, on the French coast. They're trying to get them home across the Channel."

"The Germans have won, then?" Brock said, glancing at Plunger. He felt a curious sense of betrayal and loss. The Germans hadn't needed IRA help after all. And if the Irish hadn't helped in the victory, then could they expect any rewards?

134

"They haven't won just yet," the doctor said grimly.

"But if the British have been chased out of France . . ."

"France is one thing. England's another, entirely. Let Mr. Hitler try to come over here, and he'll get a very bloody nose." The doctor, a comfortable-looking man with a paunch, tried to look martial, but failed. Brock guessed he had been a general practitioner, more used to delivering babies than caring for shipwrecked sailors, before he was called into the Navy.

The ambulance's bell was ringing now to clear a path. Brock looked out of a window and saw they were out of the dockyard and moving at speed down a residential street.

"Where are you boys from?" the doctor asked.

"Dublin," Plunger said.

"The Irish haven't been very helpful."

"What d'you mean?"

"The neutrality you're insisting on. A lot of ships have gone down in the Atlantic because Ireland won't help us."

"And why should we help you?" Plunger began angrily. "Just when have you helped us, except with soldiers to show us to our graves? . . ." Brock, sitting next to Plunger in the swaying vehicle, jammed his knee against his companion.

"Don't listen to him, Doctor," he said. "He's all wound up because of finding this young fellow in the drink. You'll find most of the Irish are in sympathy with Britain, whatever the politicians may decide."

"Politicians," the doctor agreed in a disgusted voice. "Take Chamberlain, now. We're well rid of him, and that's no mistake. Churchill's a different matter altogether. A leader, not a compromiser. A bit of an old pirate, but that's what we need at the moment. As for allies, I think we're better off without them. You know where you are when you're standing on your own two feet with nobody else to worry about."

"It's not much good standing on your own two feet if your army is being chewed up in France," Plunger said, ignoring Brock's warning look.

"Don't worry about them," the doctor said. "Everything

135

that'll float has gone across to pick them off the beaches. Paddle steamers, trawlers, shrimp boats, even little yachts. They'll bring them back, no mistake. Well, here we are."

The ambulance stopped, and the doors were opened. There was a flurry of attendants and nurses, all in starched blue and white. With efficient and practiced speed, the stretcher and its occupant were carried out of the ambulance and into the hospital. The doctor had already vanished.

Brock and Plunger looked around them. They were in a yard outside a door, above which was the inscription "Emergency." Nobody seemed to be paying them any attention. "Come on, my hard man," Plunger said, turning toward an archway beyond which they could glimpse a quiet street.

"Wait," Brock said. He had spotted a guardhouse just inside the archway, and through the window he thought he saw a uniform. "That bastard might want to know who we are," he said. "He's probably seen us get out of the ambulance. We can't just walk away."

"We'll tell him the ambulance gave us a lift," Plunger said lightly.

"We're going into the hospital," Brock said. "Come on."

He walked to the doorway before Plunger could protest further, and after a moment Plunger went after him.

"Walk as if you own the place," Brock said. He wanted to find the hospital's main entrance, which he thought would come under less scrutiny than the emergency entrance with its uniformed gatekeeper. But he could see no exit signs.

They were marching down one long corridor when suddenly a young nurse appeared before them, a look of horror on her snub-nosed face.

"What are you doing here?" she demanded. "Don't you know this is out of bounds to visitors? Who are you anyway?"

"Ah, then, we're truly sorry," Plunger said, exuding heavy charm. "It's ashamed we are for our foolishness. You see we were looking for the main entrance. We've been visiting our dear old uncle, who's in a bad way with his heart, and now we're away home to tell our dear old mum all about it."

136

She looked at them doubtfully, then said, "All right. Now go back the way you came, turn right, then right again, and you'll be at the main door." She paused, then blurted, "Wait a moment. It's not the visiting hour. Who are you?"

An older nurse appeared down the corridor. "Stop gossiping, Nurse, and come here," she called. Her voice was filled with aggrieved authority.

"Yes, Sister," the young nurse said, turning away from Brock and Plunger. "I was just telling these gentlemen they couldn't come down here. . . ."

"Come here, Nurse," the sister said in irritation. "I don't want to hear your excuses."

As the nurse hurried toward the voice of seniority, Brock and Plunger smartly turned and headed away. As they turned right, Brock muttered, "Did you have to play the stage Irishman like that, for Christ's sake? 'Our dear old uncle and our dear old mum.'"

"It worked didn't it?" Plunger grinned. "A bit of the old Irish blarney never hurts anybody. I think she took quite a fancy to me. Come on, there's the main door."

"You shouldn't be out without a keeper," Brock said, but he found himself grinning. Partly it was because of the sudden exuberance he felt. They were walking out of the main door into the fitful sunshine, and nobody was giving them a glance. Down a short driveway bordered by nasturtiums, they walked through the main gate, and then they were in a narrow street filled with cars and buses and shoppers. They were at large in England.

Plunger was as high-spirited as Brock. As they strolled among the women with their baby carriages, the old men killing time in front of shop windows, he gave a little whoop.

"D'you realize something, my hard man?" he said. "We've pulled it off. And who do we have to thank for it? The Royal Navy. The bloody wonderful Royal Navy. If the rest of it goes this well . . ."

"I'm just wondering if there'll be anything for us to do," Brock said, sobering. "If the Army is trapped at Dunkirk,

137

London will try to do a deal with the Germans. Try to make peace. And then where will we be?"

And yet, looking around him, he felt a stab of bewilderment. The street scene was too peaceful, too ordinary. There were no signs of panic, not even of concern. If the Germans were hammering on England's door, these people didn't seem to hear them. They stopped at a newsstand, and Brock bought a paper.

ANOTHER 47,000 RESCUED FROM DUNKIRK, the headline said. THE SAGA OF THE LITTLE BOATS. ENGLAND FIGHTS ON.

"It's a land of wishful thinkers," Plunger murmured, staring over Brock's shoulder.

"Bloody marvelous, isn't it?" said a little man in a cloth cap to the storekeeper. "Fooking French let us down again."

"Fook 'em," the storekeeper said. "We don't need them anyway. My boy Billy says all they do is lie around and drink wine."

"Have you heard from Billy, then?"

"Not for a couple of weeks." The storekeeper pointed at the headlines. "He's probably sitting on the beaches with the rest of them. Sunbathing, I shouldn't be surprised." He managed a laugh, but it was without amusement.

"Which way is the train station?" Brock asked.

"Turn right out of the shop," the man in the cloth cap said. "Then, first right, and you can't miss it." If he caught Brock's accent, he didn't comment on it. They were used to the Irish in Liverpool.

Brock and Plunger bought tickets for a London express which stopped at Birmingham, where Plunger had been instructed to make his first contact. They had to wait more than an hour in the station, killing the time with a breakfast of stale sausage rolls and weak tea served in chipped cups. Then they walked up and down the platform.

"We'll not be seeing each other for a while," Plunger said. "I wish it was me going to London. You'll be having a good time while I mope around Birmingham. There's a city that's as jolly as a funeral procession."

"We're not over here for a holiday, Plunger."

"I know it. Still, Birmingham. . . ." His voice was so lugubrious that Brock grinned.

"Perhaps they'll let you come down for a night out with me," he said. "You can let me know through Maggie." They had been ordered to stay out of contact except through her. No letters. No phone calls.

By the time the train pulled in, the platform was crowded. Half of the waiting passengers were in uniform, men and women.

Brock noted sardonically that while the officers' outfits were well-cut out of fine cloth, the uniforms of the lower ranks were made of serge so thick that it looked as if it would stand up on its own. The soldiers, the sailors, and the airmen had to cram into the grimy third-class compartments while their officers had plenty of room in the first-class carriages.

"Democracy in action against the Fascist beast," he murmured to Plunger.

"I'd like to have seen the Internationals in Spain putting up with it," Plunger agreed. They found places in the crowded corridor of the train, clutching the rail that ran across the window.

The London express left the station a few minutes after noon.

Chapter 12

London
May 28, 1940

IF Liverpool seemed nonchalant, London was a city of caution. There were the sandbags. They were piled around doorways, in front of windows, on top of air raid shelters. When Brock came out of the lavatory at Euston Station, he walked

139

into a wall of them because the station was so meagerly lighted.

In the streets, cars and buses used hooded headlights which gave so little radiance that they were forced to move in a tentative dawdle alongside the curbs. The streetlighting came from masked bulbs which allowed only a pinhead of illumination. Windows had been blacked out with paint, cardboard, or blinds. Pedestrians tried to find their way with dimmed flashlights. The enemy wasn't here yet, but London was a city under siege.

The journey south had been punctuated by long delays, so it was dark when the line of carriages halted at the London terminal. Brock debated taking a taxi; then, because there didn't seem to be any, he traveled by bus and tram to the Kings Arms.

On the top deck of a swaying tram he thought about the torpedoed merchant seaman. Luck had been with them, but Plunger had been right nonetheless. The seaman, whatever his condition, should have been secondary to their mission. It was not a question of condemning him to death. He might still have survived if they had slipped ashore before getting help for him. Yet Brock had risked everything for the sake of a man he had never seen before. An Englishman. He remembered Plunger's expression of astonishment. He remembered Plunger's later question: "Are you changing your mind, then, Michael?"

Brock had been irritated. If it had been somebody other than Plunger, he thought, he would have hit him. Instead he had said shortly, "Perhaps I've seen enough dead men," and they had been silent for nearly half an hour.

It was nine o'clock when he reached the Kings Arms. It was a majestic name for an ordinary-looking pub within sight of Clapham common. It was bounded on one side by a small parking lot and on the other by a Y-junction of two roads. It was built chiefly of red brick with some traces of wattle, as if the architect had attempted a mock-Tudor exterior and then given up. It was as dark as every other building in the area.

Brock opened the door into the saloon bar, drew aside the

140

blackout curtain, and walked in. Inside it was cheerful enough. A few chairs and tables, a red carpet, horse brasses and beer mugs hanging above the bar. There were about a dozen customers, most of them gathered at the bar, listening to a radio. Brock judged them a mixture of middle-class local residents, office workers, and skilled artisans. He ordered a pint of bitter from a fat man in a brown suit who had carefully combed the remaining strands of his hair across a shining pate. Brock guessed from his manner that he was the innkeeper.

The pint was put in front of him, and as he paid, the man in the brown suit nodded at the radio. "It's Priestley giving it to them again," he said.

Brock recognized the north-country voice of the BBC commentator, J. B. Priestley. The broadcaster was talking about Dunkirk and the effort to rescue the troops from the beaches.

"We've know them and laughed at them, these fussy little steamers, all our lives," Priestley said. "We have called them the 'shilling sicks.' We have watched them load and unload their crowds of holiday passengers—the gents full of high spirits and bottled beer, the ladies eating pork pies, the children sticky with peppermint rock.

"She's gone, the *Gracie Fields,* pride of the Isle of Wight ferry service, sunk in the Channel. But now, look, this little steamer, like all her brave and battered sisters, is immortal. She'll go sailing proudly down the years in the epic of Dunkirk. And our great-grandchildren, when they learn how we began this war by snatching glory out of defeat and then swept on to victory, may also learn how the little holiday steamers made an excursion to hell and came back glorious."

When he had finished, there was a silence in the bar. Finally a customer called out, "Give me another one, Barnaby."

"He talks well, that Priestley, doesn't he?" said a man with a cross of sticking plaster on his neck.

"They say they brought another forty thousand off the beaches today."

"That's just guessing. How can they tell how many got back today? It's too early to count them all yet."

141

"Funny way to run a war, if you ask me," said a little woman with a hat like a chimney pot on her dank curls.

"They know what they're doing," the man behind the bar said. "We don't want any despondency in this house, thank you very much."

Brock moved down to the other end of the bar. A few moments later the fat man appeared in front of him. "Ready for another one, sir?" he said, "I'm going to close in a couple of minutes."

"D'you have any Irish whiskey?" Brock said.

The innkeeper looked at the other customers, still gathered at the radio, then back at Brock.

"Irish whiskey is hard to find these days," he said.

"It depends what brand."

"I prefer Jameson's," the innkeeper said. Then, looking again down the bar, he said, "I wasn't expecting you until tomorrow."

"I got an express down from the north."

"What's your name?"

"Bell. Michael Bell."

"Call me Barnaby."

"D'you have a room here for me?"

"There's an attic. I've put a bed in it and an electric fire. I don't like this at all. Not in the middle of a war."

"If you want to back out, tell me now."

"I made a promise, and with me a promise is something you keep. There's only one thing I want to know. Did you do it?"

"Do what?"

"Did you kill that copper? The plainclothesman in Dublin?"

"No," Brock said. "I was there, but I didn't kill him."

"That's good enough for me. Now, you wait here a minute, and I'll get rid of these people." He moved away from Brock, and a few minutes later he started calling, "Time, gentlemen, please. Time now, if you please." He moved around from behind the bar and began to shepherd his customers through the blackout curtains and into the street.

"All got your torches, have you, then?" he called. "Mind

how you go." He closed the door behind the last straggler and locked it.

"I think I'll have a drink now," he said.

He reached under the bar and pulled out a glass and a bottle of milk. "Ulcers," he said. "Little bastards, they give me hell."

"You run this place on your own?"

"Now I do. My wife ran off with a vacuum salesman."

"I'm sorry to hear it."

"She'll come back. She always does. How long will you be here?"

"I don't know. A few months. Until they've stopped looking for me in Dublin."

"I'll give you three quid a week and your room. You work behind the bar lunchtime and evenings. Sunday nights off."

"Suits me."

"Keep your fingers out of the till and we'll have no problems. You'll get a few free drinks when the customers are in the mood. I wouldn't do it except I owe Paddy McGovern a favor."

"At three pounds a week, you're not getting a bad bargain."

The innkeeper suddenly burst into a roar of laughter. "I know it, lad," he said. "Oh, to be sure, I know it. We'll get on just fine."

As his laughter died away, there was a knock on the door he had locked. "Somebody forgot something," Barnaby said. "You watch them try and wheedle another drink out of me." It was a policeman. He took off his helmet as he ducked through the door and put his flashlight on a table. He stared at Brock.

"It's after closing time, Barnaby," he said.

"It's all right, officer. This is my new barman."

"Oh, is it?"

"Yes, he's just over from Belfast. Got in tonight, he did."

"I've come down to be near my sister," Brock said. "She's ill."

"In the Battersea General Hospital, she is," Barnaby said. "Would you like a drink, officer?"

143

"I'm here on duty, Barnaby. It's that doorway of yours. We're still getting complaints about the light coming out. There's an old woman across the street who reckons you're signaling to the Jerries so they can come and drop a land mine on her house."

"I don't know what more I can do. I put that curtain up."

"Well, you just warn your customers to be more careful when they're using it. You could lose your license, you know." He looked at Brock again, put on his helmet with imperial deliberation, picked up his flashlight, and went through the curtain. The next moment, his helmeted head reappeared.

"You tell your customers to close the curtain before they open the door," he said. "Like this." He closed the curtain, and then they heard the door open and close.

"Officious bastard," Barnaby said. "Never did like coppers. Come on, I'll show you your room."

Brock first noticed her on his third night behind the bar. Barnaby was leaving more and more of the work to him. He would perch himself on a stool near the radio like an affable Buddha, talking to his favorites, making sure that Brock was wiping the counter clean, keeping an eye on the till. Even so, for Brock it was not burdensome labor. There were times, especially early in the evening, when there were only a couple of customers to be attended to, and he could read a newspaper.

This third night he was scanning the *Daily Mirror,* which was full of the Dunkirk evacuation. BLOODY MARVELLOUS, said the headline above the editorial.

A man and two women came in. While the women sat at a table, the man ordered a beer and two sherries. He was middle-aged with a plump, dissatisfied face and a mincing manner. Brock guessed he was an office worker, for his hands were soft, the nails well-kept. One of the women, her hair obviously dyed blond, drank with exaggerated gentility, a little finger raised from the glass to signal her refinement.

It was the third customer who drew his gaze. She was a full-bodied woman, perhaps in her mid-thirties, wearing a cher-ry-red suit which matched the lipstick on her slightly pouting lips. Her dark eyes were boldly direct, and she stared at Brock with a frank interest that verged on arrogance. The customers made an unlikely trio.

Occasionally watching them as he dealt with new arrivals, Brock decided the man and the blonde were brother and sis-ter, the dark-haired woman probably the man's wife. Once, he saw her put a hand on his arm as she leaned forward to say something. Whoever they were, they didn't stay long. The man had only half finished his beer when they got up and pre-pared to leave. Standing now, the dark-haired woman looked again at Brock, smiled more to herself than at him, then led the way out.

On another night, a Saturday, he thought he saw her walk into the saloon bar, look around, and then leave. But he could not be sure, because the bar was crowded, and he was busy try-ing to cope with the shouted orders for drinks.

Across the Channel the Germans were ranged along the French coast, while in London, Winston Churchill, predicting a Battle of Britain, called on the British to brace themselves for their "finest hour." And still there was no word to Brock from Dublin. More than once he was tempted to place a tele-phone call but then thought of Peter Donovan's warning that he must follow orders even if he did not understand them. Maggie would contact him soon. Britain was at bay as she had never been before. One more blow would finish her.

There were other reasons for his impatience. Barnaby, it now seemed to Brock, was a more complicated man than he at first appeared. Beneath the bland surface there were currents. Occasionally Brock would find the innkeeper watching him with a speculative eye. In spite of his professed dislike for the police, Barnaby could well be an intermittent informer, both to ensure the safety of his license and to put a little extra cash in his pockets.

If Brock were merely on the run from foreign pursuers, then he would be of little value to the Metropolitan Police. But

145

if Barnaby thought there was more to Brock than that, then he might well display his good citizenship by putting in a call about his new barman to the local police station. It could be, Brock thought, that he was merely waiting for developments.

Dublin was letting him dangle like a man on a cliff. Why, he thought angrily, had they not made sure that his host, whoever it was, had the full loyalty of a Volunteer? Why didn't Maggie get in touch? June was giving way to July; nearly a month gone, and nothing. Unbidden, the thought came of past Army bungling. The compulsion to put plans on paper, which too often was seized. The conflicts among the leadership. He even had no way of knowing whether Sean Russell was alive.

Contending with his doubts, Brock spent his spare time wandering the streets of London, strolling through its parks. In the blaze of summer the city was lovely, as if flowering into a final peacefulness before the test ahead. During the day, only the occasional high cirrus broke the monotony of deep blue skies. At night stars glittered: "bombers' weather," according to the pessimists.

The telephone call came early one evening when sunshine still spilled into the bar through open windows and door. Barnaby answered it, then called to Brock, "It's for you."

Brock expected Barnaby to admonish him against receiving phone calls during working hours, but the innkeeper said nothing. Brock noted, however, that he remained within hearing distance. Brock picked up the receiver. It was Maggie.

"Where are you?" he asked.

"I'm at Paddington, Michael," she said. "I only have a moment. My train's leaving. . . ."

"I have to see you," he said. "I have to know what's going on."

"What's the matter, Michael?" she asked. "Everything is going as planned. You sound funny. Can you talk? Is there somebody with you?"

"Yes, there is."

"I understand. Listen, I just wanted to let you know that everything's all right."

"Why haven't you called before?"

"I'm not allowed to. I shouldn't be calling you now. They want you to just sit tight until you get your orders. You understand?"

"Yes, but listen . . ."

"I've got to go now. I love you, Michael, and I'll see you soon." She hung up the phone. He turned and found Barnaby watching him.

"Trouble?" Barnaby said.

"No. Everything's fine. A friend, that's all."

"A lady friend, it sounded like to me," he said with a fat chuckle. Brock went back behind the bar, more dissatisfied now than if Maggie hadn't called. He wondered how long she'd been in London, where she was going. Once again he suppressed the rising fury at being abandoned without directions. Events were moving to the crisis point. He knew it, and he was being ignored.

He thought back over his words to Maggie. There was nothing there for Barnaby. He had been very conscious of the innkeeper's attentiveness.

Four days later the dark-haired woman walked in again. It was early on a Saturday evening, and this time she was alone. She came to the bar and asked for a sherry. She was wearing a flowered silk dress, cut close enough to suggest the heaviness of her bosom. He could imagine the slippery smoothness of the material under tactile fingers. Her voice, when she asked for the drink, was tinged with huskiness, as if she smoked too much. This time, though she smiled pleasantly, she seemed to lack the interest in him she had displayed the first time he had seen her. He was confounded by a sense of being slighted, as if he were entitled to her absorption. Perhaps it was this irritation that made him speak.

"Your friends not coming in tonight, then?"

She picked up her glass, looked at him as if noticing him for the first time, and said, "No, not tonight." She went and sat at one of the tables, sipped her sherry, and fifteen minutes later, as the bar began to fill, she left.

147

On July 10 the Luftwaffe launched attacks on ships passing through the Strait of Dover. The Spitfires and the Hurricanes rose to meet them and, according to the BBC, destroyed twice as many German planes as the British lost. On July 19 Hitler told the Reichstag that unless there was an accommodation with the British, "A great empire will be destroyed." London rejected the appeal for peace. The great battles in the skies above southern England began. Still there was no word from Maggie.

On the evening of August 8, while the RAF was claiming over the BBC the destruction of sixty Luftwaffe fighters and bombers, the dark-haired woman walked into the saloon bar again.

Again she surprised Brock. She was wearing the blue uniform of the ambulance service, her slim feet looking incongrous with her heavy low-heeled shoes. This time, as if accepting the masculinity of her uniform, she stood at the bar while she drank her sherry.

"No, I didn't bring my friends," she said. "As you can see."

Barnaby passed behind Brock and said, "Hello, Mrs. Wyatt. How are you tonight?"

"Very well, Barnaby," she said without warmth. Barnaby moved onto his perch at the end of the bar.

"Going on duty?" Brock asked.

"Yes. It's very dull. I need a drink to give me the strength to face it."

"Where are you based?"

"Down the Common."

"You may be busy soon."

"I hope not." She sounded uninterested in the trivialities of their talk. He wondered where her husband was, if the delicate-looking man was her husband.

"There's a party next Saturday night," she said, "if you'd like to come."

"Can't," he said. "I'll be working here."

"Perhaps after you finish here," she said, and putting down

148

her empty glass, she walked out. He enjoyed the easy swing of her hips.

Four days later the Luftwaffe launched attacks on airfields and radar masts. In one day, Goring's pilots flew nearly fifteen hundred sorties. Still there was no message from Dublin. Brock found he was getting increasingly edgy, snapping more than once at customers until Barnaby warned him. Interspersed with his internal raging toward Dublin, however, were thoughts of the woman called Mrs. Wyatt. He wondered what her first name was.

He thought of asking Barnaby about her, then decided against it. The less Barnaby knew about his interests the better. Saturday arrived, and she did not appear in the bar. He decided she had forgotten her invitation.

But as Barnaby was about to call "Time, gentlemen," the telephone rang. It was for Brock. He expected it to be Maggie, and the frustration of his long wait fled at the thought that she might have his orders. Picking up the receiver, he turned his back on Barnaby, again hovering nearby. It wasn't Maggie.

"It's Victoria Wyatt." In the background he could hear voices and laughter which seemed to match the sounds in the saloon bar as Barnaby urged his customers home.

"Who? Oh, yes, how are you?"

"I'm very well, thank you. And how are you?" She sounded amused, and he guessed she was past her first drink of the evening.

"How's the party going?" Brock asked.

"It's moving along very nicely. Are you going to come?"

"I can't get away for a little while. I've got to clear up here a bit."

"Well, you do a good job of clearing up, and then you come along." She gave him an address on the north side of the Common and hung up the phone.

"My, you are popular with the ladies," Barnaby said. Brock wondered if he had recognized the dark-haired woman's voice.

"It's the old Irish charm," he said, and he began to pick up the glasses that the departing customers had left scattered around the barroom.

It was nearly an hour later when he found the address she had given him, a modern apartment house looming over the trees of the Common.

An Army captain with slightly unfocused eyes opened the door. His jacket was open, and Brock could see that he was wearing a pair of red suspenders. "Come in, old boy," he said. "The more the merrier." The room was filled with noise and smoke and people, most of the men in uniform. There were a couple of WRENS and half a dozen members of the auxiliary ambulance service. A gramophone was playing "Begin the Beguine."

The captain abandoned him in favor of a thin blonde wearing an unsuitable brown velvet dress. Perched on her head was the squared cap of a Polish army officer. Brock went in search of a drink. The apartment was large and well-furnished, with a bedroom, bathroom, and a spacious kitchen which served as the bar. He decided that Victoria Wyatt had money.

"Only beer and gin, I'm afraid," she said, suddenly appearing in front of him. She wore a black evening gown. "The Navy drank all the brandy. I'm glad you could come round. By the way, what's your name? Mine's Victoria."

"Michael Bell."

"What can I get you?" He asked for a beer, then watched her as her attention was claimed by a cadaverous man in civilian clothes who was suffering noticeably from a cold. Brock poured himself a beer from a group of bottles standing in cold water in the sink and wandered back into the living room, where the captain and his blonde were bumping their way through the throng, trying to dance to a recording of "Stormy Weather."

"Seen you before somewhere," said a burly man in an ill-fitting blue suit. "Let me think for a moment. . . ."

"Probably in the Kings Arms," Brock said quickly, apprehensive that the man might be from Ireland. He had increased his vulnerability by coming to the party.

"That's right," the man said, adding in an aggrieved tone, "You should've given me a chance. I'd have remembered. Never forget a face. P.C. Robinson. I'm the bobby on this beat." Brock relaxed. It was the policeman who had complained about the light from Barnaby's door.

"Odd mixture here tonight," Robinson said. He was drinking beer out of a wine glass. "I think she's invited everybody she meets, whether she knows them or not."

"D'you know who she is?"

"Works at the MAP, I understand." Brock looked baffled. "The Ministry of Aircraft Production, Beaverbrook's lot. Some sort of a pen pusher, I expect. How's your sister?"

"Not so good, I'm afraid."

"Sorry to hear that. Well, I must be on my way. I'm on duty in the morning." He finished his beer and pushed his way through the crowd to the door. Other people were starting to put on coats and wraps. The bleary-eyed Army captain was hunting through a pile of records, but his dancing companion had vanished. Brock went looking for the hostess.

She was sitting in a corner, talking to the man who had brought her into the Kings Arms the first time Brock saw her. He got up as Brock approached, and Brock heard him say, "Well, I'll run along now, Victoria. Take care of yourself." So it wasn't her husband. He nodded at Brock and went away with mincing steps.

"Who's that?" he asked.

"My chief," she said. "He's a dear, but he's very shy. He doesn't really like this sort of thing. It's stark courage for him to put in an appearance."

"I saw him at the Kings Arms."

"Yes, he was trying to cheer me up. He felt that was his duty, too, so he did it."

More people were leaving now, some coming over to thank their hostess, some just leaving with a wave of the hand.

"It's a bit of a mess," Brock said, looking around at the full

151

ashtrays, the empty glasses, the mess of potato crisps that a careless foot had ground into the carpet.

"You're Irish?" she said, ignoring his remark.

"Belfast."

"Shipyards and linen and King Billy."

"You're well-informed." He was admiring the drape of the black material over her long thighs. Her legs were crossed so that the flesh bulged perceptibly, round and full. He became aware that she was watching him with that same expression of inward amusement that he had noticed in the pub.

One of the WRENS walked over, martial and efficient-looking in her dark blue, and said, "D'you want us to help you clean up, Victoria?"

"Thanks awfully, Angela," Victoria said, "but Mike here is going to give me a hand."

He waited until the WREN had moved away, then said, "Why me?" He felt a little surge of excitement.

"Well, I might say you're the expert at washing glasses, or I might say I want to get to know you better. . . ." She laughed and stood up. "Perhaps a bit of both. Come on." She took his hand and led him to the kitchen.

"You start in here," she said, "while I see the rest of them out." While he worked at the sink, he could hear the last farewells, then silence, broken a few minutes later by music from the BBC's Home Service.

By the time they finished it was after midnight, and Brock knew a little more about her. She lived alone, a widow, spending her days in Whitehall, some of her nights in the ambulance service's sandbagged dugout at the other end of the Common.

"Nothing but false alarms, so far," she said. In the living room again, he saw a photograph of a fair-haired young man in football clothes and knew it was her dead husband. "Shot down over Amiens three days after the war broke out," she said. "He lived for a few days, but the burns were too much for him. They buried him over there."

"I'm sorry," he said.

152

"So am I. But then, the Germans would have killed him eventually anyway. He was a fighter pilot." She picked up the photograph, stared at the smiling face for a moment. "I'm over it all now," she said, "although some of my friends like to believe I still weep, and they think they have to rally round poor old Victoria. But, you see, I'm not poor old Victoria at all. I refuse to be." She put the framed picture on a table, face-down, murmuring, "You mustn't see everything that goes on in my life, Tommy dear."

Then she looked at Brock and smiled. A brilliant smile.

"D'you know one reason I invited you here and then asked you to stay? It was because I knew you wouldn't be in uniform. God, I'm so sick of uniforms. London's full of them; and all those young men wearing them, they think they're so smart and gallant parading around. And when I look at them, all I see is skulls grinning out from under the caps; and when they salute each other, I don't see hands, I see bones with the flesh burned off." She was still smiling, but the smile was strained, the dark eyes too bright. For the first time, he noticed faint lines around her eyes and mouth.

"I don't wear one," Brock said.

"No, there's no conscription in Ulster, is there? I'm glad."

"But you're a volunteer with the ambulance service. You wear a uniform, too, although you don't have to."

"It helps fill the time. And when the time comes, I'll be helping, not hurting. Come here." He was very conscious of her white arms and the full body underneath the cling of the black dress.

"Why me?" he asked again.

"Does there always have to be a reason for everything?"

"There usually is."

"All right," she said lightly. "You seem to be a very with-drawn man. I thought I'd see if I could draw you out. A challenge, perhaps, I don't know. Now, come on." She turned and walked into the bedroom. He followed her, thinking that he had never had an Englishwoman.

The room was all reds and blacks, but the coverlet of the

153

bed was lacy white. On the walls were photographs of her in different costumes, and he realized she must have been an actress. The dressing table and its mirror were spotlighted by a lamp set into the wall.

"D'you have any money?" she asked.

"A little. Why?"

"I feel whorish tonight. Before you leave, I want you to pay me. Put it on the table over there. Just a token."

"Whatever you're worth?"

"Oh, no. I'm sure you wouldn't have that much." She rumpled her dark hair forward over her eyes and smiled at him through the strands, and he realized she was playing a role, just as she would on a stage. Accepting the part assigned to him, Brock felt the surge of excitement again.

"Take off your jacket," she said. "The customer should feel at ease." As he slipped it off, she moved forward and began to undo his tie. He put his arms around her and pulled her hard against him, but as he tried to kiss her she jerked her head back.

"No," she said. "A *poule* never kisses a client. It's a business arrangement, nothing more." In spite of the rejection in her words, she was still smiling, holding him firmly by the hips while he smoothed the material over her buttocks. She put a hand between his legs and grasped him with easy familiarity.

"Splendid," she said coolly. "Now you must undress me." He had already found the zipper, and he pulled it down until the dress peeled open. Underneath the stylish shell, as if clothing her second secret personality, there were the whore's working clothes: stockings, garter belt, transparent slip, and lace brassiere, all black.

She knelt at his feet to take off his shoes and socks. He stared at himself reflected in the dressing-table mirror. As she stood up again, one of his arms went around her shoulders, the hand cupping the heaviness of her breast. This was an Englishwoman busying herself with him, he thought briefly, one of the enemy; but then the thought vanished as she stripped him of the rest of his clothes.

154

She took him by the hand and led him to the bed, and for a moment he remembered walking dripping wet into the Dublin hotel room with Maggie. He wasn't in Dublin, he was in London, he thought, and to hell with Maggie and her failure to call him. Victoria unclipped her brassiere and tossed it on a chair. Released from their confinement, her breasts, nipples erect, sagged into their natural carriage.

She stepped out of her slip and said, "Would you like a drink, darling? No extra charge." He nodded and watched her walk into the living room, her breasts and buttocks shifting languidly. When she returned he was under the covers.

"The black underwear. . . . Is that what you wear under your ambulance uniform?" he asked.

"Don't you like my exotic undies?" she said, grinning. "No, I must say I usually wear more serviceable items. These are for special occasions. Like you. A drop of mother's ruin, darling?"

She put the bottle and two glasses on a bedside table, then with a sweep of her arm pulled back the bedclothes. "I'm in charge here," she said, "and I like to see what's going on." She joined him, murmuring as he seized her and ran his hands over her.

"You're in charge?" he said. "I thought the customer was always right."

"Some customers," she said, rising to kneel above him, "need a little guidance." She briefly touched the scar below his groin but said nothing, and then she bent forward from the hips, her hands easing under him to capture his buttocks, and her tumbled hair swirled around his loins, and he gave himself up to lazy ravishment.

The gin remained untouched. Their movements became more urgent, and the subtlety of her perfume was being overtaken by the pungency of their sweat when she suddenly reared up and, in one movement, straddled him, her fleshy thighs gripping his sides hard. "I think we're ready for a gallop to the finishing line," she said breathlessly.

"Make sure you don't lose your seat," he grinned, watching her eyes become intent with pleasure as she sank onto him.

155

She rode him lying forward on his chest, like a jockey at full stretch, their sweat-slick torsos sliding together; and when he took her shoulders to pull her even closer, she put her lips to his, as if now, at last, the whore had fled, and this was just two people racing to complete their bout of lust.

He groaned into her mouth, bucking furiously. Her loins shuddered in response, and she whimpered in quick little spurts of sound until she joined him in quietude, lax and sweat-drenched and content.

"What difference does it make whether a man wears a uniform?" he said finally. "In bed, he'd be naked anyway."

"He has to get there first," she said, lazily lifting her head and rolling off him.

She lay on her belly. He ran a hand lightly over the amplitude of her buttocks. The sheet beneath him was damp, soaked through in places.

"You've worn a uniform, haven't you?" she said.

"I have."

"That wound. Was that when you did?"

"Spain," he said.

"Which side?"

"Do I look like a Fascist?"

"I'm sorry. I'm afraid I don't know much about that foolishness."

"You thought it was foolish?"

"Only as foolish as this one. All wars, all killing, whether on a battlefront or on a gallows, are stupid, as far as I'm concerned. There are so many nicer things to do."

"In some wars men believe they fight for principles, and they might even be right."

Her stomach heaved with laughter, and she said, "Oh, my God, if you knew how pompous you sound. There's one thing about women: Silly as some of us are, we could never be as pompous as a man."

"Beliefs often do sound pompous," he said.

"Oh, I'm sorry, darling," she said. "But it is absurd, you know. Do you think it matters one little damn, now, what the

156

principles were at the Battle of the Somme? I'm sure there were brave men on both sides who believed utterly in their war aims and got killed for it by the hundreds. And does it really make any difference today?"

"You don't believe in struggling for what's right, then?"

"I'll tell you what I believe in, Mike, darling. I believe in beautifully cooked food and Gielgud playing Shakespeare and mist on a Leicestershire meadow and a man and a woman in bed together and wine from Bordeaux and a seat in the stalls at the music hall."

She turned on her back, alongside him, her breasts swaying gracefully with the movement. She reached over and pushed the damp hair back from his forehead.

"I also believe that the world has no need for guns and shells and men who make speeches to spur young men to go and pick up those guns and load those shells in an effort to kill other young men who would be far better off in my bed, or indeed any woman's bed. And what d'you believe in, my Irishman from Belfast who has an accent straight out of Dublin?"

He had been staring up at the ceiling. Now he turned his head and saw she was smiling again, directly into his eyes. Her lipstick was smeared.

"What d'you know about accents?" he said.

"A little. I was on the stage before I got married," she said. "Accents are an actor's business."

"I lived in Dublin for a long time," he said. "I expect I picked it up along the way."

"I see," she said, seeming to lose interest. "Would you like a drink now?"

They had one. She went to the windows, pulled back the curtain, and opened the windows to the soft night air. "I know it's only fitting," she murmured, "but it smells like a brothel in here."

She stood there, staring out, until he said, "Come back to bed."

"Call me Victoria," she said. "I'm tired of playing the harlot."

157

"Come to bed, Victoria," he said, wondering if she had dismissed the idea that he was from Dublin. Her words had stirred thoughts of that city, of Sean Russell, of Donovan, and of Maggie. And there was, he said to himself, no profit in that right now.

"And take off the trappings," he said. She still wore her stockings and garter belt.

The glimmer of light that announced the dawn was showing through the open window when he left the bed and dressed. Victoria was lying on her side, her hands between her thighs, and he thought she was deep in sleep.

But as he made for the door, she spoke. "Don't forget the money," she said drowsily. "Put it on the table."

Chapter 13

London
September 11, 1940

BLOOD stared through the window at the black spaniel. This time the dog approached the goalposts alone. It sniffed the base of the pole, then moved alongside and lifted its leg. Blood wondered what had happened to its master. Perhaps he was ill and had sent the spaniel out for a run on his own. A detective, he thought, should consider all possibilities. The dog might have run away, slipped out while its master's back was turned. Perhaps the owner had moved out of the district and abandoned the pet. Unlikely, for the dog looked sleek and composed.

Blood gave a grunt of laughter when the dog ran to his right and its owner strolled into view. He had just let the spaniel off the leash for a run across the playing field. So much for deduction.

He was back at his desk when Bryant came in. The RUC

man had some files in his hands, and Blood sighed. He was sick of files and of Irishmen who pursued a dream while the world went up in flames. He felt repelled by a country whose neutrality contributed to the deaths of poorly paid seamen whose only crime was sailing the ships that brought food and supplies to a beleaguered island. He had not heard from his son for three weeks, and he had to keep telling himself it was a good sign, that he would have heard if Peter's ship had gone down.

"I've had copies made of the dockets on the IRA possibilities we selected," Bryant said. "They'll go out to the appropriate department."

"And be filed away and forgotten," Blood said.

"You told me to, sir," Bryant, said, his voice hurt.

"I know, I know. It has to be done. It's just that sometimes the bureaucracy gets on top of me. I'm more used to following one case at a time."

"We haven't been doing too badly, sir. There were those two we picked up at Holyhead; and Bourke, he's a good one to have behind bars."

"I know, Bryant. The trouble is just that, though. The fact that we picked up that pair means that they're still sending them over. God knows how many of the bastards there are over here, just waiting for the time to move. It gives me a creepy feeling, and I don't like it."

"You're right, of course, sir. There's something else. Read this." He handed the colonel a file, which Blood took with obvious reluctance.

"Do I have to read it?" he said. "You tell me what it amounts to, and I'll just sit here with my eyes closed, letting my keen intelligence do its work."

"Yes, sir," Bryant said, unable to decide whether to laugh. Blood's sense of humor baffled him at times.

"It's a curious business," he said. "It started with an old freighter called the *Maria Fairclough* being torpedoed off the Irish coast. There was only one survivor, chiefly because it wasn't part of a convoy. Apparently the skipper was one of those crusty old hellions who professed a great contempt for the Royal Navy and wouldn't accept orders from the Admiralty. He sailed on his own, and he took a torpedo below the waterline." Bryant moved to a chair and sat down. He found it disconcerting to talk to a man apparently in deep slumber.

"The survivor," he went on, "was a man called Hunter. Comes from Bootle. It seems that he was thrown overboard by the explosion. He clambered onto a piece of the wreckage and held on to it for nearly three days until he was picked up by a small Irish fishing boat not far from the English coast."

Blood opened his eyes, readjusted himself in his chair, and closed them again. He wished the story didn't involve the torpedoing of an English freighter.

"On the fishing boat they did what they could for him and then put into Liverpool, where the Navy took over and rushed him off to a hospital. He was in a bad way, and at one time they thought they'd have to amputate one of his arms. In the end it wasn't necessary. When he'd recovered a bit, he told a naval investigator about the torpedoing, and then he started going on about the men on board the Irish fishing boat, the people who'd rescued him."

Blood stirred restlessly. "When is this going to get interesting?" he said.

"Now, sir. He was lying there on the deck, a bit delirious, I imagine, when he says he heard two of them arguing about whether they should take him into Liverpool immediately or whether they should go ashore at some quiet spot first.

"Hunter was a bit pissed off, sir, because he knew he was in need of hospital attention, and one of these Irishmen was saying he didn't care about him, whether he lived or died. Now listen to this, sir. He remembers, in particular, one of them saying, 'We've come to destroy the English, not rescue them.' And he remembers the other one saying he only wanted to get him to a hospital because he'd gone into the water after him and he didn't want his efforts wasted."

"Do we know he was delirious at this time?" Blood's eyes remained closed even as he asked the question.

160

"No, sir. That was my guess."

"Better not to guess."

"Yes, sir."

"Did he have a description of these men?"

"Yes, sir. A very good one."

"Doesn't sound as though he was delirious then."

"No, sir. The thing is, I'm pretty sure I know who those two were from his description."

"Do we have them on file?"

"Yes, sir. If I'm right, they're a really vicious couple of bastards. Gunmen. Killers, bombers. The Dublin people have been looking for them for a long time, and so have we. They killed a Special Branch man during a bank robbery in Dublin earlier in the year."

"Let's see the files." Blood opened his eyes and sat up as Bryant pushed two dockets across the desk at him. He saw from the notation that they had already been selected by the RUC man as likely agents in the United Kingdom.

Patrick (Plunger) Cronin. Michael Wolfe Brock. Both veteran members of the IRA. Both wanted for murder in the Irish Republic. Both believed to be armed at all times. Both served on the Republican side in the Spanish Civil War. The two files were strewn with cross-references relating to the two men.

"They nearly always work together," Bryant said. "Wouldn't be surprised if they don't have a bit of a homosexual thing going."

"Any evidence along those lines? Direct evidence?"

"No, sir."

"Very well."

Blood studied the descriptions. Cronin, he thought, must be a giant. There were photographs of both men, head shots, probably taken with a box camera, but the pictures were so poor as to be almost useless. He didn't ask where the photographs came from. He was more interested in the later stages of the dockets.

"This bank robbery," he said. "When was it?"

"The middle of February, sir. It's in the file."

161

"Does that add up? We know the Germans are paying the Irish agents. If Cronin and Brock were to be used in England by the Abwehr, why would they rob a bank? They'd have money from Berlin."

"Perhaps not enough, sir. The IRA's always looking for more money. Some of it goes into the pockets of the leaders. It's a real gangster setup."

"What happened to Cronin and Brock when the fishing boat docked?"

"We don't know, sir. They vanished. The lieutenant who went on board is at sea, and we haven't been able to talk to him yet; but the doctor, who also went on board, says they both came ashore in the RN launch that brought Hunter to the dock. His description of the pair of them coincides with the seaman's. He says they went in the ambulance with him to the hospital, but he didn't see them after that."

"So that's all we've got? A pair of Irishmen, who may or may not be Cronin and Brock, at large in England. What about Dublin? Can your grapevine there do anything?"

"I'm working on it, sir. But they've tightened things up. One of my best informants cleared off to America a couple of weeks ago. Bastard. We paid him well, and then he decides he's had enough. Probably spending that money in a New York bar right now."

"All right, let's get copies of these photographs off to the police. You never know, although I can't see any bobby recognizing them from those snapshots. They could be of anybody."

"There's one thing, sir. You can bet they'll be together. The bastards work together like Siamese twins."

"Very well. Make a note of that in the captions."

"They'll be armed, too. If the coppers spot them, they should approach with caution."

"Better yet. Tell the police not to approach; tell them to keep our friends under surveillance and alert us. We want them alive and healthy and able to answer questions."

"I'd like to be in on any interrogation," Bryant said.

Blood tossed the files back. "The screw is tightening," he

162

said. "It seems those earlier messages we had about the movement of small shipping into the French channel ports have been borne out. The latest word from MI Six is that the Germans have at least five hundred barges massed in ports from Ostend to Le Havre. They have enough to launch an invasion force of fifty thousand men. And there's evidence that's just what they plan to do. We've picked up five German agents, and under . . . uh . . . questioning, they said their mission was to report on troop movements in the region bounded by Oxford, Ipswich, London, and Reading. That's where General Brooke has his reserves. It can only mean that Adolf is getting ready for the big jump."

"The RAF is doing well, sir," Bryant said. "They're knocking the bastards out of the sky like pheasants before the beaters on a Scottish moor."

"Yes, well, there may be a little exaggeration there, Bryant. The fighter boys are doing well, but not quite as well as the official communiqués let on."

"Even so . . ."

"Even so, the truth is that in the last two weeks we lost two hundred ninety-five Spitfires and Hurricanes. Complete write-offs. And another hundred seventeen were badly damaged. During that same period, the airfields were supplied with only two hundred sixty-nine planes. Simple arithmetic gives you the answer to what will happen if it goes on much longer. We're running out of pilots, too."

Bryant smacked a hammy fist into the palm of his other hand. "And you can bet those fucking IRA killers are part of the German plan," he said. "I'd just love to get my hands on Cronin and Brock. Give them to me for a few hours and I'd find out what the Irish are up to."

"We've got to get them first, and their other pals," Blood said. "So long as the RAF holds on, Hitler is going to wait. He can't afford to launch his barges while the Navy owns the Channel and the fighter boys control the sky above it. But if he can destroy the RAF, I think he'll go ahead. So does the Chief of Naval Staff. Great men think alike, eh, Bryant?"

"Yes, sir."

"Yes, well, he's just put out a memo saying that if the *Boche* can seize the Dover defile and capture its gun defenses, then, holding these points on both sides of the Channel, they'd be in a position to deny those waters to our naval forces. With that accomplished, they'd be in a situation where they could bring in the panzers and create real havoc. It's possible our Irish friends are going to be used around Dover. It's worth bearing in mind. Anyway, we've got to track them down, whether they're in Birmingham, Dover, or Little Snodgrass."

"We'll know what their plans are as soon as they get word over their radios, sir."

"We will," Blood said. "The trouble with that is that it may be too late."

Chapter 14

London
September 13, 1940

BROCK visited Victoria's bed six times before he heard again from Maggie. In that bed the Englishwoman was wildly inventive, ranging in her fantasies from slave girl to medieval queen, as if she preferred any period, any role, to that of an office worker in wartime London who spent hours sitting in a sandbagged ambulance station waiting to go out and pick up shattered bodies. Brock guessed that in spite of her assertions she still mourned the fair-haired young man in the photograph in her living room. That also was something from which to escape.

For Brock, too, the fantasies were an escape, a refuge from his growing impatience and anger at the men in Dublin who had sent him to carry out a vital mission and then left him in the midst of his enemies to wait and wait. It was strange, he thought, that with Maggie, a woman who believed as he did, thought as he did, he could couple but never gain full release. Yet with Victoria, an Englishwoman with no interest in ideals, unconcerned with social or political beliefs, he could utterly lose himself in a world of flesh and of the senses. When he plunged into Victoria's body, there was nothing else: no mission, no thoughts of killing, no memories of guns and bombs. It was only when he left her tumbled bed that the connection with Dublin and the past reasserted itself. Sometimes he wondered if the link to that past was growing weaker. But he brushed aside the intrusive thought, telling himself that it wasn't true, and then, if it was, whose fault was it but Sean Russell's and Donovan's and the others' sitting comfortably in Ireland?

He and Victoria were using each other, he thought, but was there any relationship where one wasn't using the other? It worked and was called love, mutual love, when both parties won what they sought from the other. Well, he was getting what he sought from Victoria—the pleasure of her flesh—and she, too, must be content with what he offered, for she invited him back. Sometimes he wondered if something deeper was developing, but that also was something to be brushed aside.

Once, as they lay together, their bodies cooling after a violent coupling, her hand in possession of his shrinking phallus, she asked him why he had gone to fight in Spain.

"Ireland," he said, "was dull." And he thought that perhaps there was some unexpected truth in that evasion. Shootings and bombings can dull the senses if they never end. "Besides, I was a Socialist."

"Was?"

"I am."

"And what did you think of it, the maiming and the killing and the sadness of it all?"

"The wine was good."

"But it changed nothing, the fighting, did it?"

"It changed nothing. Did your husband's death?"

He knew it was a mistake the moment he uttered the words,

but they were said. Her warm hand left him, and she turned on her side, her back toward him. The movement had dropped her black hair like a curtain over her face so that he could not see her expression even when he leaned over her. He touched the hollow of her back.

"I'm sorry," he said. "I shouldn't have said that."

She was crying. It was a silent weeping at first, but then her shoulders began to shake, and he could hear her, a low keening of despair that seemed to wrack her body. He let her cry, gently tracing his fingers over the whiteness of her back. She turned, finally, her hair sticking to the tears that had poured down her face, and he pulled her close and held her.

"Oh, Mike," she said, "I'm such a little fool." Her face was pressed into his chest now so that the words were muffled.

"Don't talk," he said. "Be still."

"I encouraged him," she said. "I sent him off and told him that he was fine and brave, and they killed him."

"It wasn't your fault they killed him, Victoria."

"Oh, but it was. He didn't have to go and fly those devilish machines. I could have persuaded him to wait until he was called up, and he'd be alive today." The tears had stopped now. He left her to go to his clothes and find a handkerchief. Giving it to her, he said, "I'll go and make a cup of tea."

When he returned with the tea, she was lying on her back, staring at the ceiling. She had pulled the bedclothes up to her neck.

"He was such a lighthearted boy, Mike," she said. "He never took anything seriously. I think I fell in love with him because he could make me laugh. He had this theory that a man who can make a woman laugh can always get her into bed." She sat up to take the cup he handed her, and the bedclothes fell away from her breasts to drape around her hips.

"We went to Norway for our honeymoon, to a little town called Ulvick on the Hardanger fjord. God, it was beautiful, Mike: the green of the fields, the white of the blossoms, and the sparkle on the fjord waters. It seems a long time ago, now. I never saw so much milk and butter and cheese and fish. We did nothing but eat and make love. He was very good in bed. Oh, don't worry, Mike, no better than you.

"And then this big liner sailed up the fjord and anchored near our hotel. It was German, on one of those Strength Through Joy cruises. They used to do exercises on deck all day, and they used to sing marching songs, the sound bouncing off the mountains. They were preparing, I suppose. Tommy thought they were hilarious. He lay in the grass and roared with laughter as those beastly songs came across the water at us, songs about battles and death and victory. I laughed with him, but they won their victory over him all the same."

"How old was he when . . ."

"He was twenty-four. He didn't have much time to enjoy his laughter did he?" She put down her cup, her breasts moving with an independent grace. Even in the aftermath of lust, Brock thought, her torso was astonishingly beautiful.

"He was just going to join his father's stock brokerage firm when Hitler marched into Czechoslovakia. For once he was serious about something. He said he had to do somthing about it. I agreed. Oh, yes, I agreed. I told him that there'd be a war, that there were some things worth fighting for, and that he should go and fight for them."

She said bitterly, "I suppose I had some ridiculous vision of him as my knight in goggles, flying off to . . . oh, God, I was so stupid."

They were both shot-up cases, Brock thought, veterans of disillusion. But while he continued along the path of violence and death, she had turned to life, turned her back on the grinning skull, the beckoning fleshless finger.

"I feel as guilty as if I had ordered his execution," she said.

"You said yourself that he'd probably have been killed later anyway," he told her roughly.

"It doesn't do any good, Mike," she said. "Oh, you should have seen me marching him around in his uniform to show him off to my friends. I always made him wear his uniform. He used to laugh at me; he only took the actual flying seriously, but he humored me. I used to polish his buttons and the wings on his chest. Once, I was playing at a theater in Brighton and he came over and buzzed it in his Hurricane. Then he was ordered to France. I saw him off at Victoria Station. He used to call it Victoria's Station."

She was dry-eyed now, but her eyes were wounded. Brock realized he had been shaken by her emotion. He was used to emotion, but it had always been directed at a goal: at the enemy, England. In his life it was never spilled out for individuals. They were expendable. He thought that perhaps he had been starved of humanity, but that also was something to be brushed aside. And yet . . . he felt a warmth in Victoria that he had never found in Maggie. He wondered if Victoria was undermining his faith, and immediately he was disconcerted by a rush of fear. He told himself that she was English and therefore the enemy, but it did no good. She was a woman who wept for her man, and that had nothing to do with nationality. He wondered if Maggie would weep for him. He wondered if Victoria was Maggie bereft.

"I kissed him, and the train moved off with him hanging out of the window, waving his cap at me," Victoria said. "I waved at him and felt so proud, and that was the last I saw of him. You know what I think now, Mike? I don't think there's any difference between declaring war and commiting murder. It's just that a nation does it instead of an individual."

"It's not that simple."

"That's always the answer."

"There are times when you have to fight."

"I'll tell you, Mike," she said. "I think men like to fight, and they like to kill."

Maggie's call came on September 13, just before Barnaby opened the doors of the Kings Arms for the lunchtime customers. This time she had even less time to talk. She gave him a telephone number and told him to call it from an outside phone at three-thirty P.M. He was to ask for Margaret. The exchange indicated the number was in the Swiss Cottage area.

After the pub had closed for the afternoon, he went out into the sunshine and telephoned from a kiosk on the edge of the

168

Common. As he dialed, he could see the sun striking splinters of light from a barrage balloon moored high above the grass and trees.

A man with a cockney accent answered. Brock asked for Margaret, and a moment later Maggie came on the line.

"Oh, Michael," she said. "It's so good to be able to talk to you again. Dublin wouldn't let me call you before this. How are you?"

"I'm very well, for a puppet," he said, trying to contain his anger.

"What on earth d'you mean?"

"I mean I feel like a puppet, dangling in ignorance until I feel the jerk of my master's string."

"You knew you'd have to wait for orders."

"It's been three months. Three months of waiting for orders that never come, for information that is never given." She was silent, and when she spoke again, it was with a hard edge of irritation.

"You're a Volunteer," she said. "There are hardships entailed, as I'm sure you know. It must have been very tough for you, hanging about in a pub with the whole of London to enjoy. Probably with a soft pair of thighs to get in between. Oh, I'm sure it's been terrible."

"Listen, Maggie," he began.

"No, you listen, Michael Brock. D'you think I've been enjoying myself? Well, I'll tell you, I've been cooped up in a room with a radio tuned to Hamburg for company, and right now I think I prefer it to you. It's efficient, it does what it's told, and it doesn't act like a spoiled child." This time it was Brock who was silent until she said, "Michael, are you there?"

"I'm sorry, Maggie," he said. "I didn't mean to blow up at you. I know you're obeying orders, too. It's just that I'm used to action. I want to do something. That's what I was sent over for, and I'm going out of my mind waiting to find out what's happening. Also, I want to see you. I want to finish here and take you to a big bed and do some of the things that I've been thinking about."

"You believe all you've got to do is mention bed and I'll go

169

soft as a cat's breath," she said. "Well, it won't work, Michael Brock." But he knew her vexation now was simulated.

"I think it's your behind I like best," he said. "The way it waggles impudently when you walk, showing a complete disregard for your stern mouth and disciplined mind."

"You bastard," she said, the smile coming through with her voice. "I long to see you, too, Michael. But I can't. Things are beginning to move."

"Tell me."

"You'll get two keys in the mail," she said. "One is for a deposit box at Victoria Station. In the box you'll find a small suitcase, and that's what the second key is for. Handle it carefully."

"What's in the case?"

"A gun and some ammunition. Also a radio transmitter."

"I don't know how to use a transmitter; you know that, Maggie."

"You don't have to know. Just take it to your room and look after it. You'll be needing it soon. I've got to go now."

"When will I hear from you again?"

"I don't know, Michael. Truly, I don't. I just follow my orders."

As if to verify Maggie's promise of action, less than two hours later the Luftwaffe attacked London. Hundreds of Junkers Eighty-Eights, and Dorniers broke through the fighter defenses in daylight to drop incendiaries and high explosives on the East End. Billowing pillars of smoke—white at the center, black at the edges—rose from the Royal Arsenal at Woolwich, from factories and houses, from the docks at West Ham and Thameshaven. The East End was so ablaze that as night came the German bombers needed no other guide than the gusting flames already leaping from their targets. The bombardiers merely scattered their explosives into the midst of the inferno until Londoners thought the world was on fire. It was the beginning of the agonizing test of them and their city.

For Brock it was the beginning of a burden of ambiguity. While part of his mind applauded the destruction and fear the bombers brought to the English, he couldn't forget that this was the same breed of Germans who had been the enemy in Spain, the architects of Guernica, the men who had taunted broken prisoners in the streets of Saragossa. And there was the fear, for these bombs didn't discriminate between the English and the Irishman in their midst who wanted London smashed as much as the men who launched the blitzkrieg.

Brock went to Victoria Station the day after he received the keys. The suitcase, cheaply made of brown leather and cardboard, was no more than two feet long and eighteen inches wide. It weighed about fifteen pounds. He pulled it out of the deposit box and carried it back to the Kings Arms. Barnaby was sleeping, as he always did in midafternoon, and Brock got it to his room unobserved. There he opened the case.

The gun, wrapped in a soft rag, was a nine-millimeter Luger PO 8, functional and deadly in spite of its clumsy handgrip. There were a dozen nine-millimeter parabellum slugs, each individually wrapped in tissue paper. Brock turned two latches and lifted a hinged cover to find the radio transmitter cleverly built into the base of the suitcase. The notations around the dials and switches were in German and meant nothing to him. He replaced the cover and the gun and the ammunition. Before locking the case, he left a matchstick in the folds of the rag so that it would fall out if the gun was disturbed. He put the suitcase under his bed, resting another matchstick on top of it so that it, too, would fall off if the suitcase was moved.

He thought about Barnaby. The innkeeper had shown no interest in Brock's room. He left it to Brock to clean it or let the dust gather.

For the first time since he had been at the pub, he locked the door of his room. Even if Barnaby became curious and found a way into Brock's room, the suitcase was locked and he would have no way of opening it. Even though the suitcase looked poorly made, the lock was sturdy enough.

Night after night the German bombers returned to London, guided by the bomber's moon, which turned the snakelike twisting of the Thames into a silvery summons to destruction. Brock saw little of Victoria. She was out with her ambulance in the fiery streets, carrying victims to hospitals that sometimes were shattered shells when she reached them. But early in November she telephoned Brock at the Kings Arms. She sounded strained.

"I've got tonight off," she said. "They tell me I've got a whole night when I don't have to look at blazing buildings and blood and people dying under tumbling houses."

"I'll come round," he said.

"Please," she said. "I'm going to get into my bed, and I'm not going to leave it tonight if they drop a land mine in the street outside. I just want to lie there, and I want you with me."

"I'll be there," he said.

The sirens were at full pitch when he walked across the Common to her apartment. The blackness above was already being intersected by the searchlights, which never seemed to find their targets. He reached her door as the first sound of the bombers' engines, rising and falling, took over from the moan of the sirens.

She was wearing a lime-green nightgown, and he could smell the perfume on her. But she was smoking a cigarette with quick, nervous puffs, and her eyes were swollen with fatigue. The lipstick at one corner of her mouth was smeared a fraction, as if she hadn't been able to control the shakiness of her hands.

She was holding a glass of gin, and he suspected it was not her first. The apartment looked slightly disheveled, as if she did not have the time or could not be bothered to straighten it out. Her ambulance uniform lay rumpled on a chair, where she must have dropped it the night before. Even indoors Brock could hear the steady rise and fall of the bombers' engines overhead. As she handed him a drink, the thumping of bombs and ack-ack guns began.

"Oh, Christ," she said, "I'd give my immortal soul for one night of peace and quiet."

"It will have to end soon, one way or another," he said.

In bed he lay holding her, feeling the tension in her body as the separate explosions of guns and bombs began to merge into a single, never-ending roll of thunder. It was as if she were permanently wincing, he thought, staring up at the ceiling.

When a bomb dropped so close that the building shook, the glass rattling in the windows, she whimpered softly, pushing her head into his chest. The confidence which had clothed her so securely when they first met had now fled. He thought this must have been how she was as a little girl, holding on to an adult for comfort.

"I'm taking you down to the basement," he said. "It's going to be a bad one tonight. . . ." But before he could finish, the telephone rang.

"I know who that is," she said, and went into the living room to answer it. He could hear her talking, then replacing the receiver, but she did not return. Naked, he padded after her and found her putting on her uniform.

"I was right," she said, "it was the control center. They want me to go and pick up an ambulance. It seems I won't get a night off, after all." With her uniform back on she sounded calmer, as if the blue serge of officialdom had restored her strength. "You wait here, Mike. I'll be back later."

"I'll come with you," he said, moving to pick up his own clothes. She didn't argue, and they went out together into the night of brawling guns and bombs. They needed no flashlight to make their way down the Common to the ambulance station. To the east the night sky reflected the red glow of a hundred fires and explosions. The very air seemed to be heated by the inferno in the East End and along the south bank of the Thames. Once, as they hurried along, they heard the spatter of shrapnel falling into the roadway.

The ambulance station was deserted, a solitary telephone ringing. Victoria went to answer it. As she listened, she reached for a pencil and pad.

"I've got it," she said finally. "Saxton Street. Number ten or twelve. I'll take care of it." She put down the receiver and turned to Brock. "I've got to go out immediately," she said. "There's been an incident."

173

"An incident?"

"That's what they call them. A bomb on a house or a hospital or a church. An incident. It's somewhere near the Clapham South underground station."

"I'll come with you," he said.

"Yes, you might be able to help." She grinned, astonishing him with the transformation from a frightened woman into a self-assured civil defense worker. "You're always providing service for me, one way or another, aren't you, Mike?" she said. "Come on."

They went out past the piled sandbags and turned to a small yard behind the ambulance station. The ambulance was a van that might well have carried groceries in quieter times. It had been adapted for rescue work by the addition of two stretchers which could be slid in and out through the back doors.

"Things must be bad tonight if everything else is out," she said.

They drove east down deserted streets. Inside the entrance to the Clapham South underground station they found a steel-helmeted policeman, who gave them directions to Saxton Street. "Mind how you go," he shouted as a bomb landed a few streets to the north, and he retreated farther into the shelter of the entrance.

"That reminds me," Victoria said. She reached back and found two blue helmets. "Put this on," she said, and drove on in search of the incident. She seemed completely in control of herself.

Saxton Street was a small residential cul-de-sac lined by semidetached two-story houses dating back to the early thirties. At first the empty street looked untouched. Brock guessed that most of the residents had gone to spend the night on the deep-planted platforms of the underground station. The authorities, fearing a massive disaster if a heavy bomb should hit one of the stations, had at first refused entrance to Londoners but had finally surrendered to their insistence.

In the middle of the cul-de-sac they found the house. Except for blown-out windows, it looked whole at first glance.

174

But then Brock looked up, and he saw that most of the roof was gone, the bare rafters standing out against the blue-black sky. There was a smell of gas. As Victoria pulled up, a man walked out through the open front door. He, also, was wearing a steel helmet, the word "Warden" painted across the front.

"We're too bloody late," he said. He had a thick drooping mustache and angry eyes. Brock guessed he was in his late sixties, an old man.

"Anybody inside?" Victoria said.

"It came through the roof at the back," the man said. "Took the middle of the house out like the core of an apple. There's at least one body inside. A woman. Dead."

He spat into the gutter. "Didn't have a bloody chance," he said.

Brock walked toward the front door. "I wouldn't go in there, mate," the warden said. "I reckon the whole bloody house is ready to come down." But he followed Brock through the door. The smell of gas was worse inside, gas mixed with dust and plaster. There was a narrow hallway, the walls still holding. Stairs came down from the right, and looking up Brock could see the naked rafters and the sky beyond. The floor was littered with rubble, which crunched under their feet.

The warden shone his flashlight down the hallway. "She's along there," he said.

The woman must have been sheltering in the closet under the stairs, a favorite bolt-hole of Londoners who had no basement shelter and could not reach the underground station platforms. The theory was that the stairs, and consequently the closet under them, would remain intact even if the rest of the house came down. Sometimes the theory was borne out; in this case it was not.

She was lying on her face, halfway out of the closet door, her arms stretched forward as if she had been blown forward. She wore a brown flannel robe.

"No pulse," the warden said. "She's gone."

175

Brock bent down and grasped the woman under the arms, trying to pull her clear of the closet.

"Her foot's caught," the warden said.

"Well, Jesus Christ," Brock shouted, "help me get her out of there."

"All right, all right, temper doesn't do any good. There's a bloody great beam over her ankle." Brock found that by twisting her foot he could release the leg from its trap.

As they got her clear, Victoria called from the front door. "Anything I can do?"

"No," Brock shouted. "We'll bring her out."

He turned the body over and stared in horror. He had to fight down a rising bubble of vomit. The woman must have been in her twenties, possibly a pretty woman who had once drawn admiring glances. Now she was a hideous, distorted caricature of a human being.

Some projectile had taken off the bottom section of her face, leaving a bloody mass of mangled bone and flesh below staring brown eyes. She seemed to be roaring with red, pulpy laughter.

"Oh, my God," the warden said. And then they heard a low moan from the closet. The combination of the shattered woman and the noise from behind her was enough to bring up the hairs on Brock's neck.

"Someone else in there," the warden said unnecessarily.

"Get her out of the way," Brock said. He began to pull at pieces of debris piled in the closet. The moan came again, and then more rubble fell from above, as if the house were determined to block his efforts.

It took him twenty minutes to reach the boy. The youngster, no more than seven, was hunched against the far wall under an old-fashioned sewing machine table which had shielded him from the full force of falling bricks. His eyes were open.

"We'll soon have you out," Brock said. "What's your name?"

"My leg," the boy said. "It hurts." Tear marks had drawn runnels of whiteness down his dust-smeared cheeks, but now he wasn't crying. He had red hair.

176

"See if you can crawl out," Brock said. The warden had his flashlight shining over Brock's shoulder. The boy inched forward, now on his knees. Brock could see a deep gash high on his temple, still oozing blood.

"Give me your hand, son," Brock said. As he spoke, the steady wail of the all-clear siren sounded, and he realized that the fury of the bombs and the guns had long since diminished and stopped. He had been too occupied to notice.

The boy took his hand, and Brock tried to guide him out; but the youngster couldn't move. "It's my leg," he groaned. "I can't feel it." There was an ominous shifting of the structure above them, and Brock thought, My God, the warden was right, the whole thing is about to come down on us. He reached forward, grasped the boy under his armpits, and forcibly dragged him clear. The boy in his arms, he lurched to his feet and turned.

Immediately he saw that the woman was still on her back in the hallway, the nightmare features that once had been a face still visible in the glow of the warden's flashlight. "You bloody fool," Brock said, swinging around so that the boy wouldn't see. He was too late. The youngster was twisting in his arms, twisting so that he could see the woman.

The scream came ripping out of his young throat, and as it did, the slim body writhed in Brock's arms as if gathering every last bit of physical energy to continue the scream until doomsday, until the face was made whole again and there was no more torn tissue and bone. Brock, fighting the straining body of the boy, stumbled along the hall and out the door. As he walked out, the child's shriek died away, and suddenly the boy was crying in great gulps of anguish.

"Give him to me," Victoria said. She took the sobbing youngster and carried him down the garden path to her ambulance.

"I couldn't find anything to cover her with," the warden said. "It must have been his mother."

"Let's get her out," Brock said, and together they dragged the corpse down the hallway. They put her on the tiny patch of lawn, face down, and Brock went for a blanket.

"I've given him an injection," Victoria said. "What happened?"

"He saw his mother. She's dead, and her face is a mess."

"Well, she shouldn't have got herself in the middle of a fight between men who have different beliefs, should she, Mike?" She was looking at him with a curious expression which, after a moment, he realized was dislike.

"I didn't kill her," he said. "Have you got a blanket?"

"In the back, on the top stretcher."

He found the blanket and went to cover the body on the lawn. The warden was standing sentry near the front door. "I'll stay here to make sure nobody tries to go in," he said. From inside came the sound of falling bricks and mortar.

When Brock returned to the van, Victoria was at the wheel. "I'll take the boy to the rest center," she said. "I'll drop you off on the way."

Twice she had to follow detours, once because of a barricaded crater in the middle of a main road, once because another road was blocked by fire trucks which had just dealt with a row of houses set afire by incendiaries. They did not speak until they were approaching the Kings Arms.

"The woman is dead, and the boy's mind may be affected for the rest of his life," she said.

"Women and children die in all wars," he said. "They've been dying in Ireland for centuries."

"I don't care about other centuries," she said. "I care about now, about tonight. I don't think I can stomach another corpse, any more blood. And I don't think I can see you again, Mike." As she spoke, the warning siren moaned into life again. Again the searchlights poked their white fingers into the night sky.

"Why can't you see me again? What's happened?" He thought she must have overtaxed her resources, slipped into some kind of hysteria, perhaps; yet her voice was calm enough.

"Do you remember, once, I said you were a withdrawn man, and I found that to be something of a challenge?" she asked.

"I remember."

178

"Well, we've spent time together, Mike, and I know nothing more about you now than I did when I first saw you. I want more than that. I want to know about you, but you don't want to let me in."

"I don't talk easily."

"That's not true. You do talk easily. But you don't say anything about yourself when you talk. You've defeated me, and that makes me wonder."

"Victoria, you're exhausted. Why do we have to talk about this now?" To the south he could hear the unmistakable rising and falling note of the bombers' engines.

"I think you're an IRA man," she said. "I don't know what you're doing over here, and I don't want to know. But I think you're on a mission for the IRA, and I think that it probably involves killing."

"You're insane," he said, his thoughts racing.

"Sometimes I feel a bit insane," she agreed, "but not now. I'll tell you something else. I think you've killed for your organization, and I think you're ready to do it again when they order you."

"Where do you get such crazy ideas?" he demanded.

"I've had enough of death, and the smell of death is on you, Mike, whatever you may say."

"I'm not a member of the IRA, and I'm not here on any mission. I'm here because my sister is ill and she needs me near her."

"In the Battersea General Hospital, you said."

"That's right."

She pulled up to the curb outside the Kings Arms and braked.

"I telephoned the hospital," she said, staring ahead through the windshield. "There are no patients in that hospital except for bombing victims."

"You checked up on me?" he said. "You telephoned to find out if I was telling the truth?"

"I did."

"Well, you weren't very clever. She's in a special section, a ward where they only look after people with her disease. And

179

that ward was evacuated out of London nearly a week ago to Devon. I'm going down there this weekend."

"Mike," she said, "it's no good. I telephoned that hospital soon after we met. You're lying. You know it, I know it, and it's no good going on with it."

"What did you mean, 'the smell of death' is on me?"

"I don't really know," she said wearily. "You're right, I'm very tired, and I'm not always sure what I'm saying or even thinking. But I'm sure of one thing: A man who kills as a way of life is tainted. He may think it's over and done with, at least until the next time, but he's marked by what he's done and what he's going to do. Call it the smell of death, call it the mark of Cain, call it anything, but it's inescapable."

"Are you planning to take your suspicions to the authorities?"

She stared at him, and again he saw distaste in her expression. "I'm not interested in your activities, because I'm not interested in killing and destruction," she said. "No, Mike, I'm not going to tell anybody. We'll just forget we ever knew each other. You'd better go now. I have to take the boy to the rest center. I think he's got a broken leg."

He climbed out of the van and closed the door. She looked at him once, let out the clutch, and drove forward. The guns were thumping again, and he could hear the crump of high explosives. The East End was catching it again.

Chapter 15

CANARIS put down the long-range weather forecast and signed his initials in the margin. Canaris didn't believe in weather predictions any more than he believed in Hitler's astrologer, who was proving a far worse hindrance. Arguments could overwhelm the weathermen, never the astrologer.

He suspected it was the damned horoscope merchant who had persuaded the Führer to allow Göring to switch his attacks from the airfields and radar stations to London. A few more days of concentrated pressure, he thought, and the RAF would have cracked. All his reports pointed to it, but now the chance was gone. The bombers were flying in the dark now, almost free of fighter interference, but all they were achieving was the temporary disablement of a few factories and the deaths of civilians, not soldiers.

All gone to waste, he thought. The seven hundred barges brought so laboriously to Ostend, Calais, Dieppe, and Boulogne; the ninety thousand men ready to board them with their artillery; the Kriegsmarine, which, with the destruction of the RAF, would have controlled the Channel, turned it into a German lake; all gone to waste. The paratroopers would never take off now to land in Kentish orchards and hopfields; the 17th Sturmbock, the battering ram division, would never establish its bridgeheads around Hythe, Dungeness, Rye, and Seaford.

Canaris picked up his in-house telephone and dialed an extension. "Lahousen?" he said. "Please come upstairs for a moment."

Lahousen was in uniform, for he had just returned from the funeral of a friend, a bomber pilot who had been mortally wounded during a sudden attack on his plane by a night fighter over the Sussex coast. The death had hurt the colonel badly. He had gone to school with Rudi. Together they had drunk and played and whored. There was a time when Lahousen thought he would marry Rudi's sister, but in the end she married a fat businessman from the Ruhr.

"The Irish agents," Canaris said. "Are they in position?"

"We are still moving them over," Lahousen said, "but we have at least half a dozen ready for action. Some of them have been waiting months."

"They are free of surveillance?"

"It appears so. We allowed the British to pick up a couple of men who were expendable so that they will believe their security system is in good order. However, I have word that some of those who have been implanted for the longest time are getting a little restless, Admiral."

"They will soon have action. What about radio contact?"

"It is in good order. Also, the radio transmitters are in the hands of four of the agents."

"Yes, I saw your report on that. Good, Lahousen. Now, where are the agents with the transmitters at this time?"

"There is one in London, another in South Wales, a third near Portsmouth, and the fourth is in North Wales, within easy reach of Manchester. None of the transmitters have been used yet."

"I know. The weather has been in our favor. The Thames in the moonlight is better than any transmitter. However, the weather cannot hold, and the autumn approaches. We must be ready."

"We will be ready," Lahousen said.

"Very well. Now, we have been considering targets. There were a number of options. Birmingham was tempting. They call it the city of a thousand trades, and many of those trades are vital to British war production. But it is too large for our purpose. We need a smaller city, but one which is still of overriding importance. We discussed Portsmouth for its dock facilities; Bristol for its connection with aircraft production; Sheffield for its steel production; Liverpool, Manchester, and Newcastle. We considered all the options, but inevitably it came down to one city. One city which is perfect for our needs."

Canaris unrolled a large-scale map of the British Isles and spread it on his desk. He studied it for a moment, then moved a finger to indicate a point between London and Birmingham. With the movement the map refurled itself, and Lahousen came forward to help keep the parchment flat. This accomplished, he could see where Canaris was pointing.

182

"Coventry," Lahousen said.

"It has a cathedral," Canaris said. "It also is the home of the Alvis Aeroengine factory, the Daimler Motor Works, the Standard Motor Company, the British Piston Ring Company, the Coventry Radiator and Press Company, and Armstrong-Whitworth, the armament firm. It is the largest concentration of war industry in Britain, and it has to be destroyed. If we can knock out Coventry, the English war effort will take such a damaging blow that it might never recover. Göring is beginning to realize that his attacks on London, although they make a good subject for Goebbels' broadcasts, achieve nothing but the killing of civilians and the smashing of some docks which are not essential to war production. Now he wants our help."

"The Irish and their transmitters?"

"Exactly. The Irish and their transmitters. The British have been bending the beam of *Knickbein*."

Knickbein, or "crooked leg," was the system of radio beams which intersected over the target. From their bases in the Netherlands and France, the bombers of Luftflotten 11 and 111 flew down one beam until a different note coming through their earphones told them they had reached the intersecting beam. They knew then that they were in the approximate area of their target.

"The scientists have produced something else that is not so easily affected by the British," Canaris went on.

He let the map furl and pushed it away from him. "They call it the X-apparatus, and they claim it cannot be interfered with by the British. But the original problem remains. The bombers need the final guidance from the ground."

"The Irish transmitters."

Canaris picked up a slim booklet from his side table and tossed it across to Lahousen. "You might read this," he said. Lahousen looked at the title: COVENTRY—PAST AND PRESENT.

"It gives a little history of the city," the intelligence chief said, "and describes some of the points of interest." Below the

183

title was a pen-and-ink drawing of the three slender steeples which dominated the town.

"One of the steeples belongs to the cathedral," Canaris said. "I'm told they started building it in 1373."

"If the bombers hit the cathedral, it will have a bad effect on world opinion" Lahousen said. "The British propagandists will make the most of it."

"I'm aware of that, my dear Lahousen," Canaris said coldly. "We are past the point where we can afford to worry about world opinion. If the British put their war plants around a famous old cathedral, well, that is their problem, not ours."

"What is the population?"

"About three hundred thousand, most of them engaged in war production. Strangely enough, there are a number of Irish workers in the factories of Coventry. I believe they're making very good money."

"I remember a little more about Coventry now," Lahousen said. "Isn't there a legend about a woman riding naked through the streets?"

"Lady Godiva," Canaris said. "She was trying to persuade her husband not to levy punitive taxes, I believe."

"Yes, I remember. And there was a Peeping Tom."

"A pretty little story, but that's not our concern now. Our immediate concern is to give Goring's men the guidance they want so that they can set the whole city alight and smash those war factories. You will set things in motion?"

"I will, Admiral."

Donovan was in high spirits. The British had been forced back into their own islands. They had lost thousands of men, tons of equipment in France. Their former allies on the Continent were under German control. Not even their empire could save them now, he thought. There were reports that the Canadians, the Australians, and the South Africans were not so eager in this war to come to the rescue of the mother country. And now the German Air Force was breaking up the great capital that had been a symbol of power, of domination. It was, he thought, only a matter of time.

It was a damned pity about Russell, that he would never see the lifting of the occupation of the Six Counties. But he was only one of many Irishmen who had given everything for the cause of freedom.

Russell, in spite of his illness, had insisted on going to Germany to discuss the future of Ireland with the men who would soon control London. He had held talks with Ribbentrop and his Irish affairs adviser, Dr. Veesenmayer; with the Abwehr chief, Wilhelm Canaris, and his assistant, Lahousen. But the IRA would never know what was said at those meetings. On August 8 Russell sailed for Ireland aboard a U-boat under the captaincy of Commander Helmut von Stockhausen. During the voyage his illness worsened. There was no doctor on board, only a medical orderly who could do little to help the stricken Irishman. Six days after leaving Germany, with the submarine one hundred miles west of Galway Bay, Russell died. He was buried at sea, and von Stockhausen turned back for home.

But the loss of the chief of staff wouldn't slow the momentum of IRA actions in Britain. Even though the Army Council still had to meet to select a new chief of staff, the plans set in motion by Russell would continue. Anyway, Donovan thought, there was damned little chance that anybody but Peter Donovan would be selected for the post.

Maggie was there. She was standing on the corner of Dawson and Nassau streets, looking toward Trinity College. A fine figure of a woman, Donovan thought, slowing his pace. His eyes, deceptively sleepy-looking behind the twinkling spectacles, ranged quickly up and down the streets, his gaze pausing at doorways and windows. The Special Branch was being as obnoxious as always. Maggie gave no sign that she had noticed him, but he knew she was aware of his approach.

"I was just thinking about a pal of mine who's a priest, Maggie," he said as they began to walk down Nassau Street together. "He was driving along through County Wicklow when he ran out of petrol."

"It's one of your awful jokes, isn't it, Donovan?" she said, taking his arm.

"Not everyone thinks they're awful," he said, aggrieved.

"Go on, then. What happened?"

"Well, a traveling salesman happened by and saw his plight. He offered to siphon some petrol from his motorcar and give it to my clerical friend. The thing was that the only container the priest had was a bedpan, so they had to siphon the petrol into that. Then the salesman drove off, leaving the priest to pour the petrol into his car. Just as he was putting the petrol into his tank, a policeman cycles by. He sees the priest using the bedpan, and he calls out, 'Father, you'll forgive me saying so, but that's what I call faith.'" Donovan's lined face took on even deeper creases as he laughed out loud. "'That's what I call faith.' Now that's a pretty good one, wouldn't you say, Maggie?"

"It's terrible," she said, laughing.

"Ah, well, I'll be appreciated when I'm gone," he said. "Did you have a good trip over?"

"No problems. I came on the old *Ulster Monarch,* Liverpool to Belfast."

"And what's the news from England?"

"Mostly good. They're taking a beating."

"It must be dangerous in London."

"It's not as dangerous as rotting in De Valera's prisons."

"You're a brave girl, Maggie. There's another transmitter ready to be taken over. This one's for Plunger Cronin. Can you manage it?"

"They didn't search last time. Once we get it over the border into the Six Counties, I think we're all right. They don't seem to bother to check anybody sailing from Belfast."

"How's your Michael?"

Maggie hesitated, and they slowed, finally stopping to stare into a shop window. It was full of men's suits on vapid-faced dummies. Donovan could see her face reflected in the glass.

186

"He's restless," she said. "He wants to be active."

"McGovern's nephew is worried about him," Donovan said.

"Who?"

"The landlord at the pub where Michael's working. In London he calls himself Barnaby. He's been working for us over there for years. A good man."

"And why is he worried, I wonder?"

"Brock's been spending a lot of time with an Englishwoman. An ambulance driver."

She took her arm from his and began to walk back the way they had come. Donovan had to trot to catch up with her. Her back was stiff, and she wouldn't look at him when he reached her side. She was taller than he, and he had to look up at her set face.

"I had to tell you," he said. "It was a necessary thing."

"For the good of the organization, I suppose," she said.

"For the good of the organization," he agreed.

"Well, damn the organization to hell," she said.

"You don't mean that, Maggie." She stopped now, and they faced each other. There was moisture in her eyes, and he thought that was a good sign. It was when they were dry-eyed and bitter around the mouth that they were difficult.

"The work is what matters, Maggie," Donovan said softly. "Everything must give way to that. Personal feelings, sorrow, everything. You know I'm right. I wouldn't have told you. I'd rather have bitten my tongue out, but Barnaby seems to think she's had an effect on him. Made him softer."

"What's her name?"

"I don't know. She's a widow, and she drives an ambulance around London. That's all I know. It's just a suspicion on Barnaby's part, a suspicion that he might be losing interest in his work because of her. He told me about it, and he was right to do so."

"I don't care if he's putting a hundred Englishwomen on their backs," she said. "He'll do his job, and then he'll come back to Ireland. I know Michael better than you do, or anyone else, for that matter."

187

"Of course, you're right, Maggie. But we can't afford to take any chances. It's an important mission, and there must be no mistakes."

"I'll go and see him."

"You'll do no such thing." Donovan's voice now was hard and direct, buttressed by his authority. "I'm taking him out. We'll handle this some other way, with some other Volunteer."

"No!" Maggie's voice was agonized. "That would finish him. Please, Donovan, if you pull him out, we'll lose him; the organization will lose him. You can't do that. You owe him too much, you and all the others."

Donovan was silent. Words never revealed motives, he thought; they were used to cover them. Maggie's real fear was that she would lose Brock. Emotions were always getting in the way. And Donovan needed Maggie in London just as she needed Brock. Well, there was a way; there were other Volunteers unweakened by mawkishness. There were others who would make sure the job was done.

Maggie was staring at him, pleading with her eyes like a defendant in front of a judge.

"Very well," Donovan said. "But you'll not go and see him. You'll talk to him, but it'll be on the telephone to give him his instructions when you get them from Hamburg. Do you understand, and do you promise to obey your orders?"

She took his hand in mute gratitude. Donovan thought, If I were interested in such things, I could take her straight to my bed as a reward; it means that much to her. She would tell herself it was for Brock and his future, never thinking that it was for hers, too.

"He'll not let you down, and neither will I," she said. "We'll repay your trust tenfold."

"And you'll not go and see him?"

"I will not," she said. "I won't say anything about this. It'll be between the two of us. Oh, Peter Donovan, how long do you think it'll be before we're finished and we can come home to Ireland?"

188

"It'll not be long; I can promise you that, Maggie. And the work that you're doing, you and Michael, will hasten the day. But first we've got to get that transmitter to Plunger Cronin." He paused, then added, "At least we don't have to worry about Plunger."

Blood finished his study of the radio messages. There was no doubt that they were becoming more frequent. Whereas the previous traffic had been on a basis of no more than once a week, in the last few days contact was being maintained on a daily basis. He picked up the latest message, received only three hours earlier and decoded within the hour.

"Coventry," he said thoughtfully. "Liquorice and Carrot to Coventry by A.M., November 14."

Now, what the hell was that supposed to mean? Presumably Liquorice and Carrot were the code names of IRA agents working for the Germans. They were to be in Coventry before noon of November 14. Coventry, he thought, meant factories, armaments, airplane engines, tanks.

It had to be sabotage. Yet it didn't make sense. What could two men do, however determined? Suppose, however, that agents were already planted in the factories, waiting for Liquorice and Carrot to bring them explosives. That could be it. Perhaps the explosives were already inside the war plants, only awaiting the arrival of Liquorice and Carrot to order their activation. But if that was the case, why were two men needed to carry the instructions?

It was the first time the radio messages from the Abwehr had mentioned Liquorice or Carrot, and Blood swore softly at the thought that perhaps the code names referred to something other than agents. Maybe the words referred to a unit of agents. It was all very well, he thought, for the whiz kids from Oxford to break the Abwehr's coded messages, but there could still be codes within codes.

He left his desk and wandered, still musing, to the window. No sign of the spaniel or his owner. Give me a good ax murder, Blood thought ruefully. Or even a tricky little poisoning case. In criminal cases there were always clues of some sort, however meager. To start with, you had a body, and a body could tell you a lot. He wondered where the spaniel had got to. There had been a few bombs dropped around Wormwood Scrubs, and animals were just as susceptible to high explosives as humans.

He turned back to his desk. At least he had heard from young Peter. Only a postcard from Swansea, but that was enough until the days went by and he started worrying again. He recalled his earlier theory that the IRA men were no different from any other criminals, and thus to hell with their motives. He had been wrong.

He was trying to catch a criminal before the crime was committed, and his only clues were radio messages from people he didn't know to other people he didn't know. In a search for a needle in a haystack you knew what a needle looked like. . . . Hell, he thought, I do know what the needle looks like. There was every chance that his needles were in those damned files that Bryant was so fond of. And the haystack in which to look for them was a town called Coventry.

Blood looked at his calendar. November 14 was four days away. Suppose photographs of the men in Bryant's files were sent to Coventry and the coppers up there were told to be on the lookout for them, especially on the thirteenth and the fourteenth. That was the sort of leg work that produced results in ordinary criminal cases. An extra-special watch at the station and at the bus depot. Keep a sharp eye out for men carrying anything heavy. He could send Bryant up there, perhaps, to put a bit of ginger into the effort. In the meantime he would have to provide heavier security at the factories, try to persuade them to put on a full-scale search for hidden explosives, set up an investigation of their personnel files.

Damn it, he thought, now I've got to find out who controls the security at those factories. He picked up his telephone and prepared to plunge into the maze of bureaucracy that organized every second of Britain's finest hour.

Then something else occurred to Blood. Jesus, he thought,

the date might mean nothing. It could be that the Germans had set up a code within a code so that November meant December, so that the fourteenth meant the fifteenth. He might be searching the right haystack at the wrong time. But it was useless, stupid, to look for problems where there might be none. He began to dial.

Chapter 16

London
November 11, 1940

BROCK left the Kings Arms early. He knew that Barnaby slept until nine A.M., when he would rise and make a breakfast of toast in the kitchen they shared. At seven-fifteen A.M. Brock put a razor, an extra pair of pants, and a jacket into the suitcase containing the radio transmitter and locked the case. He was wearing flannel trousers, a thick polo sweater, and a worn sports coat with heavy brown brogues. The rest of his clothes and belongings he left in his room. The case was heavy but manageable. Once, it banged against the wall as he was passing Barnaby's room, and he waited in strained silence, but there was no sound from the landlord's room.

He slipped down the stairs and out through the side door into the street. It was drizzling, for the glory of the summer months had given way to the misery of a London November, and early workers were hurrying, heads down, toward the underground station. Brock went across the dampness of Clapham Common, hunching his head against the splashes of rain draining off the leafless trees. At the telephone kiosk he had to wait until a man in a thick overcoat had finished shouting into the receiver about quotas and shortages, asking his listener if he knew there was a war on. Finally the businessman finished and stamped off into the rain.

Brock dialed the Swiss Cottage number. The same cockney voice answered, but when Brock asked for Margaret, the reply was that she was away, wouldn't be back until the next day.

"Where is she?" Brock demanded.

"No idea, mate," came the bland reply. Brock didn't believe him.

"This is important," he said. "I must find her."

"Sorry, chum. She'll be back tomorrow," the cockney said, and he hung up the phone.

Brock hesitated, about to dial the number again. Finally he swore and left the clamminess of the kiosk. He took an underground train to Charing Cross. He felt a mixture of anger and the same dissociation that had overwhelmed him during the interview with the American reporter. He was riding through the entrails of a besieged city with a radio transmitter and a gun in a suitcase and, he thought suddenly, hundreds of pounds in his pockets. Remembering his debates with other Volunteers about the necessity of taking the battle to England, he found now that his arguments had lost their force. He had been thinking of milord and milady in their manor house, of the politicians bleating their hypocrisies in Parliament, of the red-faced officers in their London clubs. But they had nothing to do with the pallid workers sitting across from him in their cheap clothes, tired faces signaling the sleepless survival of another night of guns and bombs. The old men, the poorly fed girls in their off-the-rack dresses, the women thinking and worrying about their families—they were no different from the Dubliners of the back streets riding their buses and trams to another dreary day of work.

The money. He hadn't thought about that for a long time. Perhaps he would go to the Savoy or one of those expensive hotels on Park Lane, for he certainly had enough. He entertained the notion for a moment like a wealthy guest: a luxurious suite, expensive sheets, a spacious bathroom. But knew he wouldn't do it.

At Charing Cross he took a taxi to Southampton Row and found a hotel of the type favored by commercial travelers. Asked how long he would be staying, he said perhaps a couple of nights, perhaps longer. He was lucky to find a room, he was told, because London was full of people. He was asked for a deposit to cover two nights.

In his room, he took the gun from the case, loaded it, and slid it between the waistband of his trousers and his belly. With his sweater pulled down and his coat buttoned it was concealed, though it pressed uncomfortably against his stomach. He went out and ate at an inexpensive restaurant on Oxford Street. The food was poorly cooked, the portions meager, for the U-boats were steadily chewing at the lifeline across the Atlantic. He walked for a while, then saw a film in which a whimsical Leslie Howard spirited refugees out of Europe. Brock fell asleep, coming awake when the lights came on during a break in the program. He went to a pub off Leicester Square and began to drink. The place was noisy with uniformed men and their cheaply dressed women, but Brock so clearly craved his own company that nobody approached him.

At eight P.M. he walked out, found a telephone booth, and telephoned Victoria. She knew his voice immediately.

"You've been drinking," she said.

"I have."

"What d'you want, Mike?" Her voice was strained.

"I want to see you."

"No. It's no good, Mike. It's over."

"I need you. I need you now."

"I'm going to put the phone down."

"Please," he said. "Please listen to me, Victoria."

"Don't you realize you're hurting me, calling me up like this?" she said. "I want it to be over. I want to forget it, and damn it, now you're making me cry." He remembered her weeping at his side in her bed, the dark hair mingling with her tears.

"Can I come and see you?"

"No. Please, Mike, go away and leave me in peace." Now he knew the tears were coming. "Please, Mike."

"Some of what you said about me was true. I want to talk about it. Face to face. I've thought about it so much."

"I won't see you, Mike."

"I need your help. I want to talk about it, Victoria."

"About what?"

"You've made me see some things differently."

"The thing you're going to do?"

"Perhaps." Suddenly he was wary, sensing the precipice ahead. But he had already gone too far.

"You're talking about killing people, aren't you, Mike? You're talking about blood and death and your part in it."

"It's not that," he said helplessly. "I just want to talk."

"Don't do it, Mike," she said. "I beg you. Not for me, but for yourself."

There it was. The decision. He felt beset by doubt as if by a storm. He remembered working in the corner store in Dublin as a youngster. He remembered the little scales on the counter. Most of the children could afford only a few toffees or chocolates. He would place the little brass weights on one tray and spill the candies onto the other tray until they balanced. If Mrs. Regan wasn't watching, he would allow a few extra candies to slide onto the tray and then snatch them up and empty them into the tiny paper bags.

His father's death. The cruelties and stupidities of the English. The rage at the injustice of it all. Those weights had been heavy enough to keep him steady on his course. But now the doubts, the heretical thoughts, were bringing his scales into perilous balance.

"Please," she said. She was crying again.

"I don't know what you're talking about," he said. "All I want is to see you."

"No."

"Why not?"

"Because I don't trust you, and I don't trust myself."

"You're a lot stronger than I am," he said, and he hung up on her tears.

He returned to his hotel room and slept until the air raid siren awoke him shortly before midnight. He sat at the window of his room and watched the searchlights and listened to the crash of bombs. Once, the hotel structure shivered from the impact nearby of a concussion bomb, but Brock stayed at the window, staring out.

He telephoned the Swiss Cottage number at nine A.M. This time Maggie answered.

"You shouldn't have telephoned until you were instructed," she said. "Are you in a public kiosk?"

"Oxford Street," he said. "I have to see you."

"What's the matter, Michael?"

"Somebody's onto me. I had to move out of the Kings Arms yesterday."

"You should have told Barnaby where you were going."

"What d'you mean? D'you know Barnaby?"

"Never mind that now. Can you come to . . . no, that's no good. I'll see you in an hour on the little bridge over the lake in St. James Park. Do you know it?"

"I'll find it."

"Bring the transmitter," she said.

He went back to the hotel, recovered the suitcase from the locked closet, paid his bill, then took a taxi to the park. He looked at his watch and saw he had ten minutes to find the bridge.

She was waiting for him, leaning forward to watch a couple of ducks in the water below. He thought that she looked prettier than he remembered. He paused for a moment, studying her intent profile and the flow of dark hair falling around her shoulders. She sensed him and turned to face him.

"Hello, Michael," she said. "Let's walk." She made no move to embrace or kiss him. They walked over the bridge and down to the water's edge, their eyes on the oriental skyline of the Whitehall buildings. The weight of the suitcase was pulling at his arm.

"Why did you want me to bring the transmitter, Maggie?" he asked. "Am I going to be put to use at last?"

"It looks heavy," she said. "D'you want to sit on the grass?" Instead they found a bench, deserted at that time of morning.

"What happened?" she said.

"The night before last. I discovered that somebody I know

195

guesses I'm a Volunteer. They believe I'm in England on a mission for the organization."

"They?" She was staring ahead, her hands clasped tightly in her lap.

"Somebody I met."

"Somebody who drives an ambulance?"

He stared at her, trying to force her eyes toward him, but she continued to gaze across the grass.

"You've been spying on me," he said. "You couldn't see me for a moment, but you could spy on me and then throw what you learned in my face."

"I haven't been spying," she said wearily, and now she turned toward him. "Barnaby, at the Kings Arms, is one of our best men. He told us, not because he was spying on you but because he couldn't help but notice it. Have you been having a good time with her, Michael?"

"It's none of your business, Maggie."

"How did she discover what you're doing over here?"

"It was a blind guess. She said she wouldn't do anything about it, but I couldn't risk it. I walked out of the Kings Arms the next day."

"She is my business, you know, Michael. Anybody you see, anybody you talk to, is my business."

"We're not engaged; we don't even have an understanding."

"You bloody egotistical fool," she said in a hiss, then fell silent as a bowler-hatted man in striped trousers walked briskly by. "I don't give a damn if you jump into bed with every woman in London," she went on. "She's my business because I'm your control. I give you your instructions because I speak for Dublin, and you do what I say because I speak for Dublin."

"I know that."

"Oh, Michael," she said, "I wonder if you do. This is different. This isn't an ambush outside Ballycastle. This is the future we're dealing with, and much of it depends on you." She looked at him, and he saw tears gathering in her eyes. "We'll deal with our personal problems later," she said. "When we're both back in Ireland."

196

He pulled out a handkerchief and sat silently as she snuffled into it for a few moments before handing it back.

"Put the suitcase on the bench," she said finally. "All right, now open it." He looked around, saw that there was nobody within a hundred yards, and unlocked it. His clothes covered the dials of the radio transmitter. She lifted the jacket so that he could see part of the housing of the machine.

"It's been preset," she said. "You see this switch in the bottom right-hand corner here? Push it forward, like this, and the radio is transmitting."

As she spoke, the radio came to life, needles in the dials swinging crazily for a few moments until they steadied. She studied each dial, gave a murmur of satisfaction, and pulled the switch back. "The batteries seem to be giving full power," she said. "Everything is in order, Michael."

And then she told him about Coventry. Told him that the bombers would home in on his radio beam to destroy one of Britain's greatest arsenals in a stroke that could finally bring down Mother England.

"It's beautiful," she said. "Some of the guns and some of the Crossley tenders and armored cars that were used against Ireland were made in that little city in the Midlands. The owners of those factories have made their millions from Irish blood and Irish submission, and now an Irishman comes to bring down the revenge from the skies as if the gods themselves will tolerate it no longer. Michael, it's beautiful."

He said nothing. It was cold, and he hunched his shoulders, feeling the pressure of the gun on his belly.

"Those millionaires," he said finally. "Will they be in their factories when the bombs come down?"

"What sort of a question is that?" she demanded. "It doesn't matter where they are; it's their devilish workshops that matter."

A woman walked by, a little boy tugging at her hand. "I want to see the ducks, I want to see the ducks," he was saying. When they had passed, Brock said, "The millionaires won't be there, but the workers will. The bombs will come down on ordinary men and women."

"Ordinary men and women," she mocked. "Did those ordinary men and women ever protest that what they were making was bringing death to ordinary Irish folk? Like hell they did. They worked away and picked up their pay packets and went home whistling. Are we to weep for them now when they never wept for us?"

"When is it to be?" he asked.

"Three or four days, perhaps," she said. "When you get to Coventry, telephone me at the number I gave you. Call me each day at noon."

"I'm to go there today?"

"Today," she said. "Call me at noon tomorrow."

He suddenly laughed. "Here I am worrying about the factory workers," he said. "And I don't have a thought for myself. With all those bombs coming down, Michael Wolfe Brock is just as likely to get blown apart as they are."

She laughed with him. "I wondered when you'd think of yourself, Michael."

"If I don't, it's sure that nobody else will."

"Indeed?" she said lightly. "D'you think that's how it is, that I don't care what happens to you? Well, you're wrong. I do care, even if you have a bad habit of getting into the wrong bed every so often."

They stood up and began to walk toward Whitehall. "I could steal a car to get out once the bombs start falling," he said.

"Or a bicycle. It's not a big city." He fell silent, thinking of other times he had used a bicycle. All those other times, when he had used bicycles and guns and bullets, had drawn him inexorably to the moment just ahead when he would help destroy a city. It was as if his whole life had been nothing but a preparation. He wondered how he would feel after it had been done.

"Where do I go? Afterwards, I mean," he asked.

"Back to Barnaby's place."

"Oh, yes, Barnaby. And perhaps you would be kind enough to explain why I couldn't be told that Barnaby was one of us?"

198

"He wanted it that way, Michael. He can't afford to have many people know about him. That's how he's survived so long. His value to the Army is his anonymity."

They parted at Trafalgar Square. "Take care of yourself," she said, and now she put her arms around him and kissed him. The pressure of her body pushed the hard angles of the gun against his stomach.

Every seat on the train from Euston was occupied. Brock stood in the corridor, his suitcase at his feet, and stared out at the flat fields, the red-brick cottages, the leafless trees. Occasionally the train would follow the meanderings of an overgrown canal, but most of the time it rumbled north between featureless fields, one seeming no different from the next.

If his whole life had been programmed for what lay ahead in Coventry, he thought, then where did Michael Collins fit in? What had been the point of their encounters? Staring out at the twilight creeping across the fields, he wondered if Collins had felt a sense of accomplishment in the last days before the bullets tore into him on that lonely country road. Though neither of them knew it, Collins had only three days left to him when they last met and talked. Brock was on the run following the debacle of the Four Courts, and Collins, once the most wanted man in Dublin, was then the commander in chief of the Irish Free State Army, entrenched in Dublin Castle.

The free staters had caught Brock in a house on the Ballybough Road and taken him to a police station where he was lodged alone in a small cell. They kept him there for six hours before the tall figure of Collins loomed in the doorway. Brock never knew if it was chance that led Collins to find out where he was or if orders had been given that, in the event of his capture, Collins must be notified. It didn't really matter. He was in custody, and now Collins had come to see him. The victor.

He was wearing a uniform with a Sam Browne belt and red tabs on the collar. He looked tired, even more tired than when he had been on the run himself, every Tommy on the alert for him. Brock looked at him and said nothing.

Brock was sitting on a narrow wooden bench. Collins took off his cap, tossed in onto a table, and sat beside him. He leaned forward, his elbows on his knees, and rubbed his eyes. Finally he sat back, his head canted against the wall behind him.

"You're a faithful man, Michael Brock," he said. "You're wrong in what you're about, dead wrong; but I know that for you it's a matter of faith, and I can't find it in my heart to blame you. Between us, you and me, and those who feel like you and me, we're tearing this country apart, and I don't think there's anything either of us can do about it. Perhaps in a few years, but not now."

"We've always had our traitors," Brock said. "It's nothing new, and it will make no difference when the end is reached."

"Oh, Michael, Michael," Collins said wearily. "Let's not use the old words, for they lose their meaning from overuse. To you I'm a traitor. To others I'm a hero. And all of you are wrong. I'm just a poor fellow trying to find a road away from death and grieving, and not doing very well at it."

"There's death aplenty for men like Cathal Brugha and mourning aplenty for his family with you in Dublin Castle."

"D'you remember the post office in 1916, Michael?" Collins was looking at him with something like a plea in his eyes.

"I remember," Brock said.

"D'you remember me warning you there about men who grow too fond of killing, men whose lives become nothing but the planning of murder and the carrying out of their plans?"

"I remember," Brock said. "It has nothing to do with what's between you and me. There'll be an end to killing when Ireland's free, and that's an old word that will never be worn for me by overuse."

Collins said, "We have nearly won that battle. Give us the time and you'll see. We'll get all the things we talked about when we first met."

"Everything you've won is at Mother England's sufferance. We fought for the unshackling of the whole of lovely Ireland, and you say it's a victory when you'd still take the oath of loyalty to the King of England and leave the North in the hands of those corrupt men in London. It makes my stomach churn."

Collins was silent for a moment, struggling for control of a temper famous throughout Dublin. Finally he said flatly, "Wars that don't end in settlement end in utter destruction."

Brock, staring straight ahead, his hands in his pockets, said nothing. He felt as if he were sitting in judgment on the big man in the green uniform, and he took no pleasure from it, not with this man who had represented all the hopes and dreams for a risen Ireland.

"Something has gone terribly wrong," Collins said. "To you and the Volunteers with you it must seem so simple and easy. It's a hundred percent or nothing at all. And I can't make you see that nothing is neat and clean when you're dealing with men and their power."

"You showed me a letter once, written about a place called Skibbereen," Brock said. "In Skibbereen it was very simple. Irish men and women and children were dying because they had no freedom."

Collins stood up abruptly and reached for his cap. His face, when he turned and looked at Brock, was tight with anger. "For God's sake, Michael," he said, "I don't need you to tell me about the history of this country. I know it far better than you. But I'm telling you now that the path you are treading will take you only to violent death."

"It's no good, is it?" Brock said.

"No," Collins said slowly. "It's no good."

For a moment they looked at each other. Now the anger had left Collins' face, and he looked younger, more like the man of 1916. In that instant it was as if Brock were again the eager boy, Collins the laughing revolutionary, and a warmth came to both their faces. Collins raised his gloved hand in a gesture that was almost a salute.

"Good-bye, Michael," he said, and he turned to the door.

Outside, Brock heard Collins talking to the men who guarded him, but the voices were muffled by the heavy door, and he couldn't make out the words. Finally he heard the sound of re-

201

treating footsteps, and there was silence but for the drip of a faucet into the tiny washbasin.

Thirty minutes later the door opened, and a young lieutenant appeared in the doorway, his eyes resentful.

"Come with me," he said. They went to a room where a sergeant sat at a table on which was a pile of Brock's personal belongings.

The lieutenant nodded at the worn wallet, the handkerchief, the small amount of cash. "Take it," he said, "and count the money, for we wouldn't like you to think you've been robbed while enjoying our hospitality."

Brock knew they were going to let him go, and he knew that only one man was responsible.

"You'll not get back the gun we found in the house," the lieutenant said. "Not even Michael Collins could order that. Now get out of here, for you and your sort disgust me."

"You can go to hell," Brock said, and a minute later he was out on the street.

Two days later Brock was on his way to join a flying column operating around Crookstown in County Cork, an area violently opposed to the Treaty. He went unwillingly, for it seemed to him that the action groups in the countryside were peripheral to the conflicts in the larger towns. If the Irish Free State were overthrown, the dynamic would be in city streets, not in hit-and-run ambushes along country lanes. But he went.

He found his contact drinking with half a dozen Volunteers in a Crookstown tavern. The group consisted of untested ploughboys and clerks, and Brock felt a mixture of uneasiness and irritation at being among them. Finally their leader, a worried-looking schoolteacher from Fermoy named Tom O'Kane, said it was time to go. They were planning an ambush of a convoy expected to pass through a valley called Beal na mBlath.

Brock was given an old revolver, which he had no chance to test, and a bicycle, for they planned to cycle to the site.

Even though it was dark, Brock was astonished to see some

202

of the men openly carrying their rifles on their backs, others bearing axes which they would use to cut down trees to block the road. When he asked O'Kane about it, the schoolmaster said, "Oh, don't worry about that, now. There's not a man in the whole of County Cork who would say a word to the authorities." The attitude seemed to Brock typical of the apprentice style of his fellow fighters.

When dawn came, the trees had been felled; and now Brock saw there were at least forty men in the ambush party, for more men had arrived during the course of the night. The light of the new day showed the terrain. The narrow road was contorted by zigzags, which resulted in a series of blind corners. On one side of it was a swampy, watercress-laden stream. On the other, alder and low shrubs hemmed in the pavement before giving way to the green slope of a hill. The column, on the streamward side of the road, had a clear field of fire, and Brock was forced to admit to himself that they seemed to have chosen a good site for bloody work.

But as the morning advanced and the men waited in the knee-high grass, he wondered if their intelligence reports were on the same level. Except for a farmer in an old mud-spattered car and a couple of boys on bicycles, nothing passed along the road. By the afternoon, impatience had taken command of the column. In spite of the pleading of their commanders, men began to drift away, picking up their bicycles and pedaling off down the road along which their victims were expected. Some cited work they had to do; others declared that the convoy would not come.

Brock lay in the grass, a little apart from his comrades. He wanted to test-fire his revolver but knew he could not risk a shot, which might alert an approaching convoy. Once he asked what would be carried by the trucks, but nobody seemed to know or even care.

A little after four P.M. they heard a rumbling of wheels and scattered to their positions. But it was nothing more than an ancient four-wheeled brewer's dray driven by a grinning boy, a cloth cap on the back of his head. O'Kane was evidently expecting it, for he went down to the road, motioning for some of his followers to join him. Together they greeted the boy, and then they released the nag pulling the dray. Half a dozen men lined up on one side of the dray, put their shoulders under it, and after a few attempts managed to tip it over onto its side. Bottles spilled into the road, smashing as they went.

"The trees are too small," O'Kane said in explanation as he passed Brock. "They're not much more than saplings, and the convoy could have pushed through them. They'll not get past the dray, though."

Three hours later, when less than a dozen men remained in ambush, the convoy appeared. From their positions they could see it before those in the convoy could see the roadblock. First came a motorcyclist, then a Crossley tender and a touring car followed by an armored car. Brock immediately realized that this was not a supply column but a military grouping against which the handful of ambushers would be impotent. Again he wished he were back in Dublin.

The Volunteers opened up through the hazy twilight. The stutter of machine-gun fire was interspersed with the crack of rifles. Brock didn't even raise his revolver, for at this distance it would have been as useless as a peashooter. From the armored car, guns returned the fire, supported by rifle fire from the Crossley tender and the tourer. The whole thing, he thought, was a debacle too typical of the fighting outside Dublin. Even if the ambushers were victorious, and there was little chance of that, they would gain nothing more than a few weapons and the deaths of some soldiers.

Ten minutes after it began the ambushers started to pull back. Some of them headed for a white farmhouse with a gray slate roof which stood behind them on the brow of a hill.

Brock went with them, following a fold in the hill which had given them cover. As he approached the farmhouse, the firing died away, and, half-crouching, he looked back. The motorcyclist had taken cover behind the armored car, leaving his machine on its side in front of the barricade. The occupants of the car were behind the Crossley tender, while the guns of the

204

armored car pointed uselessly at the hillside, unable to elevate enough to reach the farmhouse. The roadway was littered with broken glass from bottles which the dray had carried.

As he stared down, a man appeared from behind the armored car. He was carrying a rifle at high port across his chest, and as he looked around him, he appeared oblivious to the danger of the guns on the hillside. There was no mistaking that tall figure in the peaked cap and the Sam Browne belt, no mistaking the erect carriage. Brock thought that even in the twilight he could see a grin on the full lips, but that must have been imagination; for Collins was at least a hundred yards away, and the light was going fast. In the moment that he recognized him, Brock thought of the contradiction in the gun in Collins' hands. As a man on the run Collins had declared proudly that he never carried a weapon. Yet, now that he was facing his old comrades in arms, he was bearing a rifle, and Brock didn't doubt that he had used it. He seemed to be reloading it.

Brock shouted at the men above him, withdrawing to the farmhouse. "It's Michael Collins," he cried, but even as his voice echoed down the valley, a single shot blazed out of the farmhouse. Brock knew what he would see before he turned.

Collins was down, the left side of his head a dark smear of blood. He didn't move. It was that swift. One moment he was standing in the middle of the road as if in defiance, the next he was a sprawled, lifeless figure on the rough pavement. Brock gazed down the hill in horror, his lips forming the word "No," but no sound coming out. Immediately more shots, rifle and machine-gun fire, broke out, but he remained upright, his eyes unable to leave the sight on the road.

"Come on, you bloody fool," a man said, tugging at his elbow. "The orders are to scatter and get back to Crookstown."

Brock stared at him blankly.

"D'you hear? We have to get out of here at once, for there'll be reinforcements along that road in a minute."

"Leave me alone," Brock said. "Let me be." The man hesitated, uttered a muffled exclamation, and turned to run head down past the farmhouse. Brock stayed where he was. He sank onto his belly and peered through the grass at the road below. The firing from the hillside and from the convoy had stopped, giving way to a silence unbroken even by the calls of birds. An invisible mourner, he watched the soldiers emerge cautiously from their vehicles and approach their fallen general. They grouped around him, and Brock could see them crossing themselves, now ignoring the hillside from which the ambushers had fled. One soldier went down on his knees and seemed to be cradling the head of the corpse.

Brock didn't move. He watched them carry Collins to the tourer in which he had been riding. He watched the soldiers push the dray to one side and clear the fallen trees so that the convoy could move forward. He remained there on the hillside long after the convoy had gone, when the only signs of the futile battle were the barricade pushed to the side of the road and the blood on the ground.

Traveling north now to Coventry, Brock remembered the sense of loss that overcame him after the time in Beal na mBlath. He had continued the work, but something had gone from it. It became a thing of the mind, not of the heart; for it was Collins and Collins alone who had talked of the risen Ireland as a joyful, buoyant experience in which they would reclaim their true heritage, build a new nation that would astonish the world.

Brock had told Maggie that the numbness at his core must have been the result of his precarious life, but he knew it had more to do with the death of Collins. After Collins, it seemed to Brock, his emotions had been deadened as if he had taken an involuntary immunization. It had something to do, as well, with the new leaders on both sides. They were humorless mediocrities, men concerned with meaner ambitions.

De Valera. Well, his time had come, as it might not if Collins had survived. He had won an independence of sorts, an independence for the Church and the shopkeepers and the censors; and the "wild geese" still flew to America and to poor-paying jobs under Mother England's skirts, and the Six

Counties remained a fief of London. So Brock had fought and killed. He had met men who killed for the pleasure of it, as Collins had warned, but he didn't believe it was true of Michael Wolfe Brock. Now he was going to kill a town, and he got no pleasure from that thought any more than he had enjoyed the sight of the woman in the house in Clapham, the sight of the little boy staring down and screaming in terror. It would happen in Coventry, too; and it was right that it should happen, for it would take Ireland a step closer to the freedom that must come. And yet . . .

Brock found that it was not the broken body of the woman that disturbed him; it was the shriek on the lips of the red-headed boy. He stared out the grimy window. They were through the outskirts of the city and heading into the center, the train slowing as it made its way past the backs of row upon row of working-class houses. On a patch of rough grass he saw a group of boys playing football, using their coats on the ground for goalposts. Brock wondered if he was their executioner coming to call.

Chapter 17

Hilversum, Holland
November 13, 1940

THE room was long, low-roofed, windowless. Sixty desks faced the platform at one end of the chamber. At the desks sat the pilots and bombardiers of Kampfgruppe 100, the pathfinders for the planes of Luftflotten 11 and 111 based in France and the Low Countries.

Every man was equipped with a pair of headphones. In front of each pilot was a mock-up of the controls of the Heinkel He 11p-6; in front of his bombardier partner were a black switch and a small red bulb. The aim of each pair was to make its bulb light up. It was like something out of an amusement park, Lahousen thought.

General Hugo von Sperrle, commander of the Condor Legion in Spain, director of the air assault on Amsterdam, moved to a table on the platform and tapped his pencil sharply for attention.

"Gentlemen," he said, "we will now proceed. We do not have very much time. We shall go through it once more, and then we shall see how well you have learned your lessons. It is really very simple, and there is no reason why a single bulb should fail to light. The key is concentration, concentration, and again, concentration.

"Now, it is essential that in the split second that the pilots see the needle on their gauges moving, in that split second they must react. Traveling at more than two hundred miles an hour, you could pass the beam and lose it unless you react immediately. Let us begin."

The bleak unshaded lights were switched off, and the airmen were allowed five minutes to readjust to the only remaining illumination, the soft glow of the gauges in front of them.

"Remember, gentlemen," Sperrle said, "here you have ideal conditions. In the skies over Britain there will be flak, possibly night fighters harrassing you. We will begin."

The pilots immediately heard the familiar tone which meant they were traveling along the signal beamed from the radio station at Oostburg. They stared in utter absorption at the gauges, their hands tensed on the controls. After three minutes it happened. The needles, resting at the midway point, swung violently to the right, and at the same moment, a faint high-pitched note interrupted the steady tone of the Oostburg signal.

The pilots manipulated their controls to make their imaginary planes turn left. Too much, and the needle would swing past the desired midway point. Too little, and it would fall short. Just the right amount, and for a few seconds the high-pitched note of the signal from the ground, growing in intensity, would break up into a staccato *brr-brr*, almost like the ringing of a telephone. That was the bombardiers' moment. If they pressed their switches while the *brr-brr* continued, their

208

red bulbs would light up. If they followed the same pattern in the air over Britain, their bombs would find their targets.

Throughout the room the bulbs were lighting up, casting an eerie glow on the triumphant faces of the pilots and bombardiers.

"Very well," Sperrle said, "let us have some lights."

As the airmen took off their headphones and leaned back in their seats, some lighting cigarettes, they stared around, trying to see whose bulbs had failed to light.

"Whose bulb remained dark?" Sperrle asked. Two reluctant hands went up.

"General, I think my bulb is broken," said one of the failures, a youngster with an infectious grin. A whoop of laughter went up from the other pilots and bombardiers.

"Perhaps so," Sperrle said. "All the same, you and your bombardier will remain for more practice. And the other gentlemen at the back of the hall whose aim was less than perfect. The others may go."

A few minutes later Lahousen and Sperrle sauntered through the dusk toward the officers' mess.

"My men will be ready, Colonel," Sperrle said. "I hope your man on the ground will be equally ready. If he is not, all this work will have gone for naught."

Lahousen said, "Don't worry, sir. The beam will be operating. The Abwehr has had very few failures." He wanted to add, "Compared with other branches of the services," but because of Sperrle's rank, he didn't dare. During the practice sessions he had found difficulty in concentrating. His thoughts had been back in Berlin.

Was it possible? Canaris conspiring against Hitler? Two days ago he would have laughed out loud at such a suggestion. Yet he couldn't laugh away the implication of Canaris' words. They were a veiled invitation to Lahousen to join him and his fellow plotters. He had gone over the conversation time and time again, and he had realized it was not the words so much as the tone, the expression on his chief's bleak face. There was no doubt about it.

He realized that Sperrle was talking to him again. He caught the word "tomorrow."

"I'm sorry, General, I didn't hear you," he said.

"I said, it looks as if the Coventry raid will be tomorrow. We will know by noon. Does that present a problem?"

"No, sir. If a decision, one way or another, is made at noon, we can alert our agents to be in position. They are waiting and eager to hear the engines of your bombers."

"It will be an important test. If we are successful with Coventry, we will go on to other cities outside London, the cities where the war production of the English is sited. Will the Abwehr be able to transmit from these other cities?"

"We have agents across the length and breadth of England," Lahousen said. The Luftwaffe generals did not know that the few radio transmitters were in the hands of Irish agents, that most of the German operatives had been arrested. It wouldn't matter, Lahousen thought, for one agent alone could move about the country to guide in the bombers. Again he wondered if Canaris was awaiting the outcome of the war-production raids before deciding whether to strike against Hitler. If they were successful, the Abwehr chief might decide to abort the conspiracy. It was Hitler's failures that had driven Canaris to thoughts of conspiracy, not any philosophical or political views. Tomorrow might alter the course of the Third Reich. His, too, he thought.

Chapter 18

Coventry
November 14, 1940

BRYANT leaned against the wall of the railroad station, waiting for the London train. It was already ten minutes late, and he could see people in the crowd on the platform leaning forward to stare down the tracks past the cattle pens. He felt a similar impatience. After inspecting the passengers alighting from the London train, there would be the express due in from Birmingham, and then he could seek some lunch. He was hungry. Still, he thought, it was better than sitting in his office at Wormwood Scrubs, staring at files and moving bits of paper around. He could feel a return of the old excitement at the thought that he might get his hands on an IRA killer.

Liquorice and Carrot. Perhaps they were men he had known from the old days. That would be a double pleasure. He moved away from the wall as the train appeared down the curve of the track and rumbled into the station. The waiting passengers were restless now, jockeying for the best position to climb aboard and claim a seat. As the train stopped, the doors opened, and suddenly the platform was a mass of surging people, those leaving the train pushing through the crowd trying to board it. Bryant retreated to a position where he could see the arrivals surrender their tickets and walk out into the station yard. His battered features seemed impassive, but under his bushy eyebrows his eyes studied every man and woman. The last few passengers were passing through the barrier when he heard the train from Birmingham pulling into the station on the other side of the London train. He swore. A constable had been assigned to the other side of the station, but Bryant didn't trust him. He had seemed slow-witted and uninterested.

Swiftly, he dismissed the last group of passengers moving past the ticket collector, hurdled the barrier in spite of the official's protest, and raced to the bridge which led to the other platform. He was breathing heavily when he came down it on the other side.

A crowd of people from the Birmingham train was passing through the barrier, watched somnolently by the constable. There were fewer passengers on this side of the station, and Bryant reached the policeman in a few strides.

"Anything?" he demanded.

"Nobody I recognized," the constable said.

"Anybody similar to those pictures we gave you?"

"No, sir. Well, there was one. But . . ."

"Where is he?"

"He's gone, sir. Went through in a fair hurry, he did."

"You bloody fool. Get me through the gate."

"Very well, sir." The policeman moved solidly forward and said, "Everybody stand back, now. Make way for this gentleman to get through." It was hardly necessary. Bryant pushed past the few remaining travelers and headed out for the street. He saw the man almost immediately, abut fifty yards up the road. He saw the pale hair, the broad back, the suitcase swinging in his powerful grip.

"Plunger Cronin," Bryant said softly. He realized the constable had come up behind him.

"Get back to your post," he said. "I'll handle this." He began to walk after the big man. He could feel the sweat of excitement gathering in his armpits.

Brock telephoned the Swiss Cottage number at noon. It was the third time he had called Maggie as instructed, for now he had been in Coventry for more than two days.

The acceleration of the war machine in the Midlands city had brought in people and money, especially money. The stores were jammed, the cash registers singing a refrain of swift-moving money. The war, it seemed, had been good to Coventry.

It was a curious hybrid of a town, the busy factories ringing its medieval heart and at the center the mass of stone that was the cathedral. Brock had spent his time strolling the streets and alleyways, his suitcase locked in the room he had rented at the grim-looking Ansell's pub on the Northampton side of the city. He found himself studying the faces around him, as a hangman might gaze upon the face of his approaching victim. The faces—some laughing, some somber, some impassive— made him uneasy, as he'd never been before in England. He would visit the cathedral that afternoon, he thought; it would be quiet there.

212

As soon as Maggie came on the line, he knew. Knew it would be today. Her voice had a tremor to it, a shakiness that came from exhilaration.

"Are you well, Michael?" she said.

"I'm fine," he said, wishing he could share her excitement.

"It's tonight," she said.

"What time?"

"Are you in a call box?"

"Of course, Maggie."

"You must be transmitting at seven o'clock. Everything is scheduled for them to arrive at seven-fifteen. They may be later, but they'll be no earlier than seven-fifteen."

"Very well," he said. "At seven o'clock.

"Where will you transmit from?"

"The cathedral," he said. "I think it'll be there. If not, then I'll be just outside. It's in the center of the city."

"Will you be able to get away after the bombing starts, Michael?"

"I'll make arrangements."

"Be sure you do, my darling, for they'll turn that place into an inferno. There'll be incendiaries first to set it afire, and then they'll drop their explosives into the fires. Berlin says you've got no more than half an hour to get out before the explosives come down."

"I'll go west, toward Warwick. It's away from the factories. It's the residential side of the town."

"Leave the transmitter," she said. "They want the transmissions for as long as possible. Until it's destroyed by the flames and the explosives."

Brock went to the cathedral. It was a little to the east of Broadgate, the core of the city. The great pile of pink sandstone was dominated by a steeple supported by flying buttresses as tall as the cathedral was long. Inside, Brock saw there were guild chapels along the north and south sides of the building, but it was the five-sided apse containing the chancel and sanctuary that drew his eye. A lone cross forged from silver stood on the altar, the light from perpendicular

213

stained-glass windows pouring onto it as if from floodlights. One of the windows depicted a winged cherub on wheels, which he supposed was appropriate enough for a city that drew its fortune from the wheel.

He sat in a pew in the great nave and stared around at the soaring arches of stone which supported the carved oaken roof. The beams were sculpted to represent the vault of heaven. It was very quiet. Occasionally the footsteps of a visitor would echo through the vast interior, but mostly it was still. As a boy he had prayed to a God who had won his belief; but that was many years ago, and now, after all the years of blood and death, he could no more pray than he could wear the clothes of the boy he had been.

He sat there in the cathedral for an hour; perhaps more, for in that great building there was little sense of time. He thought of Maggie and Donovan, of Plunger and the time in Spain. He thought of the man executed against a country wall outside Dublin, the man who had shouted that it was all in their grasp if they waited. Mostly, though, he thought of Michael Collins, and though he tried to fix his thoughts on the man of 1916, the picture that would not go away was that of the sprawled body in the dirt of the valley called Beal na mBlath.

Finally he stirred and stepped out into the aisle. An old man in a clerical collar and dark gray suit was walking slowly toward him, his white hair catching the rays of light pouring through the west windows. He was using a walking stick, and the *tap-tap* of its tip punctuated the softer noise of his footsteps.

"I was watching you," the old man said. "You've been sitting there a long time."

"It's a good place to rest."

"And to pray," the old man said.

"I wasn't praying."

"Then you were thinking. Sometimes that's a form of prayer."

Brock didn't want to discuss such matters. He had had

214

enough of priests in Ireland. Still, there was a benignity to the old man's features that made Brock tolerant of him.

"Does the cathedral stay open all night?" he asked.

"All day and all night. The cathedral is always here for whoever needs it."

"It's magnificent. You must be proud to carry on your ministry in such a building."

The old man laughed. "God bless you, young man," he said. "I don't serve in the cathedral. I'm just a country vicar with a parish in a village outside the city. I have no connection with the cathedral except through God. Indeed, I often disagree with the bishop, good man though he is."

He gazed around with the deep affection of a man looking at his familiar home. "I come here to pray," he said. "It's silly, I know, and my lord bishop wouldn't approve; but I believe my prayers will be heard more clearly from this place."

"I'm afraid I don't understand."

"No, neither would my bishop; and I expect you're both right," the old man said.

A line of schoolgirls had entered the great doors behind them. Their chattering and the admonitions of their schoolteacher rippled through the church and then were lost in the immensity of the arches.

"You see," the old man said, "this building was for centuries just a splendid parish church. But then, in 1918, the church authorities decided that it should become a cathedral. It was selected for that glory, not built for it; and therefore it is a special place to me. It is called the Cathedral Church of St. Michael, and it's my whim that God might hear a prayer said here just a mite more clearly than one said in my own little church."

Brock said nothing. He had difficulty in following the old man's logic. "Don't misunderstand me," the clergyman said. "My church is a handsome house of worship, more than two hundred years old, with a pretty clock tower, though I do wish the people in my parish would better remember its purpose on Sunday mornings."

215

"Certainly there is an awe attached to the cathedral," Brock said. He was in no hurry, and the old man's ramblings passed the time.

"Exactly. That's the word I would use. Awe. That's one reason I come here to pray. And to think. But then I'm afraid I have something of a reputation for eccentricity. You sound Irish. You're a Catholic?"

"I was brought up as a Catholic."

"It's strange how age changes attitudes," the old man said. "There was a time long ago when I took such distinctions seriously. Now I'm ready to die, and it doesn't matter much. But this cathedral matters, this marvelous old place and what it represents. It's not just wood and stone. It's the sweat and thought and love that went into it." He touched the flagstones with his cane and shook his head.

"People don't matter to me anymore. Not very much. Is that a terrible thing to say? I suppose it is. But I find that as death approaches me, it's this building that comforts me most. Not the people around me. When I come here, I feel small and yet part of something noble and therefore, somehow, comfortable. You, now, you don't look comfortable in yourself."

The remark, only half-heard amid the meanderings of the vicar, came at Brock like the probing of swordsman's foil.

"I mean that you look troubled," the old man said. "Ah, now, don't worry. I'm not one of those priests who intrude where they're not wanted. I know that you have to work things out for yourself. Everybody does."

"Tell me something, Father," Brock said suddenly. "If you had to make a choice and you had the power, would you save this cathedral at the expense of the people of Coventry? You say you love this building above all else. Would you let the city die if the cathedral could thus be saved from destruction?"

The old man was disturbed by the question. He hesitated, then said, "I would never answer anything like that, because the situation could never arise."

"But if it could?"

"This is pointless."

216

"It's nothing more than a philosophical point, Father. Accepting that, which would you save?"

"No, it's foolish even to discuss it. It's like the question, Which of your two sons would you save if both were drowning? You'd do your best to save both, of course."

"But if you could only save one—the city or the cathedral?"

The clergyman stared at Brock. It seemed to his inquisitor that the faded blue eyes were frightened. The thin lips were trembling. "I won't talk about it," the old man said. "It's an evil question."

"You won't answer it?"

"I must be going now. I have an appointment. I'll wish you good day, sir."

"I'm talking about people's lives, Father," Brock said. "I'm asking if you would sacrifice the lives of ordinary people who have committed no great sin so that an idea, an ambition, a building like this, if you like, could live on. It's a simple question, isn't it?"

But the old man was walking away down the aisle, his walking stick striking a hurried counterpoint to his progress, his shoulders bowed. He stumbled once in his hurry, and Brock thought he would fall; but he recovered and moved on, a small bent figure in the immensity of the cathedral.

"It doesn't matter," Brock said softly. "It really doesn't matter, Father."

He thought, I know the reply. It's the same as Peter Donovan's would be. The priest was just an older version, a softer version, of a man in Dublin who thought that lives were nothing more than impediments in the way of what he wanted.

For a moment there was anger, anger such as he had seen in the face of the informer condemned in County Kildare. Good Christ above, he thought, I've lived all my life with men and women who would do anything for an idea, an ambition, an ideology. And suddenly, here in this cathedral marked for destruction by them, I could vomit at the very thought of them and all their futile blood letting.

Finally, after the purge of anger, he thought, I know what I

217

need to know about the priest and about Donovan and the rest of them in Dublin; and now I know what I need to know about myself and what I must do. The black storm of doubt and anger had passed. The decision had been made, and he was content. Was that, he wondered, how Collins had felt when he signed the treaty?

He left the cathedral through a side door and went in search of a telephone. If Maggie wasn't at the Swiss Cottage number, he would leave a message with the cockney. He owed that much to her and to Donovan and the others in Dublin. There would be plenty of time for him to decide what to do with the rest of his life.

Chapter 19

Soesterberg, Holland
November 14, 1940

AFTER his duties had been completed, the meteorological officer planned to attend a dance at the Luftwaffe group headquarters in Utrecht. To save time he was already wearing his dress uniform. The white jacket gave him the appearance of a musical comedy star as he stood in front of the huge curtained board, but the assembled pilots and navigators did not smile. They cared only about his words, for the weather could separate life from death.

"Northwest Europe," he said. "The high pressure continues. It covers Holland, Belgium, France, and Denmark. And England."

Among the crews there was a rustle of barely suppressed satisfaction. The navigators were taking notes.

"You will find some stratocumulus at five thousand feet, but not in any great amount, nothing to bother about. There's a cold front moving down from Norway with associated thunderstorms, but it's not expected to reach our area until shortly before noon tomorrow. The later flights, however, should bear it in mind, since they will still be returning at dawn." He continued talking, giving more details about the approaching cold front.

A navigator in the second row put up his hand and received a nod from the Met man.

"Lieutenant, what about the target area?"

"As I told you," the weatherman said with some irritation, "clear, absolutely clear except for the possibility of minor stratocumulus at five thousand feet. Also, prevailing westerly winds at no more than five to ten miles an hour. This applies to the entire British Isles, from the Orkneys to the Scilly Islands."

He had lost his audience now, but still he droned on. Finally he gathered his papers and moved away to allow the general, von Sperrle, to take his place in front of the curtain. Normally the intelligence officer would have followed him, but this would not be a normal operation. The crews, who had been whispering to each other, fell silent.

The general reached for the cord at the side of the board. He pulled it, and the curtain parted with a rattle of metal rings.

Somebody among the crews said "Coventry." But they all had seen it. Sometimes the marker pencil on the plastic that covered the enormous map of Northwest Europe would depict a zigzag pattern, starting with the assembly points near the coast and then tracing angular routes whose object was to avoid the flak and the night-fighter stations.

But the route to Coventry was straight. "Assembly will be here," the general said. He had picked up a long schoolmaster's pointer, and the crews immediately recognized the area on which the tip of the pointer rested, ten miles inside the Dutch coast. They had gathered there for their last raid three nights earlier.

Oberleutnant Joaquim Trettner, Staffelkapitän of the lead section of Kampfgruppe 100, stared at the assembly area and

219

thought that it was at just such an area that a pack of wolves might gather before plunging down on an isolated settlement. Inside their own territory, yet within range of a roving enemy. The notion pleased him.

"There will be no evasion tactics," the general said. "You will fly directly to the target. As it happens, this route does not approach the English antiaircraft concentrations. There is a possibility of night-fighter attacks—you all know where they are stationed, here, here, and here—but without the guidance of searchlights they will have their usual difficulties."

There was a murmur of amused agreement as he went on. "I don't believe any of you have ever seen one. You wouldn't know what they look like. You will have no trouble with night fighters. No, you will fly directly to your target, using your new radio apparatus. I know it will be a clear night, but you will still use the equipment. This is most important. Much will depend on your reports on its efficiency."

Outside the briefing hut, ground crews were laboring in the weak sunshine. Although they were well inland, the air smelled of the sea, damp and pungent. Superintended by armorers, the men were maneuvering silver incendiary bombs into the bellies of the dispersed black Heinkels. Among the incendiaries were a small number of high explosives. Their purpose was to bring down roofs and walls so that the phosphorus of the incendiaries could set fire to fallen timbers and wooden slats. The third type of bomb being loaded from the trains of tractor-drawn trolley was markers. These would explode in showers of yellows and blues and whites, visible for miles, to guide in the following heavy bombers with their loads of HE.

Some of the heavy bombers would be carrying canisters weighing up to eight thousand pounds that could bring down whole city blocks.

"This will be an important run," the general told the crews. "As you were told at Hilversum, you'll be using the X-apparatus for the first time. This equipment can mean the difference between winning the war against the English and losing it. You must prove its efficiency so that we can retain it for our

220

bombers. Thus, the English will find that no clouds, no storms, nothing, can deter us from reaching our selected targets."

Trettner hunched his neck into his zip-up leather flying jacket, waiting for the moment of melodrama that the general allowed himself at the end of each briefing. It always embarrassed Trettner, yet he couldn't ignore the prickle of excitement that ran up his spine at such moments.

"Thank you, gentlemen," the general said. "We fly against Coventry. *Heil Hitler!*"

"We fly against Coventry," the crews shouted back at him. *"Heil Hitler!"*

Chapter 20

BLOOD had not seen McGregor for twenty years, but he recognized him immediately. The widow's peak was gray now, the skin had lost its freshness, and deep lines dragged at the corner of his mouth. The eyes, though, the eyes were still the same: that extraordinary shining green, as if there were a cat gazing out from the well-shaped skull.

"Forgive me if I don't get up," McGregor said, reaching out to take Blood's hand. Blood saw that a walking stick hung from the edge of the desk.

"I heard about the wound," he said. "Bit of bad luck. Belgium, wasn't it?"

"Holland," McGregor said. His tone didn't encourage further inquiry. "Take a seat," he went on. "We don't have much time."

Behind the Scotsman's head, through the window, Blood could see the cenotaph and the tops of London buses trundling up and down Whitehall. The central location of the office, in the heart of the war-making machine, made him feel like a provincial come up to town from his outpost in Wormwood Scrubs. A picture of the King in air force uniform hung on the beige-colored wall to his right. An old-fashioned, yellowing clock next to it showed three forty-five.

"Go ahead," he said. "Flanders was a long time ago. We can talk about it some other time."

"At least," McGregor said, "I can fill you in a little on what I've been up to over the years since we last met. For some time, now, I've been with the air department of the Secret Intelligence Service. A big name for a fairly small organization. Anyway, as a result of that service, I've been cleared for most secret information not available to your boys at MI Five. In fact, it's been confined to a very small group indeed."

He paused, opened a drawer in his desk and withdrew a black revolver, which he placed on the blotter in front of him. Blood's astonishment must have shown.

"The Scots," McGregor said, "are supposed to be a dour, realistic people, and that may be true; but I'm using a bit of melodrama with the gun because I want to impress something on you."

Blood said nothing. The gun on the table was pointing almost directly at him.

"I've brought out the gun because I want you to know, Blood, that I wouldn't hesitate to use it on you at this moment if I thought that what I'm abut to tell you would go any further. I would pull the trigger without compunction. It's a harsh thing to say to somebody who fought at my side on the Somme in that other war, but I mean it. I mean it, I assure you."

"You've made your point," Blood said. His voice was level but there was an anger in him that McGregor had thought the demonstration necessary. McGregor, he thought, had always taken himself very seriously.

"Have you ever heard of Ultra?" McGregor asked.

"Ultra? No, I don't think so."

"Good. If you had said yes, you would have been arrested." Blood's irritation could not be held down.

"McGregor," he said, "I don't know how many years you've been in intelligence, but it seems to have had a weird effect on you, and I don't like it. Good God, man, we were lieutenants together on the western front. Have you forgotten?"

McGregor ignored the outburst. "Ultra," he said, "is the name given to a cipher machine now in our hands. Originally called Enigma by the Germans, it is used by every German command to decode messages from Berlin. Equally, it is used by the German high command to decode messages sent from the field. The story of how it came into our possession doesn't concern you now, but I can tell you something of its value."

Blood detected a trace of excitement in the Scotsman's voice now, as if the thought of Ultra and its implications still held awe for McGregor.

"With Ultra," he said, "we know what the Germans are planning: how many divisions they expect to use, the disposition of their forces from corps down to company, what they think we will do, how they will react to our moves. We know exactly what is going on in their Teutonic minds. Blood, it's like playing cards—poker, if you like—with a complete description of the other fellow's hand in your head. Ultra is, in fact, our trump card."

"You'd better go ahead and arrest me," Blood said. "I know about the broken code."

McGregor remained undisturbed. "No, you don't," he said. "You know that we have broken the lower-level code used by the Abwehr to direct their agents. That is not what I'm talking about. Ultra is above and beyond that, far beyond anything that has ever been accomplished in any way at any time. But it creates difficulties."

"And now you have a difficulty."

"We have. That's why you're here. It's the matter of Coventry."

"You know about Coventry?"

"I have all your reports here," McGregor said, resting his

223

hand on a buff folder. "Carrot and Liquorice and all the rest of it. I can tell you some things which might help you find those two but I'm afraid it'll do you no good. First, we know what the Germans plan for Coventry. As a result of information given by Ultra, we can be pretty sure that Carrot and Liquorice are part of that plan."

"What's being planned for Coventry?" Blood demanded. He was astonished that his reports had reached Whitehall so swiftly and further astonished that the separate branches of intelligence were meshing so efficiently.

"Ultra is not perfect," McGregor said, the reluctance of his admission showing clearly. "For example, a message might go out that a certain place is to be bombed at a certain time. Usually there is a code within the code, so that the actual name of the target is concealed even from Ultra. Our problem is that somebody in Germany made a mistake and sent out the actual name of the target."

"Coventry," Blood said. "When?"

"Tonight."

"It could be a trap of some sort. Why would they make a mistake like using the real name of the city?"

"It could be," McGregor said. "But we don't think so. Even the Germans can trip up sometimes. The link between the Ultra message and the Abwehr order to Carrot and Liquorice supports our belief."

"Carrot and Liquorice were ordered to be in Coventry November fourteenth. Today. There has to be a connection."

McGregor's eyes flicked to the clock on the wall. It was getting close to four P.M. "The raid has been ordered for seven-fifteen P.M." he said. "We think your Carrot and Liquorice will be used as signallers. Somehow they're going to help bring in the German bombers."

"I've got a man up there looking for them."

"Call him off."

Blood's expression showed his bewilderment.

"Call him off," McGregor said again. "It's an order from the

224

very top. We don't want anything to happen that might indicate to Berlin that we're onto them. If that means letting a couple of agents operate, well, we have to do it."

"You're talking about the destruction of a city, man."

"I know what I'm talking about. So does the old man at Number Ten. We received this message an hour ago. He could have tried to evacuate the city. There would have been some confusion, but we could have got a lot of them out. He's decided against it. And don't think that was an easy decision, Blood. The lives of women and children."

"It's murder not to do something."

"It's not murder. It's war. Think for a moment, Blood. Suppose we evacuate the city. Suppose the raid is called off. Suppose it's some sort of a trick. The Germans would hear about our reaction. They'd know we've got Ultra, and that could change the course of the whole war, not just the safety of a single city."

"But Carrot and Liquorice have nothing to do with your Ultra. We could still catch them and give nothing away."

"You don't seem to understand, Blood. Ultra can give us the edge in every battle we fight. It can mean the destruction of U-boats, even of the German fleet, so that our supply line across the Atlantic remains open. It can mean the saving of the lives of thousands of soldiers and seamen. One day we shall invade the Continent. Ultra will give us a spy at Hitler's elbow, telling us in advance about every move he plans, telling us what he expects us to do or not to do."

McGregor's eyes again went to the clock on the wall. He shifted in his chair, and suddenly Blood knew that in spite of his words he was thinking fearfully of the destruction awaiting the Midland city. But he continued.

"Against all that, what is the importance of an air raid on Coventry? Other cities have been bombed. Other cities will be bombed."

"So we just sit here and wait for the bombs to fall?"

"We wait, and you call off your man."

"But listen to me, McGregor. You're saying that everything must be natural, as if we don't know the raid is planned. Is that right?"

McGregor nodded, his lips tight.

"Well, it's not natural if we call off the hunt for Carrot and Liquorice. It makes no sense either way."

"I know," McGregor said. "The argument has been made and considered. As a matter of fact, I made the argument you're now putting forward. I was turned down."

There was a silence broken only by the ticking of the clock. It was after four P.M.

When the telephone rang in the stillness, both men were startled. McGregor picked it up and immediately stiffened.

"Yes, sir," he said, his green eyes going to Blood. "He's with me now. I've explained the situation." Then he was quiet, listening intently. He made some notes on a yellow pad in front of him, and his eyes ranged again to the clock. When he spoke, there was a new note in his voice, a note which Blood realized was satisfaction.

"Yes, sir," McGregor said again. "We can bring them in from Daventry. I'll get onto it right away." He slammed the telephone down, and now there was a note of exultation in his voice.

"The situation has changed, Blood," he said. "They've reconsidered my argument. It was too much for the old man just to let them smash Coventry without lifting a finger. Now, if you were an IRA man, trying to guide in German bombers, what would you use?"

"Some sort of incendiary device," suggested Blood, astonished by the sudden change of tactics. "More likely a radio beam for them to home on."

"That's what we think," McGregor said. "So this is what will happen: We're going to put spotters on the roofs with orders to look for sudden fires and to extinguish them at all costs. And we're going to bring in radio-surveillance units to monitor the area for unauthorized broadcasts. When did you last hear from your man up there?"

"Not since this morning. He telephoned in."

"Very well. Try and contact him through your people at the Scrubs. Alert him to the urgency of the situation. As for you, you're to start at once for Coventry to take charge. How long will it take you?"

"It's about eighty miles."

"There will be a car downstairs. We'll clear the way for you. Use the siren, if necessary, and you can rip the blackout covers off the headlights. There'll be a radio installed at your disposal. You can have my driver. He used to race at Brooklands. You should be there by six P.M. Plenty of time to see the bombs come down."

"Thanks," Blood said, but the irony in his voice was overwhelmed by the feeling of pleasure that at last he was going to act instead of sitting behind a desk at Wormwood Scrubs.

"We'll set up an emergency headquarters for you. All information will be funneled to it. We'll radio you the location on your way. All right?"

"I'm on my way," Blood said. It was four-fifteen P.M.

Chapter 21

Coventry
November 14, 1940

BRYANT could have taken Plunger Cronin, had him arrested neatly and conveniently, half a dozen times since he had arrived in the city. But the RUC man wanted more. Cronin had to be either Carrot or Liquorice. One or the other, but not both. That meant the other IRA agent was still at large in Coventry, and Bryant knew that eventually there would be a meeting. Carrot would link up with Liquorice. Cronin would link up with . . . whom? It must be Brock.

Bryant had been tempted. One of the air raid shelters

would have done handsomely. Let him get Plunger Cronin alone in one of those shelters. Give him a free hand and he would get all he needed to know within the hour. The IRA men, Bryant thought, were very good with the bomb, the gun, the sneak ambush, but they weren't so tough when it came to experienced interrogation with a bit of muscle thrown in. It was a temptation, but he resisted it because Blood would not have been impressed with his efforts, however successful. Blood, he thought, might have been a champ as a Scotland Yard officer, but he was out of his division dealing with IRA killers if he thought he could beat them with the gloves on. The Royal Ulster Constabulary knew better because the years had proved there was only one way: Meet force with force, violence with violence.

It was the suitcase that intrigued Bryant. Not once in the six hours Plunger Cronin had been in the city had he let it out of arm's reach. In the cafe where he had eaten he had kept his leg firmly against it under the table. Now he had taken it with him into the cinema, where he had already killed two hours.

Perhaps it held explosives for use against the Coventry factories, but it was too small to contain a significant amount. Guns? Ammunition? Bryant wanted very much to take a look inside the case, but that would have to wait until Cronin linked up with his partner.

Sitting in the cinema, half a dozen rows back from the dark figure of Plunger Cronin, Bryant again considered his options. He could telephone Blood to report that he was trailing his quarry. But what good would that do? Blood was a hundred miles away. He could call on the local police. But then he might lose control of the situation. The coppers probably would insist on picking up Cronin immediately; and though it might inhibit the IRA plan, whatever it was, Brock would still be at large with the ability to act.

The decision was taken from him. Cronin wasn't waiting for the end of the film. He was moving toward a side door. There was a flash of daylight, and Cronin slipped out, the suitcase still in his hand. Bryant went after him.

Handling the exit door gently, he eased himself out and peered along the alley that bordered the side of the movie house. It was growing dark, but he could see Cronin at the end of the alley, just about to walk into the busy street that passed the front of the cinema. In contrast to his earlier leisurely progress, the IRA man was moving quickly now, as if the time for action had come. Tension growing in his chest, Bryant walked swiftly after his prey, not bothering to conceal the thud of his footsteps now that Cronin was out in the street. Cronin was going to meet Brock. Bryant knew it. He would wait until the contact had been made. Then he would call the coppers.

Behind blazing headlights, Blood's car moved north up the A-5, the black needle on the speedometer hovering around the 80 MPH mark in open country. McGregor's man, once a racing driver, was quiet behind the wheel. The lights from the dashboard cast a yellow glow on his absorbed features; his black hair was combed tightly back, as if this man of speed were determined to be as streamlined as his machines.

At crossroads they would see the flash of swinging torches in the hands of policemen holding back cross-traffic, and Blood knew what McGregor had meant when he said he would clear the way for them. There was hardly time to see the dark figures of helmeted constables gazing at the hurtling machine. Occasionally, oncoming traffic, drivers dazzled by the unhooded headlights of Blood's car, would waver, then pull over.

They were past High Wycombe when the radio came to life.

"This is Coventry Emergency. This is Coventry Emergency," a woman's voice said. It was well-modulated, surprisingly clear.

"This is Coventry Emergency," she said again. "Come in, Colonel Blood. Colonel Blood, can you hear me?"

Blood picked up the microphone from its rest and pressed the speaker button.

"Blood here," he said. "I can hear you loud and clear."

229

"How far are you from Coventry?" she asked.

"About sixty miles," he said. "I'll be there in less than an hour. What is the situation?"

"Roof spotters are in place," she said. "Three radio-surveillance vans are moving in from the outskirts." Blood wondered who she was, this calm, efficient young woman. She gave him the address of the emergency control post, which had been set up in an art school on Ford Street. Blood began to hunt through the map of Coventry which the driver silently handed to him.

"There is someone here who wants to talk to you," she said.

A moment later Bryant's voice came into the speeding car.

"Colonel?" he said. "We've lost them."

"We've lost who?"

"Sir, Liquorice and Carrot. The code names must be for Brock and Plunger Cronin. I spotted Cronin, and I was following him."

"Then you lost him?"

"Yes, sir." Blood was silent, staring at the suddenly illuminated rear of the truck ahead of them.

"What happened?"

Bryant told him. He told Blood about the contact at the railroad station, the trailing through the city streets, the trip to the factory gates, the visit to the cinema. "He left the cinema, and I was following him through the crowds on High Street. I had him in good view, then suddenly he vanished. He must have ducked into a shop and then gone out the back way. It's the only explanation." Blood struggled to control his irritation.

"Did he know you were following him?"

"I don't think so, sir. I don't know."

"You don't know," Blood said. He considered tongue-lashing Bryant, dismissed it as a waste of time.

"What about Brock?"

"Nothing, sir. I suspect Cronin was on his way to join up with him. There's one thing, sir. He was carrying a suitcase. He kept it close to him all the time I was watching him."

A suitcase. A suitcase could hold a radio transmitter.

230

"Who's in charge there?" Blood asked.

"An army major. Major Wainwright."

"Tell him I'll be there within the hour. Is there anything coming in from the surveillance vans or from the spotters?"

"Nothing so far. What should I do now?"

"Give Cronin's description—what clothes he was wearing, and so on—to all constables on patrol. Go and look for him. Get out into the streets." Blood had decided he preferred talking to the woman.

He returned the microphone to its rest. The Irishmen. He was ready to accept that the Irishmen held beliefs which led them to think that honor and justice were on their side when they worked to destroy a city. Yet, like all men on their level, they were nothing but pawns. Great events were controlled, he thought, by men of power; and so it was with Coventry. The German high command was making the decisions, not the Irishmen. And Churchill was willing to sacrifice Coventry for greater ends.

Almost hypnotized by the glare of the headlights, Blood thought, Poor Coventry.

Chapter 22

Soesterberg, Holland
November 14, 1940

AT six thirty-two P.M., Oberleutnant Joaquim Trettner pushed forward the throttles of his Heinkel He 11p-6. In England it would be dark also, he thought, but clocks would show five thirty-two P.M. Pilots like him, bomber crews like his, would be preparing to fly, thinking about their targets as he was thinking about his.

The heavily laden Heinkel was gathering speed now, and he brought up the tail. There was the familiar, smoothly powerful push of his spine into the back of his seat, into the parachute on which he sat. The plane surged forward, its wheels barely retaining contact with the ground.

Now! He hauled on the control column, and the nose came up. A moment later the craft was staggering ungracefully into the air. The noise, the shaking of the machine, had once reminded him of the time he stood on the footplate of a locomotive. His father had been the engineer of a train running from Hamburg to Bremerhaven and, illegally, had allowed young Joaquim to accompany him. But by now Trettner had carried out so many missions, become so used to the plane, that it reminded him of nothing but sitting at the controls of his Heinkel.

He touched the rudder bar and knew he had satisfactory control. He glanced at the air speed indicator. The arrow was moving steadily up. The horizon was out of sight below the dimly visible black nose of the plane.

"Wheels up," he said.

A heavy clunk as the undercart folded into the fuselage. The obstruction gone, the plane lifted sharply, as if finding at last the real freedom of flight.

"Wheels up," said his flight engineer.

"Flaps up," intoned Trettner. He didn't look out at his wings to check. He was scanning the sky above and ahead.

"Flaps up," reported the engineer.

It was ironic, Trettner thought, adjusting the earphones over his leather helmet. For the first time, they were to use the crucial X-apparatus to home in on their target, and the night was brilliant with moonlight. No wonder the general had dubbed the operation "Moonlight Sonata." Staring down he could see the dark shadows of the dikes thrown across the flat fields and, off to the right, the mass of buildings of Amsterdam and the IJsselmeer beyond.

His crew reported in over the intercom. Fuetterer, in the rear turret, complained about the cold. He always did. Glancing over his shoulder, Trettner could see the spitting flames of other engine exhausts as his pilots brought their lumbering machines into position behind him. The pilots began to report in.

By the time they had assembled close to the coast and each plane had taken its assigned slot, the group was passing over the water's edge at ten thousand feet and still climbing.

Trettner threw the switch that would bring the nagging note of the radio beam into his cramped cabin and ordered the other pilots to do the same. Utterly unnecessary, he thought. With this moonlight you didn't even need a map and compass; you could navigate by landmarks alone. Already he could see the line of the English coast. Sperrle would have done better, he thought, if he had ordered them all to wear blindfolds or perhaps blacked out their Perspex windows.

At fifteen thousand feet Trettner leveled off and stared forward and down over the Heinkel's nose. The meteorological officer had been right: There were traces of stratocumulus at about five thousand feet, but they didn't hide the approaching coastline or the landmass beyond. From behind him came the chatter of short bursts from machine guns. The gunners were test-firing their weapons.

"All armory in order," came the report.

"Very well," Trettner said. "Navigator?"

"On course, sir."

"Very well."

Trettner's eyes flicked to the newly installed gauge on his controls, the gauge that would connect with the agent's transmission from the city ahead. Then he settled back into his seat, forcing himself to relax for the eighty-minute flight to Coventry. Softly Trettner began to hum a Bavarian folk song.

Chapter 23

Coventry
November 14, 1940

THE brown van was parked on a quiet suburban street off Warwick Road. It would not have earned a second glance except for the steady hum of a dynamo and the squared wire antenna on the roof, slowly turning backward and forward within a radius of forty-five degrees. Any schoolboy would have known that it was monitoring toward the city center, but there was nobody to see the van. The street was deserted, the houses darkened enough to satisfy the most despotic air raid warden.

In the dimly lighted interior, Sergeant Walter Pearson sat with headphones covering his ears. His eyes were on the dials of the gray monitoring machine built into the wall of the van. Behind him a corporal was holding the microphone of a two-way radio. Every few seconds the corporal spoke softly into the mike. "Nothing . . . nothing . . . nothing," he murmured, his voice an uninterested monotone.

Identical vans were parked on roads to the north and the southeast of the city. Inside them, similar scenes were being enacted. The monitoring system was called triangulation. If the rogue transmitter in the city was switched on, the three seeking antennas would home on it. A simple mathematical calculation would give the interesecting area from which the three receivers were picking up the radio beam. Then they would start to move in, reducing the size of the suspect area the closer they came to each other.

Pearson's stubby fingers played delicately with the row of knobs controlling the scanner. He wondered what the hell it was all about. An hour ago they had been in Daventry, finishing an early meal of cottage pie, talking about the movie they were going to see in the camp cinema. Then the panic had hit. The vans had been driven to Coventry at top speed, urged on by authoritative voices nagging at them through the two-way radio. Pearson could feel the first pangs of indigestion.

Behind him the corporal was still murmuring, "Nothing . . . nothing . . . nothing."

Kampfgruppe 100 passed over the English coastline between Colchester and Harwich at fifteen thousand feet. Joaquim Trettner was no longer humming. His eyes were ranging restlessly into the darkness beyond the cockpit. The English night fighters had never troubled the pathfinders before, but there was always a first time. The sound of the radio beam from Holland continued uninterrupted through his earphones.

He thought about Leutze. Ten minutes earlier the pilot, number three on his starboard wing, had turned for home. He said he was having generator trouble in one engine. He could be telling the truth, but Trettner didn't know about Leutze. He was new to the Kampfgruppe. There would be an inquiry.

Looking down, Trettner could see the flat, moonlit countryside of England. Before the war he had taken a vacation in Cambridge. He liked the English, but that had nothing to do with this mission. Twenty minutes, he thought. Another twenty minutes and it would begin.

Maggie answered the telephone so swiftly that Brock thought she must have had her hand on the receiver when it rang. The line was bad. Although he could hear her clearly, he could tell from the resonance in his earphone that his words weren't reaching her. He tried shouting, but it did little good.

"I'll call you back," she said. "What's your number?"

He had to shout it three times before she finally repeated it correctly and put down her receiver. As he waited he wondered about her reaction: anger that all their preparations had been for nothing; disgust that he was backing out at the crucial moment. When the telephone rang and he picked up the receiver again, he found that the line was free of interference. Her voice was sharp with anxiety.

"What's the matter, Michael?" she demanded. "Why are you calling? It's nearly seven o'clock."

"The time doesn't matter, Maggie," he said. "I'm not going to do it."

"What d'you mean, you're not going to do it?" He could feel her astonishment singing down the wires from London.

"I saw myself this afternoon. I saw myself in a little old priest in the cathedral, an old man who doesn't care about people, whether they live or die."

235

"For God's sake, Michael, what are you talking about? Are you all right?"

"I'm fine, Maggie. I'll get a train down tonight, and I'll see you tomorrow. I'll try to explain, face to face. I'll call you in the morning."

"You're serious, then? You're not going to do it."

"I can't, Maggie. I can't for about two hundred fifty thousand reasons, some of them children. I've killed for the organization, killed a number of times, but this time I can't do it."

"Donovan suspected it," she said.

"Suspected what?"

"That you'd back out, that you didn't have the resolution to do it. I told him not to doubt you, but he was right all the time. What will you do now?"

"I don't know, Maggie. I'll come down, and we'll talk tomorrow. Perhaps we can go off somewhere together. Remember, once, you talked about us having the whole of green Ireland to play in? Perhaps we can find a little corner instead."

Her voice was cold. "That wasn't good enough for you in the old days, and it's not good enough for me now. In Dublin they'll have a word for your failure."

He thought of Collins and the time in the police station, and he felt trapped by old beliefs, old arguments that wouldn't go away. "Well," he said softly, "I lasted a little longer than Michael Collins."

"What did you say?" she demanded.

"Nothing. Nothing at all," he said. "They can do what they like with me. But I won't have the murder of a city on my conscience. If they court-martial me, they'll court-martial me, and the city of Coventry will still stand."

"You damned fool," she cried. "Your betrayal won't make one bit of difference, not one bit. Because, you see, Donovan put another man with a transmitter in Coventry. He's already at the cathedral, doing what you should be doing."

"Who?"

"I don't know. What does that matter? I only heard two hours ago. Donovan double-crossed me, and it seems he was right to do so. He wanted to take you out, and I pleaded with him to trust you, and he said he would; but he knew you better than I did, so he brought in a backup man."

"He's from Dublin?"

"He's at the cathedral with a transmitter, I tell you, another transmitter just like yours. Oh, Michael, don't throw it all away for nothing. Go and work with him; do your duty like you always have. I'll not mention that you wanted to change your mind. Nobody will know. We'll forget we ever talked like this, and, you'll see, one day we'll have the whole of Ireland for our own."

His belly was churning now as he stared out into the moonlight that drenched the street. All his agonizing came back to mock him. While he had fretted, Dublin had bypassed him.

"The other man's the insurance, is that it?" he asked. "Making sure. Does he know he's doubling up on me?"

"He's expecting you, Michael. He was told that if you didn't appear, then he was to go ahead on his own; but he's expecting you."

Sergeant Pearson, monitoring from the southwest sector, was the first to pick up the transmission. At seven two his dials showed that a radio beam was being transmitted at eleven zero four degrees from the center of his monitoring arc. He glanced at the map at his elbow. The pirate radio was somewhere on a line stretching from the van through the center of the city and beyond. The two other vans had it almost immediately.

Behind Pearson the corporal was writing down their vectors. He turned and swiftly drew a circle on Pearson's map. It included a ten-block area in the heart of the city. Pearson noticed that the cathedral, indicated on the map by a cross, was inside the circle.

He shouted at the driver to start his engine.

To the north and to the southeast the other two vans also began to move.

It would take him at least five minutes to reach the cathedral, more like ten. Brock dropped the receiver as if it were contaminated. It clattered, dangling at the end of the coiled rubber connection. He plunged out of the phone booth and began to run.

He was at Greyfriar's Green, southwest of the cathedral. As he ran he caught a glimpse of a clock in the window of a real estate agent. After seven, nearly five past. Pounding along Hertford Street he passed a pub just as the door opened, and a man stepped out. They collided hard. The man went down, shouting, "Hey, what the hell. . . ." But Brock had recovered and was racing on. He had his hand against his belly to hold the gun tight against the turbulence of his striving body.

Gasping now, he swung right, into High Street, and almost immediately left, into the darkness of Pepper Lane, where his urgent feet on the cobbles sent echoes bouncing off the old walls. It was more than five minutes since he had left the phone booth, and still the cathedral wasn't in sight.

He heard a clock begin to strike seven. For a moment he was confused, but then he knew it must be slow. Suddenly, there it was, the cathedral, bathed in moonlight, the proud spire an admonishing finger against the cold and starry sky.

He vaulted the low stone wall that surrounded the church and ran over the grass and ancient graves until the great doors towered above him. They were locked. He beat on them in frustration, swearing as he bloodied his knuckles. He turned left and found a smaller door. His lungs still heaving, he pushed it open, and the next moment he was inside. The vast interior was illuminated only by moonlight coming at a sharp angle through the rich spectrum of colors in the tall windows above the altar. The silence enclosed him. He stood there, trying to ease his breathing.

Then he shouted, "Where are you, for Christ's sake?"

There was a movement among the pews, and Brock knew somebody was in the cathedral with him.

"Is that my hard man, then?" Plunger said. "You're late, Michael." His voice, carrying easily through the stillness of the church, was as composed as if they were meeting for a drink.

"Plunger!" he said. The word was for himself, not the waiting man. "Oh, you stinking bastard, Donovan." And yet, he thought, it had to be Plunger. Donovan would have taken a twisted delight in using Plunger as the insurance against his perfidy. Again he muttered, "You stinking bastard, Donovan," as if the IRA chief were at Plunger's side.

Moving swiftly down the center aisle, Brock saw that Plunger was sitting in a pew to the right, his head turned to watch Brock's approach. He was smiling.

"Where's the transmitter?" Brock demanded.

"Don't worry, Michael," Plunger said. "I've taken care of things, like I always have. It's turned on. I see you don't have yours. Did you lose it, my hard man?"

Even as he spoke, the air raid sirens began to sound, the opening gurgle swiftly growing into the chilling high-pitched wail of warning. One of them sounded as if it were immediately outside the cathedral. Brock stopped twenty yards from Plunger.

"Where's the transmitter, Plunger?" Brock asked again. He knew his voice was shaking with emotion. Slowly, almost lazily, Plunger got to his feet, twisting to face Brock.

"It's here," he said. "You sound strange, Michael. Are you all right?"

"The planes," Brock said. "They'll be here in a moment."

"That they will. Isn't that the idea?"

Brock's hand dropped to his belly, and he pulled out the Luger. He held it, pointed down, against the side of his leg. His finger paralleled the short barrel, did not touch the trigger.

"I'm not going to let you do it, Plunger."

"Is that a gun you've got there, Michael?" Plunger said softly.

"Where's the transmitter?"

"Why, it's right here at my feet. *I'm alive forevermore, amen, and have the keys of hell and of death.*"

"Turn it off."

"That's from the Book of Revelations."

"You think you have the keys to the death of Coventry?"

239

"Maybe I have, Michael."

"Turn it off, and we'll talk about it."

"I won't turn it off, but we can talk, if you like. You wouldn't be thinking of using that gun on me, now, would you, Michael?" He had to raise his voice to be heard above the moan of the sirens; but even so, they both caught a scraping noise on the roof.

"There's a priest up there on the roof with buckets of water and sand," Plunger said. "A couple of pals he's got up there with him. Ironic, isn't it? They're up there waiting for the incendiaries, and we're down here to make sure they drop in the right place."

"There's the women and the children, Plunger," he said. "You'll be killing people who've never lifted a finger against you or against Ireland."

"You're forgetting one thing, my hard man."

"What's that?"

"They're English."

"They're human beings."

"Would you use your gun to stop me, Michael? With no priest to hear my confession?"

Brock hadn't thought about the use he might make of his gun, hadn't thought of pulling the trigger against Plunger; but now the idea lodged in his brain like the beginning of a cancerous growth. He knew he wasn't powerful enough to hope to overcome Plunger in physical combat.

"Kill me and you make yourself nothing," Plunger said. "Stop me bringing in those planes and you turn your whole life into a hoax; for it will mean you've killed those soldiers, those policemen, for nothing. And that is murder."

There was a new sound, now, coming through the sirens when their wails were at the lowest pitch. They both listened, straining to catch the intruding sound, and they both knew what it was.

"They're on time," Plunger said. "Very punctual. You've got to give that to the Germans. Come on, Michael. Let's forget all this nonsense. Just a few more minutes and then we'll both get out of here."

"Turn it off or. . . ."

"Or what, Michael? Are you really going to put a bullet in your old mate, Plunger? Is that it?"

Brock hardly heard him. He was thinking of the old days: Plunger grinning at him as they hid in an attic, waiting for the Special Branch men to find them, while outside, the shadows of the gallows fell on the ground of Ireland. Plunger coming to rouse him from bed with a message that an informer had betrayed him. Plunger's face in the glow of a burning police barracks. Plunger in Spain, that great grin on his face, coming back into the lines with a scrawny chicken he had "found" so that they could eat something other than beans. Spain. . . . Jarama. . . .

The sound of the sirens died away as if defeated by the rising-falling note of the oncoming planes.

"I'll do it, Plunger," Brock said.

"There was a time when you thanked me for saving your life, my hard man. You said it, not I."

"I'll do it, Plunger."

"Some of them in Dublin said you'd changed," Plunger said. "I didn't believe it at the time." He hadn't stirred from his position, lounging with his buttocks against the back of the pew behind him, his hands hidden in the pockets of his raincoat.

"This isn't the same," Brock said. "Things have changed."

"No," Plunger said, his voice suddenly cold. "You've changed, Michael. How did they get to you, I wonder? God almighty, you're just another Michael Collins."

Brock brought up his gun, but Plunger didn't alter his stance, didn't look at it. His eyes were fixed on Brock's face. The blast of the gun in Plunger's pocket was a brutal roar that fragmented the stillness of the place. It wouldn't stop. The echoes flew into the farthest reaches of the cathedral and came hurtling back in a ricochet of sound, only to go and come again. A scorched hole had appeared in the front of Plunger's raincoat.

Plunger had missed. Now Brock could see the barrel of Plunger's gun poking through the seared hole. Almost simultaneously they fired, and the double explosion was a stunning

241

thunderclap insulting the quietude of the place. Plunger Cronin took the parabellum slug in his chest. The force of it carried him back over the top of the pew behind him until he was draped, his whole big body, in a sagging mass between the pews.

Plunger's second bullet had struck Brock in the right shoulder. It spun him around, off balance, as if he were a marionette whose strings had been jerked by a vicious child. His gun clattered to the stone floor.

Pivoting back on his heels, Brock went over. His head smashed against the armrest of a pew next to the aisle. It was like the time at Teruel, the same exploding pain and then blackness.

Above him the sound of the planes' engines had become a steady thunder.

The Heinkels were coming in one behind the other, streaming down the track of the radio beacon. In the lead, Trettner was having trouble with gusts from an alternating west wind which kept trying to throw him off course, but the steady note from Oostburg didn't alter.

He could see the city clearly now, but he gave it no more than a glance. His attention was concentrated on his instruments.

"Bombardier?"

"At alert, sir."

"Very good. I'm starting my run." Again Trettner touched his left rudder, fighting the thrust of the westerly. Some flak now. It was coming up on the starboard quarter but at least three thousand feet beneath the line of bombers. Trettner pushed the control column forward, and the plane dipped. Assigned bombing height was fourteen thousand feet. Descending, the Heinkel picked up speed until Trettner eased back on the throttles.

"Stand by, all crew," he ordered. Every one of them, including the gunners, was straining for the sound of the ground transmission. The flak was closer now, and searchlights moved steadily across the night sky, seeking targets for night fighters.

242

In the nose the bombardier was watching the cross hairs of his sight moving steadily across the suburban areas of the city until they intersected with inner-city factories and rows of tightly packed housing. It was perfect sight-bombing weather, but he waited. He realized he was holding his breath, so intense was his concentration, and gently he expelled it. Any second now, any second.

The first bomb to hit Coventry was an incendiary from Trettner's Heinkel. It did not explode. It might have been faulty or it might have been the recent rain. The lawn of a house half a mile from the city center was so damp that the bomb buried its nose into the grass without detonating the phosphorus inside. The incendiary was discovered the next morning by two children. They tried to attach a clothesline to the protruding fin and drag it out of the earth. Adults chased them away and called bomb-disposal units.

All the other incendiaries in the first string, however, exploded. They laid a line of fire into the heart of the city. The last bomb of the string penetrated the roof of a shop on Whitefriar's Street, not far from the city council offices. The upper timbers swiftly caught fire, and within half an hour the roof collapsed in a shower of flame and black smoke.

The incendiaries, marker bombs, and high explosives from Trettner's plane still hadn't reached the ground when the second in the parade of Kampfgruppe 100s flew into the radio beam from the ground-based radio transmitter and the bombardier pulled his toggle.

One after another, the pathfinding bombers connected with the ground transmitter and showered their loads into the city. From fourteen thousand feet the crews could see pinpricks of light steadily growing larger and joining together like expanding blobs of quicksilver. Among them were the vivid colors of the marker bombs.

Within one hour, two hundred fifty fires had been started within the city boundaries. Ammunition for the flak units around the city was already below the limit for dealing with a light raid, and it soon ran out. This was something more than a light raid. The heavy bombers pouring in behind the pathfinders delivered their loads secure from retaliation.

It was little men who were supposed to be fussy, Blood thought. But this Major Wainwright was a big man, meaty at the neck and jowls, and still he was fussy.

"How far apart are the radio vans now?" Blood asked.

Wainwright peered at his map, reaching for a slide rule.

"I don't want an exact figure," Blood said. "Give me an estimate, for Christ's sake."

Wainwright looked at him, full of reproach. "It'll be a guess, you know," he said. "I'd say there's less than a quarter of a mile between the three of them. The transmitter must be somewhere around the cathedral and the council offices."

"Call them off," Blood said. He felt exhausted. Beyond that he felt more sad than angry at what was happening. An overwhelming sadness and feeling of helplessness. Who was more to blame? He, the man who'd failed to find the Irishmen? Or Churchill? Or the IRA men or the Germans?

It didn't really matter now. Not until he could think about it later. Coventry was being murdered. They all had their justifications. They were all right. It depended on the point of view. The emergency room shook. The high explosives that had followed the incendiaries were pulling the town to pieces. Lumps of plaster were falling from the ceiling above him.

"But they're so close," Wainwright said. "Another ten minutes. . . ."

"Call them off," Blood said. "The Irishmen will have gone. They'll be looking after their own skins now, getting away as fast as they can. We're too late. It's all over."

"What shall we do with the vans? Send them back to Daventry?"

"No," Blood said. "Turn them over to the air raid defense people. They can use them to carry the wounded. There are going to be a lot of wounded."

Brock awoke to a transformed world. He stirred, moaning at the pain in his shoulder.

He heard a furious crackling. The place was so hot that his mouth was parched, and he had difficulty breathing. Holding his useless arm with his left hand, he stared up. The cathedral was filled with light. Incendiaries had pierced the lead roof and lodged among the oaken beams. The entire roof was ablaze, molten lead streaming down into the sanctuary and onto the pews.

Even as he watched, an incendiary dropped through the flames and exploded twenty yards away on the floor in a shower of incandescence, like a suddenly opened furnace. Some of the pews and chairs had caught fire, adding to the heat until Brock felt as if he were pinned on the rack of an oven. Huge beams running between the stone arches were burning and cracking apart, sending flaming shafts of wood pitching down into the interior of the cathedral. On the west wall a tapestry was on fire. The long flames, reaching upward, joined the overhead holocaust.

Brock got to his knees, one hand grasping the end of a pew. Flames were playing around Plunger's draped body. Driven by dread yet awed by the blazing spectacle, he staggered to his feet and turned toward the side door. For the first time, he heard the thunder of high explosives, felt the shudder of the ground, and knew the Germans were dropping their heavy bombs into the torched city.

Staggering, swaying, running, he was two-thirds of the way up the aisle when he heard the grinding noise above him. It was, he thought crazily, like the grinding of the Devil's teeth, a horrible gnashing together of stone against stone. He stared up. He stared up in time to see two enormous pieces of arch collapse inward, coming down toward him, gigantic, tumbling as if in slow motion. He stopped; he didn't try to escape. He gazed up as if at a wonder beyond comprehension. He gathered air in his lungs and then expelled it in a shriek, terrible, inhuman. He screamed once, the sound of it overwhelmed by the roar of the flames, the clashing of stone against stone; and then the arches plunged down on him, and he was lost in the tumbled mass of broken stone.

Chapter 24

THROUGH the big iron gates and past the lodge they came. Past the grave of Roger Casement and the big ugly monument to O'Connell. They turned right and walked along the path until they all were gathered at the site known as the Republican plot. There weren't many. Thirty-five if you included the two little boys and the baby in the arms of an old woman in a black shawl.

Donovan was standing next to the grave of John Devoy. On one side of the Devoy memorial was the word "Patriot." On the other, "Rebel." These were Republicans buried here, some of the men from the post office and some who had died in Kilmainham Jail.

A chair was brought for Donovan to stand on, and he climbed into position so that he could look down through his spectacles at his audience. He thought of the great gatherings at Bodenstown, where Wolfe Tone was buried, and again he wondered why the young men no longer responded to the call.

"I'll tell you no jokes today," he said, "but I'll tell you a story all the same." He paused while he took off his dirty raincoat and handed it down to one of the men standing at his side. It was suddenly hot in the cemetery, the sun blazing after a brief shower.

"You've all heard enough Republican speeches," Donovan said. "Sometimes I wish we were as eager to fight as we are to make speeches. Anyway, I'll just tell you a story today."

He looked at the solemn little boys and said, "It's about two men. In olden times they would have been gallant knights who risked their lives to go out and slay the dragon that tormented their anguished country. But these two men lived in modern times, when we have to use bullets and bombs instead of swords and lances.

246

"They could have lived comfortable, easy lives, these two young men. They could have had homes and wives and children to comfort them. They could have walked down the streets of Dublin with no fear in their hearts of any man. They could have grown old in safety. They could have.

"But there was a dragon to be slain, so they put all the thoughts of comfort behind them, and they went out into the streets and into the hills, and they took up arms against the dragon, whose name was England, and they offered their lives as sacrifices. These two became brothers, not by blood but by shared belief and love for each other."

Donovan paused and looked down at his meager audience. Above the O'Connell memorial, rooks were cawing as they swooped up and down in the sunshine. Donovan picked out familiar faces. Old gunmen, Volunteers who had been turning gray when they fought Michael Collins, men who would pick up their weapons once more if ordered. He could see women who'd worked alongside the action squads and the flying columns. And there was the hard core of his weakened forces, younger men in cheap clothes with the marks of poverty and privation on their faces. Too few of them, he thought, far too few.

"They did love each other, these two young men. And when the time came to carry the fight across the seas to the camp of the enemy, they went together like David and Jonathan. Now they were utterly on their own, with every man's hand turned against them! But they worked together with laughter on their lips and resolution in their hearts. . . ."

Donovan paused again, looking toward the gates and a woman walking slowly toward them. He had wondered if Maggie would come. Certainly she knew of the memorial service.

"They followed their orders, followed them to the letter, although they knew those orders almost certainly meant their deaths. Death didn't matter so much to them because they knew they were following in the glorious footsteps of Tone and Pearse and Connolly and Kevin Barry and all the rest of the Republic's martyrs."

247

Maggie was standing at the edge of the little crowd now, looking up at him, her face impassive. Donovan talked on, but his thoughts had already moved on to tomorrow and the action planned in the Six Counties.

"And so, indeed, death found them as they were striking a mighty blow for Ireland. They died together, these two, in the land of the enemy, far from the mountains and streams and green fields they loved so well. But not in vain. For Plunger Cronin and Michael Brock, the young knights, kept bright the promise and the flame of revolt, which will never go out while Ireland lies broken and in chains.

"We do not know. It may take another five years, ten years, fifty years; but the young men will still go north or across the sea to face the dragon and offer their bodies to his scorching breath. Until one day, Ireland will be whole again, and the young knights will put away their swords and think of life instead of death.

"But now, as we stand here remembering the day when Wolfe Tone died, let us also remember Plunger Cronin and Michael Brock, men whose names are only the latest to be written in the shining pages of Ireland's history." He bowed his head, and there was silence except for the raucousness of the rooks.

When it was over, he went to Maggie and took her hand. "Come," he said. "I'll give you a ride back into the city. There are things to discuss, plans to be made. We can talk on the way."

Note

BEGINNING at seven-fifteen on the night of November 14, 1940, waves of German bombers led by the pathfinding Kampfgruppe 100 attacked the city of Coventry nonstop for ten hours. At the time, it was the most concentrated air assault ever launched.

Later estimates were that thirty thousand incendiaries were used to set the target ablaze. Into that inferno the German bombardiers dropped a thousand high-explosive bombs. About four hundred planes delivered their loads into the compact city.

The defense system was shattered during the early hours of the raid. By eight-thirty P.M., more than two hundred forty fires were blazing. Destruction of water mains reduced fire-fighting waterlines to a trickle. Craters and debris made roads in the medieval city center impassable.

Over fifty thousand houses were damaged. One hundred acres of the city center were destroyed. The water, gas, and electricity systems were smashed. Six hundred people were killed and nine hundred were badly injured. German pilots reported that they could see the pillar of fire that was Coventry from the coastline a hundred miles distant.

The next day the charred smell of Coventry's agony could be detected five miles away. Observers reported refugees leaving the city in trucks and cars, pushing handcarts and baby carriages, carrying their bedding. In daylight, six hours after the last bomber turned for home, the city was still dark under a black fog.

A new word was coined: *Coventrated.* It didn't last long, for Coventry was merely a precedent for Dresden and Hiroshima.

The cathedral burned until only the stone walls and the steeple were left. It has never been rebuilt; a new cathedral was constructed alongside. The shell of the old structure remains as a permanent memorial to the violence of man.